chapter 1

JACOB MCPHEARSON ROSE slowly from his hiding place, nursing an aching back, and cursing the stiffness in his long unused legs. He'd maintained his watch there behind that row of scrub trees for the better part of two days now, and even his mind ached from the sheer tedium of it all. But with any luck, and if all went as planned, this morning would mark the end of it, and to the end of Rhen Larson as well, and the sooner the better.

Larson had come down from Illinois to farm this stretch of Kansas bottom land and build his fortune. He lay claim to more than 200 acres along the Cimarron River valley, with ample room for crops and livestock alike. The rich stand of cottonwood and wild plants which grew along the riverbank gave the place the appearance of an oasis amidst the never-ending sea of rolling grasses which ruled this part of south-west Kansas.

Already forty acres had been planted in corn, and in the straightest rows a man had ever seen. Alongside the crop stood a simple shack of a house, a sturdy corral, and a barn---well built, but only half finished.

But Jacob McPhearson was not interested in the barn, the house, or the crops for that matter He was there solely to have dealings with Larson, unpleasant dealings.

Rhen Larson had something that Jacob McPhearson considered his own, and he wanted it back.

Two days of lying prone on that hillside in the hot summer sun had given Jacob a good idea as to the daily habits of this Larson fellow. It had been an investment in dirt and sweat, but today would be the payoff.

McPhearson chuckled to himself as he watched the big man once again walk from the shack toward the barn following his breakfast. A man could set his watch by it. Soon Larson would be sharpening his hoe, preparing for his never-ending assault on the native weeds and grasses which threatened the crop. Jacob had never met the man, but by now he knew him better than most.

At nearly six feet five inches and weighing in at over 300 pounds, Rhen Larson was not a man to be trifled with. He had hands the size of sycamore leaves, and arms like tree trunks. But McPhearson had no intention of wrestling with this giant. He intended to let his gun do the talking this time, just as it had done so many times before. This was how Jacob did business.

The time had come. He had waited long enough. Now the watcher became the hunter, and throwing off the stub of his last cigar, Jacob brushed off his clothes, mounted the stolen horse, and began his carefully scripted ride down to the Larson farmstead, and to his long-awaited revenge.

Catherine Larson was just finishing up the morning wash down at the riverbank when she glimpsed her husband walking slowly from the house out toward the barn. His gait seemed slower and heavier than usual this day. Truth was, and all appearances to the contrary, the farm was not prospering as he had hoped. The burden of backbreaking labor and the increasing possibility of failure were taking their toll.

Lately he had been quiet, somber, and moody. It was nearing June, and while the corn crop had done well so far, Larson knew that in a land where grasses prevail, the kind of rains needed to sustain a seed crop might prove to be few and

CONGER'S BRIDE

Lew McKimmon

Cover Photo.---------------- cdp

Contributing Editor.------- N. Keene

ISBN: 0615833535
ISBN-13: 9780615833538
Library of Congress Control Number: 2013912842
Lew McKimmon Books, Indianapolis, IN

far between. This explained the overly straight rows he had planted to aid in irrigation, and of his daily war with the weeds that threatened to steal badly needed moisture away from the crop.

Catherine had just finished washing the clothes, and herself as well, in the cool Cimarron River. She loved to play and swim in the water, and used the excuse of the laundry to do so almost daily. She was still wet in places as she finally got dressed again and gathered up the wash. Catherine lifted the laundry basket, and humming a native tune, walked gracefully toward the clothesline which Rhen had hung between the house and the barn. She hoped that the special dinner of rabbit stew and fresh baked bread she was preparing would cheer her husband up somehow. At least the wash would dry quickly in the hot Kansas sun.

She had nearly finished her task when she noticed a lone rider approaching out of the east, his horse walking at an easy gait, but the distance was too great to make out any details. Curiosity grew as Catherine hurriedly finished up, and tying back her long dark hair, she started over to where the rider had stopped to speak with Rhen, thus sealing her fate.

McPhearson had ridden to less than a hundred feet from where Larson was standing before the big man bothered to look up at him. Rhen had seen him coming alright, but was watching him out of the corner of his eye as he sharpened his hoe. Visitors were rare in these parts.

The stranger wore eastern style clothes, complete with overcoat and string tie, and a blocked gray hat. Riding upright and proper like, he seemed more likely a gentleman, and not just some saddle bum. Rhen noticed that the man wasn't wearing a waist gun, but did have a rifle in the scabbard. This was an older man, and handsome in a dark sort of way. Rhen was sure this fellow was either selling something or wanting a handout. Still, it was possible that he might just be lost, as there wasn't anything within ten miles of this place.

So Rhen decided he'd hear what the man had to say, give what hospitality there was to offer, and send him on his way. Larson had work to do, and standing around talking to strangers, or anyone else for that matter, never accomplished much of anything.

Thus, Jacob McPhearson had passed his first test that day, representing no threat to Larson by riding in well-dressed and casual like. It would get easier from here on in.

"Good morning!" Jacob smiled his most sincere smile as he opened the conversation with the standard greeting. "I'm lucky to have found you. I seem to have lost my way ."

Larson was already tired of this gent, and would have been just as pleased if the man had not gone ahead and dismounted. He showed every indication of someone who liked to talk, and Rhen was not one for palaver at this time of the day, or any other time for that matter.

Catherine had watched the man dismount, and being more social than Rhen, was always interested in hearing the latest news. Having finished her basket of clothes, she started on over to where the two men were standing. This morning she was wearing the pretty pink dress that her mother had given her years before. It fit her a little more loosely now than it had back in Virginia. She would have had to admit that she had lost some weight and was considerably stronger nowadays, what with all the work it took to put food on the table out here in the Kansas prairie land---work that seemed never to end. Jacob noticed the girl walking their way. This was all going much better than expected. He turned slightly to hide his features. He knew the girl would recognize him, even at a distance, and needed to be sure that she was very close up before that were to happen. He had no intention of getting into a foot race with a girl that young.

"So tell me, how many acres do you have planted here?" McPhearson was stalling. He needed only a few more seconds to spring his trap. She was almost there. He had to time this just right.

Rhen thought this was all a lot of nonsense. What possible reason would this man have for wanting to know how many acres he had planted? It was doubtful that he intended to stick around to help him pick the corn in the fall. Now Rhen was convinced he was selling something.

Catherine's footfalls were close by now. She was being forced to look into the bright morning sun and didn't have all that clear a view. Folks seldom ever came by that way, as the marshland over to the east made it difficult to get there. She didn't recognize the horse, and didn't remember seeing this man around there before. Still. There was something strangely familiar about him---the way he stood…"Could you take a look at this map for me?" Jacob reached his hand into his coat. The girl was now right behind him shielding her eyes from the sun.

Rhen was a man of manners, and did not fail to make the proper introduction. "This is my wife, Catherine ."

Jacob turned his head and smiled at Catherine, and then, pulling his pistol from the shoulder holster inside his coat, proceeded to fire three shots into Larson, point blank, two to his chest, and then one between the eyes.

Catherine watched in horror as Rhen fell, and then stared at Jacob's face in disbelief. It couldn't be! Not here! Terror set in, and she was frozen for that instant, unable to move, or even know what to do.

Instinct told her to run. She somehow must command her legs to run and get away from there! Terror gripped her as she turned, unable to breathe, unable to think, unable to move.

She would not be quick enough. Her moment of hesitation, that instant of disbelief, had condemned her. She would not escape from Jacob McPhearson's deadly trap. Everything was going as planned.

Just as Catherine turned to run, her head seemed to explode in a raging fire, and then darkness. A powerful blow to the head had ended her escape. The ground rushed up to meet her, but she would not feel the impact.

It had all been too easy.

chapter 2

LESS THAN A quarter mile north and east of the Larson Farm, a lone figure plodded through knee high grass, rope in hand, with a mule tied to the other end. The man was young, early twenties to be exact, of average height and build, and sported a shock of wavy blond hair he'd had since he was a boy. The mule was brown, as would be expected, and the man wore eastern style clothes, well-sewn, but not fancy.

Will Conger was fresh out of Kentucky and heading west. This was the land he had heard about all those years, and if it hadn't been for the war, and all the trouble it brought with it, he would have been here years ago.

As it was, he had already done just about all the walking he cared to do that day, even with the day not yet half done. He knew he was feeling sorry for himself and was ashamed for it, having lived through much worse than this with the Sixth Illinois, and right now he wasn't even being shot at! At least the mule wasn't complaining any more than usual.

It had to be close to noon, and taking a break seemed like a good idea. He would have to turn south a bit to catch back up to the Cimarron, as he had been forced to swing north earlier to get around that stretch of marshland he had run into. Still, the grass was not so deep here, and the going was not all that difficult. Pulling the mule along, he started up a gentle rise leading up to a low hill just ahead, figuring that the river would be on the other side.

That's when he came across something totally unexpected. There in the middle of nowhere was a substantial pile of horse manure, known as "horse apples" where he came from. He didn't need to be a great tracker to figure this out, as he had been raised on a Kentucky horse farm, and had raked and shoveled several tons of horse droppings in his lifetime. This horse had to have stood there for quite a spell, perhaps days, to have made a pile this large. It was easy to see where the horse had been tied off, as the grass around had been grazed down almost to the soil below. Looking around at the vast empty prairie surrounding him, Will could see nothing at all which would cause someone to leave a horse in this place for any amount of time, let alone for days.

It was getting hot, and as nothing could be gained by standing there looking at a pile of horse apples, Will pulled the mule's line taut and continued up the hill, anxious to get to the cool water of the Cimarron which waited for him on the other side. His head still ached from the fall he had suffered the previous day as the result of an ill-tempered rattlesnake and a very solid rock hidden in the deep prairie grass below. His startled chestnut gelding had thrown Will straight over his nose and run off to places unknown. It was unlike that horse to spook like that, and although the impact with that rock was quite a knock, Will could clearly see his horse as it rode off at full gallop. He remembered that it almost seemed as though someone had been riding it as it ran! But there was no one in the saddle that he could see. Still, it just didn't make sense.

Conger had been on foot ever since, and his aching head was eager for a long nap under a big shade tree to wait out the hot afternoon sun. His hat still didn't fit right, and dragging that contrary mule around had just about taken it all out of him.

Just as he was about to crest the hill he saw something else that was as much out of place in this endless prairie as a pile of horse apples---a cigar butt! And not just one, but several, scattered about the hillside just under a line of scrubby little trees and bushes. It was apparent that someone had been lying there behind the brush for some time, for the grass was heavily pressed down at that spot.

Now horse apples and cigar butts don't just fall out of the sky, and their being there spoke strongly of someone waiting for someone, or watching the movements of someone without wanting to be seen. Such things usually meant trouble. Will considered Indians, but it didn't seem likely they would be smoking cigars. But then he had never had any run in with the native population out this way, so he couldn't be sure. He knew Cherokees and Shawnee, and had traded with the Oubache on the Wabash River up by Vincennes. Most of them used tobacco in one way or another, so why not? Still it just didn't seem likely. This was probably a white man. Walking a few more feet, Conger topped the rise of the hill, and suddenly things fell into place.

Below him was a farm, with fields of corn planted in the straightest rows Will had ever seen. There was a barn which looked to be about half built, and a clapboard shack with a garden out back. It was nicely laid out, and seemed like a lush green island there in the midst of this ocean of prairie grass. It also answered the question as to what someone had been up there watching. Not long from the war, Conger could appreciate the strategic advantage this hill enjoyed over the countryside. From there the entire river basin was visible. Whoever had been up there spying knew what they were about.

Spying? It dawned on Will that there was something wrong here. As welcome a sight as this farm was for his poor aching head, it would pay to be cautious in his approach. Usually someone coming unexpectedly upon a house out this way would shout out their presence, so as to avoid a bullet infested welcome. That kind of hospitality could prove down right unhealthy. With Indians and such about, having someone skulking around could easily make a fellow nervous with his trigger finger. It just stood to reason to make yourself known.

But that pile of horse apples, the cigar butts, and the impressions made on the grass were not neighborly. They showed every indication of an ambush, but for who, and why?

Conger decided to take a circular route down toward the barn, and thus stay out of the direct sight of the shack below. If there were something amiss going on down there, he'd surely find out soon enough.

Catherine found herself gently floating on crystal clear water, surrounded by a garden of fragrant water lilies. Sun beams peeked through light green willow leaves, creating diamonds in the placid water below. A lovely yellow bird chirped from time to time on a low-hanging branch nearby. It was all too beautiful for words.

But she was not alone. There was someone else nearby, someone who did not belong there. She strained her eyes to see, but the image was blurred and unclear. Slowly, the bird's pleasant chirping seemed to change into a rasping, scraping sound, not like a bird at all.

At last the figure came into focus. It was Satan himself, complete with horns and a forked tail. He held a spoon in his hand and was eating rabbits from a large red and white bowl. Their long ears could be seen above the rim, scurrying about as they tried to escape. And then the devil, with an evil smile, turned his head, and spoke to her.

"Well, it's about time. I was beginning to think you weren't coming back at all. I guess I hit you a little harder than I meant to. You must accept my apologies."

Nothing could have brought Catherine back to her senses faster than the sound of that voice. Terror struck like lightning running down her backbone. Satan was there after all, and his name was Jacob McPhearson.

She tried to get up, to run, to find a weapon. But her efforts were in vain. Her arms were spread far apart over her shoulders, and would not move. Her legs were spread apart as well. As she turned her head a shot of agonizing pain ran through the backside of her skull. Her vision was still somewhat blurred, but she could clearly see that her ankles were tied to the bedposts with heavy leather straps. She was certain her wrists suffered the same fate. Knowing the man who had done the tying, struggling against these bonds would be a wasted effort which would serve only to provide him with greater pleasure. As she expected, he had removed her clothes as well.

She lowered her head back down upon the pillow. It felt wet, as did the back of her hair. She knew at once it must be blood, her blood, and remembered the blow to the back of her head as she had tried to run away. Rhen! Her vision was clearing now, and with it, her memory. The horror was real! Rhen was dead. Jacob had shot him. She was alone now.

Jacob watched with humor as the girl struggled with her bonds and fought to regain her consciousness. He scraped out another serving of rabbit stew, the first real food he had eaten in days. It was quite good, and he was enjoying every bite. He would remember to finish the rest of it before he took his leave that day. Catherine heard the scraping sounds, and now knew the source of the chirping bird in her dream. The role of the devil was easy to cast, for that was exactly the way she saw the man she had at one time known fondly as her Uncle Jacob. This man had been her father's adopted brother, taken in by the O'Dell family after Jacob's parents had been killed in a house fire. The circumstances surrounding the tragedy were always a mystery, as only Jacob had escaped, and certain marks on the parents' skulls were hard to explain. Still, it was the back woods of Virginia, and those hills held their secrets well. It was not long, however, until the O'Dells were questioning the wisdom of taking the boy in.

Things came up missing. Chickens and young kittens were found terribly mutilated, not uncommon to be sure, but in a manner quite inconsistent with the workings of the natural predators of the area. Jacob's surly and withdrawn manner made him difficult to deal with, and he flat out refused to attend school, spending his time instead with the far more exciting crowd of hangers-on at the local taverns.

Jacob left home at the age of sixteen, and followed a dark path. Over the years he became wealthy in the slave trade which flourished in the south. He also made considerable profits from the sale of whiskey to frontier Indian tribes, the running of opium, and a highly profitable trade in white slavery as well. The kidnapping of young white girls and their subsequent sale as concubines to wealthy businessmen at home and abroad was far more widespread than would first be believed. The frontier was an excellent source of young women, with their disappearance easily blamed on the Indians. Drugged senseless, the girls would often be transported out of the country in specially prepared coffins, where no one would look.

William O'Dell inherited the family farm and later married a lovely Cherokee maiden. Her name was Flower Song, but she was known in the white man's world as Rebecca, so as to keep her native origins unknown. Great prejudice was held in Virginian society against "squaw men" and their Indian wives. But Rebecca's assumed name and persona allowed her to run in polite circles, with the explanation of her dark features being that her family was of Spanish royalty. It seems folks will believe whatever makes them feel important, and rubbing shoulders with European nobility seemed most fashionable. Rebecca's mastery of the Spanish language, along with her charming and infectious demeanor, made the ruse a success.

When Rebecca gave birth to her firstborn, a daughter, she gave the child two names, one of the Cherokee nation, and one of the white, where she would be known as Catherine. Rebecca taught her daughter the proper ways and manners of a young lady of the South, just as Flower Song taught the girl the ways of the Cherokee, their language, their customs, and the knowledge and secrets of the land around her.

As Catherine grew, her father added to her education by teaching her the knowledge of tools and firearms. She became proficient with weapons at an early age, often joining her father on overnight hunting trips, bringing home meat for the family table. Catherine quickly grew into a very self-sufficient young lady.

Then the war came. William felt compelled to join the army of Virginia. Sadly, he fell at the first battle of Bull Run, as the Yankees called it. The day's fighting had long ended when a stray bullet, which seemed to come from nowhere, dropped William in his tracks. He was buried there, with honors, along with hundreds of others, in a grave marked only by a number, its exact location forgotten over time.

It was only weeks later that long-lost Uncle Jacob came by the O'Dell farm with news of William's death, offering condolences, and his willingness to stay on and give whatever help possible. Never a man to leave things to chance, the bullet that had felled William had come from Jacob's gun.

Rebecca had been in poor health these last few months, and had pleaded for William not to go to war. Now she was a widow. Her condition steadily worsened and she was losing weight. It was agreed to send Catherine off to a finishing school in Lynchburg. Three months later Rebecca was buried. As William O'Dell's only living relative, Jacob inherited the farm. He soon used his newly acquired wealth and property to expand his sinister empire. Employing men and women known for their ruthlessness, he was now running white slaves and opium through a network of agents, both in the States and abroad.

The years passed quickly, and the North prevailed. Catherine's unexpected return home after the war put Jacob in a difficult position. Things had changed greatly at the farm during her absence. The house was now used to store illegal goods, slaves, and captives as well.

Two young white girls, Hassy and Ginny, were living at the house at the time, each having been told their families had died in a fire, and that they were orphans. They were assured that they would be relocated to fine homes where they would be well cared for by families who would love them.

They were in fact to be victims of the white slave traffic Jacob profited from so well. One of the girls, Hassy, now fourteen, didn't believe the nonsense about the fire, and had run away twice, only to be captured each time by Jacob's hunting dogs the next day. A runaway could mean the hangman's noose for McPhearson, and he knew it. Hassy would have to be dealt with.

Although Catherine's homecoming was ill-timed, the girl had potential. She had grown into quite a lady and was as lovely as her mother had been. But she had proved to be high strung and defiant since her return. Jacob decided he would take Catherine for his wife, enjoying her charms, and thus solidifying his claim to the O'Dell estate. And if she continued to give him trouble, he would simply sell her off like the other girls. She would bring a good price, especially in Europe.

That evening Jacob brought Catherine into the barn for what he described as a most important lesson in life. He bound her tightly to a chair, easily overcoming her struggles. Jacob was much too strong for her to put up any meaningful resistance. He then walked over to a nearby stall and picked up the runaway Hassy, unclothed and bound, and with every appearance of having been beaten. Her eyes were filled with terror as he tied her to a barn pole. Hassy was fully expecting to have her back whipped mercilessly, as had been the custom with runaway slaves at the time. But instead, she was tied facing out, with her bound hands hooked on a peg above her head, and her feet bound together as well, toes barely touching the ground. Jacob then turned to Catherine.

"This is what happens to those who betray me. Remember what you see here tonight, and learn." And then, removing his ivory handled knife from its sheath, Jacob proceeded to expertly slice young Hassy to ribbons. The viciousness and brutality of the attack was not lost on the disbelieving Catherine. It was obvious that he had done this sort of thing before, and fully delighted in it. Terror gripped Catherine as she realized that sooner or later Hassy's fate could very well be hers as well.

Later that evening, long after Catherine had been escorted under guard back to her room, Jacob visited her with a proposal of marriage, promising a life of luxury and happiness. She knew to refuse his offer meant a horrible death.

She had little choice but to accept his proposal. Still, using her wits, she asked Jacob to delay the wedding two days so that she would have time to prepare herself for their wedding night. He readily agreed, happy that she was so willingly obliging to his offer.

Judge Bennet, all but owned by Jacob, and partner to his crimes, hurriedly performed the ceremony as two of Jacob's hired thugs bore witness. An hour later Jacob visited his new wife's bedroom to collect his prize. It had all been so easy. Catherine wore only a loose fitting embroidered gown, open in the front. She would humor her new husband and allow him whatever he asked of her. But her mother had taught her well the ways of nature and the many uses of the herbs and plants which grew nearby. The drugged wine she gave to him quickly took its toll. Jacob fell into a deep sleep, and was not aware of his bride's late night escape upon her great black horse into the dark Virginia countryside. The dogs could not find her trail.

That had been eight months ago. And now, there Catherine lay, bound to the posts of the bed Rhen had brought with him to this prairie wasteland. Somehow Jacob had found her and as she looked upon the ivory handled knife stuck into the bedpost, she could once again hear Hassy's screams of agony, screams that she knew would soon be hers.

"You're thinner now, you know." Jacob walked the few steps over to the bed and sat down beside her. She reeled from his touch, but bound as she was, she could hardly move at all. Despite her efforts, he was going to do whatever he wished. In a last ditch effort at survival, she dredged up an old forgotten story, hoping to buy time.

"If you kill me, you'll never find the gold." Jacob smiled that sinister smile of his and she knew at once that it hadn't worked.

"You may be right of course. But your father wasn't such a clever man that I won't be able to find it sooner or later, if it even exists. You, however, are far too dangerous to me alive. You know too much. You had your chance, yet you betrayed me, and on our wedding night of all things! Did you think I would take a thing like that lying down? Did you? No, my dear, I will not! Instead, it appears you will be the one who takes it lying down, in a manner of speaking."

Jacob laughed at his own joke, pleased with his cleverness. He was in charge now. Her bonds were too tight for her to offer any resistance. He was going to enjoy this. After all those months on the hunt, vengeance was his. Her screams of agony would be all the apology he would ever need.

"At last, we're together again, my dear. And who would blame a man for wanting to enjoy the company of his beautiful bride before her untimely death? And by the way, thank you for the stew. It was delicious." Jacob removed his top coat and shoulder holster, hanging them on a nearby chair. He then loosened his trousers and climbed onto the bed. His property was his again, at long last.

Catherine's fears turned into unbridled terror. She trembled and wept bitterly, helpless before this man's assault. Poor Rhen! All his plans and dreams! She should have told him about Jacob. He was too good a man to have died that way. It was all her fault!

Her brave façade was gone, for there would be no way out this time. Catherine's mind, faced with this violation of life itself, reverted to its primal state, and drawing from the deepest vestiges of her soul, she gave one last desperate appeal to the spirits of her people, to heaven itself, and to all the angels above.

She screamed.

Coming around to the east side of the barn, Conger tied the mule to some bushes under the large cottonwood which shaded the area. He walked quietly around to the front of the barn, glad now to be wearing the moccasins he had exchanged earlier in lieu of his riding boots, which were not suited to miles of walking. His steps made almost no sound on the short green grass. He glanced into the barn, but saw nothing inside. He did however see large posts, like long corral posts lying sideways at the door, but he couldn't make out their purpose.

Somehow, this place seemed familiar. He was certain he had never been there before, but still… He shook all that out of his mind and got back to the matter at hand.

Looking down, he saw what appeared to be drag marks on the ground. Something heavy had been drug around to the back of the barn, and very recently. Will unsnapped his cavalry holster and removed the pistol. There was blood on the grass as well, and it was certain now that foul play was involved here---grass doesn't bleed.

At the back of the barn, he found his answer. A very large man lay face up on the ground. He had a crimson stain on his chest, and had been dragged there, apparently from where he had been shot. Will had seen dead men aplenty during the war, and he knew this was one of them. It did not require close examination to see that he had been dead only a short time, and that chances were that whoever had shot him was still somewhere around.

Close by a roan horse was tied up to a post, partially hidden by a second cottonwood. He thought immediately of the pile of horse apples he found below the hill, and made the connection. Will decided not to approach the roan for a closer look, fearing that it might whinny in the presence of a stranger, and warn its rider. He had already determined that the dead man on the ground had never ridden that horse, as it was far too small to have carried his weight, especially as the horse showed every indication of having come quite a distance.

Circling back toward the house, Will saw something he hadn't noticed before. There was a laundry line hung from the barn with fresh wash drying in the gentle breeze. Among the clothes on the line were dresses and other women's things he knew little about. If there was a woman here, she might be in hiding somewhere, or she might be up at the house and possibly in serious trouble. There could be other answers, too. Perhaps the stranger on the horse wasn't all that unwelcome after all, at least not to someone.

But somehow that just didn't make sense. Why leave the body out in the open like that? And why was the door to the house closed on such a warm day? Using the clothes on the line as cover, Will crept slowly over to the corner of the house. He thought he heard a man's voice coming from inside. The voice was steady and calm, but he could not make out the words. Pistol still drawn, Will was just about to call out, demanding an explanation for what had happened here, but glancing to the north he saw something else that didn't belong there---a column of dark smoke far into the distance.

Appraising the smoke, it seemed likely that some poor family had the misfortune of their home or barn to catch fire. It happened often enough. The smoke was far off, and represented several hours of riding time to get there. He couldn't ride over to help them anyway, as he didn't have a horse at that moment. Those folks were on their own.

Conger heard the man's voice again, and could almost make out the words this time: something about lying down, and then laughter. At once, Conger felt ashamed. Why there he was, eavesdropping! Whatever was going on in there was probably none of his business. But then again, there was the matter of a man dead on the ground no more than a stone's throw behind him, that plus the fact that someone had been in hiding, watching the farm. And for what purpose? Enough already. He would knock on the door and get to the bottom of it.

The matter having finally been decided with himself, Will straightened up, and overcoming his better judgment, started to knock.

Then she screamed.

William Conger had been raised a gentleman. He had been taught to treat every woman as a lady, whether she deserved it or not. He stood when a woman walked into a room, and held the chair for her until she had been made comfortable. He had never taken liberties with any woman, and stood for a woman's honor even when that honor could easily have been brought into question. Conger had given more than one man a good thrashing for lewd comments carelessly bandied about concerning the young women in this community. This was his way.

He heard the scream. He had heard screams before, from men and women alike. There was nothing within him which would allow him not to act, not to respond to this cry for help. His gun was already out and in his hand, and with his mind made up, he sprang into action, giving the wood plank door a mighty kick.

But Will had forgotten that he was still wearing his moccasins. The soft leather had little impact on the door, but the impact on his foot was intense. All he had managed to do was to create a loud booming noise, and cause himself a great deal of pain.

Still, Conger's fine Welsh tenor voice shared space with an Irish temper bred from his mother's side. The fury within him already kindled by the woman's scream now boiled over into a rage. He lowered his shoulder and viciously attacked the defiant door and the evil it protected. The door splintered under the onslaught, while Conger's momentum carried him off balance into the house, causing him to fly headlong over the table and chairs which stood in his way. Dishes and food scattered throughout the room as he landed head first onto the hard packed dirt floor, with plates and cups crashing all around him. The impact reopened the wound on his head, and he had to fight to maintain the grip on his pistol. The pain was intense.

Looking up, Conger saw a man on a bed, his features filled with a horrified venom. A quick glance sideways saw a woman on the bed as well, undressed, and with a least one arm tied off to the bedpost. The man had his trousers down, and was balancing himself on his knees as he turned to deal with this intruder.

McPhearson was stunned with disbelief by this stranger's sudden appearance, fearing at first that it was Rhen Larson raised from the dead. He had been certain there was no one within twenty miles of this place, and had felt no need to be on guard. But Jacob quickly recovered, and sizing up this new opponent, reached over to retrieve the pistol he had left hanging on the chair nearby.

Still on the floor, with gun in hand, Conger saw the man's intent and opened up, firing three shots in rapid succession. Those shots did not miss at such short range. McPhearson went limp and could not control his fall, flipping over the footboard, and landing face up with arms out-flung. His head and neck lay twisted in an unnatural position.

Conger held his gun on the man as he pulled himself up. Through the haze of gunpowder filling the room, he saw that the man's eyes were still open and active, but the awkward way in which he had landed indicated a man with a broken neck, and most likely unable to move. The man's gun belt still hung menacingly over the nearby chair. Conger moved it to a peg on the wall, away from the fallen man, just in case.

Convinced that this fellow was not going anywhere, Conger worked to summon up enough nerve to look over toward the bed. Part of him was fearful of what sort of harm the man might have done to the woman before he had managed to stop him. His other concern was that he was certain the woman was wearing nothing, and truth be told, he would be embarrassed to look upon a woman without her clothes. Gentlemen didn't do such things. Will Conger was a gentleman.

Will finally summoned up the courage, and looking over to his right, gazed upon a sight which took his breath away. She was beautiful. Bound as she was, there was no part of her which was hidden. He looked down upon her as though he had somehow known her all of his life, and that doing so was the most natural and proper thing he would ever do. He studied every line of her lovely form with reverence and awe. He just stood there and stared, not in lust, but rather in pure amazement.

For Catherine a whole new threat had just appeared. She did not know her rescuer, and for all she knew, he was just a likely to take advantage of her helpless condition as the man lying on the floor. She had to think clearly and quickly to get herself free of those bonds, and find a means of protecting herself. Still, the young man staring at her was rather good looking, and had the most gentle expression in his eyes, almost innocent, as though he had never seen a woman undressed before. She considered the possibility.

"Pardon me sir," she spoke softly, with a Southern belle accent that could fell a pecan tree. "Would you be so kind as to cut me loose from these straps that terrible man put on me? They are very uncomfortable and prevent me from showing proper modesty in the presence of a gentleman."

Will was instantly ashamed for his impudence. His mother would be boxing his ears something awful for such an unmannerly thing. Turning red, he immediately pulled out his clasp knife, and trying to avert his gaze as much as possible, went about cutting her bonds. Not thinking, he nearly lay upon her as he cut the straps holding her wrist and ankles on the far side of the bed. He saw blood on the pillow, but chose not to say anything about it right then, for fear of frightening the girl.

Catherine took his clumsiness in stride, grateful for being released, and not wanting to anger this man in her position, as he held a knife in one hand, and a pistol in the other. So far, so good.

Her bonds cut away, Will turned his attention back to the man on the floor. He had not moved, and his breathing was becoming increasingly hoarse. His eyes were starting to fade, and it was apparent that he didn't have much longer to live. The girl rose up off the bed, a bit shaky at first, no doubt Will thought, as a result of the wound on her head. Will folded his knife and offered his hand to steady her.

Wringing her wrists, she worked at getting the feeling back into her hands. Surprisingly, she made no effort to cover herself, and the look on her face was no longer that of the gentle, helpless girl who had so sweetly asked for help only a few moments earlier. Now, only fury and rage shown in her eyes.

Will stepped aside as she walked around the end of the bed and looked down at her assailant. For his part, Conger was ashamed that he had made no move to cover the man, for his pants were still down to his ankles after his fall, a sight no lady, especially this one, should be forced to see. Still worrying about her modesty, Will was justifiably stunned as the girl stood directly above the man, and pulling the ivory handled knife from the bedpost, proceeded to drive the blade deep into his lower abdomen, again and again.

"That's for what you did to Hassy." She spoke, with a voice quivering with rage, and spit in his face.

Conger stared in disbelief. He had never seen anyone do such a thing, much less a woman, and truly did not know just how to react to what he had just witnessed. The man's blood flowed freely, and his agony was terrible to witness. Conger realized that it was possible that the girl had gone mad, and that her actions reflected a sort of insanity brought about by the man's attack upon her. But she had spoken of Hassy, and had acted as that person's avenger. Apparently there was some dark history between these two, of which Will could only guess. It might not be madness after all.

The man groaned and coughed, choking on his own blood, unable to speak, but clearly able to experience the emotional and physical pain this woman had inflicted upon him. Will chose to make no effort to stop her. He would grant the girl the privilege of her vengeance, no matter how distasteful it might be. This man had it coming.

The girl then stepped over to where Will had hung the man's gun on the peg. She unholstered the pistol, and then stood over him once again.

"And this is for Rhen." She proceeded to empty the gun into McPhearson's chest, slowly, one bullet at a time, cocking the hammer and using both hands to pull the heavy trigger. Again, Will made no move to stop her. He had no idea who Rhen was, but assumed it was the big man he saw lying dead behind the barn. The bullets hit home, and the man's life was silenced. Her terrible revenge was now complete.

Conger still had his pistol out, having become so mesmerized by the act of vengeance before him, that he had given little if any thought as to what he was doing. Breaking down the door and saving the girl was as far as he had planned things out. Understandably, Will was unprepared for what happened next.

The girl dropped the gun on the floor, its power spent, Satan now destroyed. She turned around, and walking the few steps to where Will was standing, buried her head into his dirty, sweat stained shirt. She cried bitter tears, clutching Will tightly, like a little child seeking comfort from a parent.

Will just stood there, for once doing the right thing. He gently put his arms around the girl, but ever so carefully, for he was still holding the pistol in his hand. They could not have stood there together for more than a minute or two, but it seemed much longer.

Something happened to Conger when she touched him. Something inside of him changed. Something was added to him that had not been there before. It was something he felt, but couldn't understand, something in his spirit. Finally Will gathered his wits, and after a time, broke the silence.

"Ma'am, it would be best if you got dressed now. We have a lot of things we need to do here, and I'm going to need your help. Could you do that for me?" She raised her head and looked into his eyes, searching for something that only a woman would know how to find. He gently released her, and stepping back, returned his gun to its holster. Will then went over to the bed, and removing a blood stained blanket, covered the man's lifeless body. Conger had seen enough.

The girl seemed to be in a trance, unable to move, staring down at the remains of what appeared to be a pink dress which had been cut to shreds, and laid in pieces now by the side of the bed. Will was just now beginning to comprehend the terror her attacker must have put her through. Such scars could take a long time to heal. He would try once more to get her moving.

"I'm sorry I ruined your door ma'am, but I can fix it later. Right now I'll just step outside while you get dressed." Getting the girl dressed had nothing to do with modesty. Will had long since gotten used to seeing her the way she was and felt surprisingly comfortable with it all. But if he was going to get her through all of this, he needed to at least get her world back to some form of normalcy. He would see to it that burials were made and try to get her to family, or at least to a neighbor's place, where the womenfolk could help her get through this, somehow.

Conger walked out the door and stopped short. He had forgotten about the column of smoke he had seen earlier to the north. That might have been as long as an hour ago, given all that had transpired since. There were now three columns of smoke on the West Kansas skyline, each closer to this farm than the first. Suddenly a fourth smoke became visible, this one much closer. They needed to get out of there, and fast.

chapter 3

CONGER RAN BACK into the house only to find the girl half dressed, still staring at what remained of her pink dress. Her fixation testified to the humiliation she had suffered at the hand of her attacker, and of his affection for that knife of his. He had cut the dress from her, Will assumed, no doubt as a sampling of what he intended to do to her later on, after first taking his pleasure. Such a threat could explain her actions with the knife, as the man laid sprawled on the floor.

Will started to speak, but held his tongue, realizing that dressed or not, it had been a mistake for him to leave her alone with that man's body lying there at her feet. He didn't know much about womenfolk and their ways, but he had seen battle shock before, and this girl had it. He needed to take charge of things here and now, and be quick about it.

"Ma'am, we're going to have to leave here right away. The Indians are burning the farms to the north of us, and we may be next. You'll need to finish dressing while I get some things together. We only have a few minutes time." Conger had no idea how this girl might react to what he had said, but he knew he had to be blunt and to the point, and forceful if it came to that.

The girl had put on a cotton pullover shirt, the kind most farmers would be seen wearing in the fields those days. It was much too large, but covered her pretty well, but she still needed some trousers, or something. Will told her so.

Catherine was preoccupied, remembering the big day she had planned for her and Rhen together. The rabbit stew was going to be her best effort yet, and she had intended to whip up a batch of corn pudding later on. She had hoped to walk out onto the prairie hand in hand with Rhen, if just for a little while, and listen to the wind in the grass, and the call of the birds. Catherine had always felt as one with the spirits of the earth which surrounded her. She hadn't asked much of her life here in the middle of this beautiful desolation, but had somehow hoped that she could have just this one day for herself, something special, something happy. Then, somehow Conger's words sank in.

"What are you saying about fires? How do you know about fires?" She still seemed in a stupor, but at least she was talking again. Will noticed that the Southern accent was missing, replaced instead with something very different, something clipped but melodic. Who was this dark haired girl?

Will led her out through the doorway, but didn't have to point. She saw what he saw, and gasped, suddenly aware of towers of smoke where none should be. She turned slowly, and walking back inside, reached into a canvas bag which hung from a peg by the door. She pulled out a short but deadly looking double barreled shotgun, the same one she had dropped the rabbit with the day before. Turning a chair back upright, she sat down facing the door, her face wearing a look of iron determination that Will would never forget.

"Ma'am, we have to go now. It isn't safe here. Hurry and dress, there's no time." Will's voice was a little more insistent now. What was she doing?

"You go ahead sir, and I thank you for your concern. I would ask that you take my horse with you. She is in the barn. Speak to her softly and she'll be alright. Please go now." Will wasn't buying any of this nonsense. He had seen no horse in the barn, and he certainly had no mind to leave this girl behind for the savages while he ran safely away.

"Ma'am, I must insist. It is not safe for you here. We must leave and get to a place of safety. If I'm not mistaken, Fort Davis is not far from here. We need to hurry."

The girl stood up, and looked Conger straight in the eye. Even in her bare feet, she was nearly as tall as he. She seemed to be looking into the depths of his soul, representing a presence, wise and ancient, the likes of which Will had never encountered before.

"Hear me brave knight. You have rescued me from a terrible death at the hands of a man who I once considered to be my friend. His name was Jacob McPhearson, and he was my uncle. He somehow followed me here, to the middle of nothing, to take his revenge on me. I know my husband's body lays out there by the barn. I saw Jacob shoot him down. Rhen didn't have a chance. He never carried a gun. He didn't know about Jacob, I never told him, and now he's dead because of me." Conger started to reply, but she silenced him.

"Be still, and listen! Today I have been widowed and raped, and I have cut and murdered a man solely for my own personal vengeance. He was evil and vile and I have put an end to him. You sir, did not kill him, you only stopped him from doing again what he had done before. I thank you for that and for allowing me the chance to free this earth of his filth."

Will was astonished by her words. He did not recall ever hearing such powerful things spoken by the tongue of one so young. But her impassioned plea had not yet ended.

"I have done these things, and you are witness to them. I cannot leave this place. It is bad enough that you, a total stranger, have looked upon me without my clothes, and in the most compromising of positions. How am I to live in polite society, like a decent woman, with these things on my conscience? Sooner or later the truth would be known. How am I to provide for myself? I will not become some man's toy in return for a roof over my head."

"No sir, I will not leave. I would rather suffer whatever fare the Cheyenne have in store for me than the stares and gossip of the women and the leering looks of the men. I am a widow, and I have been ravaged, but I am not a harlot. I still have my pride, and I will die here alongside my husband in the house that he built for us with his own two hands. I will thank you to take your leave now sir, before it's too late, so that I won't have your death on my conscience as well." With that, she sat back down, and stared out the door, fixing her gaze on the horizon once again.

Confound it all! Arguing with a woman at a time like this was a wasted effort. It was as though she welcomed death at the hands of the Indians, to somehow free her from the torment of her past. Her uncle? What sort of family must this be? There had to be more to this story than she was telling. But to wait around here to hear the rest of it would surely mean getting his hair lifted, or worse.

Conger stalked out of the house in disgust. He took a deep breath and looked around him. What a nice little place they had built there. It had all the makings of a first class farm. Her husband had worked with great skill and vision. Will wished he had known the man.

This McPhearson fellow had left his horse tied up out back. Conger could ride it out of there right then and be done with it. She had said something about a horse in the barn, but looking over, he still did not see one. It just didn't make sense. He glanced over at the farmer's body lying there in the grass, and recalled the hundreds of other dead men he had seen on battlefields across the South. They were young and strong too, with fresh faces, many not yet even old enough to shave. Each of those men had meant something to someone, somewhere, but they would never be coming home. Mankind seems forever destined to author its own tragedies.

Conger had never been able to make sense of war, even as he himself had participated in the carnage. But whatever the case, it was for those left alive to build what was next for this world. He then realized that it had fallen to him to write the next chapter in this girl's life. Suddenly he knew what he must do. It made perfect sense, somehow.

Will walked quickly back to the house, ignoring the columns of smoke to the north, and the ticking clock they represented. He had this thing to do. If he had not intervened, the girl would most likely be dead by now, with her murderer running free. If he was indeed responsible for saving her life, it then made no sense to allow her to die so needlessly, after the fact. If this made him a fool, so be it.

He stepped back through the door, finding the girl still sitting in the chair where he had left her, but that hardened look of defiance was now missing, replaced instead by the look of a lost child, not knowing her way home, as the whole world collapsed in around her. Will bent down and touched her hand.

"Ma'am, you are too good a woman to be lost in this way. You are right in what you said about the way people would treat you. Folks can be cruel to a woman out on her own, and you have suffered enough already."

She had not yet looked up at him as he spoke, but he could tell she was listening. Will took a deep breath. What he would say next seemed impossible, but it was a thing he felt from the depth of his soul, although he didn't know why. But he could not keep it still inside of him. He was somehow wonderfully compelled.

"Ma'am, I know this is sudden, but circumstances will not allow for a proper courtship." She suddenly looked up, and seeing the sincerity in his eyes, felt her heart skip a beat. This could not be happening!

"I cannot leave you behind. I want you to come with me, and stay with me." Will's tongue was dry and his aching head hurt more than ever. Part of him suddenly wanted to excuse himself and run for cover, but he stood, and gathered himself.

"Ma'am, I am a good man, and I swear I will never harm you. If you would be willing to take a chance on me, I would very much like it if you would be my wife."

There it was. And at that moment neither one of them could believe he had just said what he had said.

They just stared at one another, neither one able to say anything. The silence seemed to last forever, but it was really only for a few seconds. Now and then time really does stand still.

There was something inside of Catherine that did not wish to die. That is why she had screamed. That is why she had run from the clutches of Jacob McPhearson back in Virginia. It made no sense to end her life now. Even after all of this, she had no real desire for her life to end. She was simply ashamed. But this man, who knew nothing about her, had offered to take her by his side, and make her his wife. How could this be?

Catherine knew that he could have taken advantage of her, tied up and helpless as she was. He could have demanded favors for her release. But he had not. She somehow knew that he was not that kind of man, and never could be. Even after all that he had witnessed, he was unwilling to leave without her. It made no sense. Nothing made sense. But it all seemed right, somehow.

"I accept your offer for marriage, sir. I will go where you wish me to go." She was amazed she had said such a thing, but she was content and comfortable with her decision. Somehow her world seemed right again.

If Conger was relieved, or happy, or anything, it didn't show. He was still too stunned by what he had just done to react. Instead, it was time to get down to business. Captain William Conger of the Illinois Sixth once again began barking orders. It was time to get moving.

"Thank you Ma'am. Now if you would please finish dressing, and tell me what you need to take along with you."

"I'll be ready in a very few minutes, sir." She had somehow already thought the whole thing out, and knew what needed to be done.

"If you would, please sir, bring my husband's body in from the yard and place him on the bed. It just wouldn't do to leave him out there like that. I realize we don't have enough time for a proper burial."

All things considered, Conger could do no less than agree to the task he was being given. She was making sense now, and he wanted to keep things on track. He walked out to where the big farmer lay, wondering to himself just how he was going to move his enormous frame. After two attempts to lift him failed, Will yielded to reality, and grabbing the man's arms, dragged the lifeless body back toward the house. It was a struggle.

By the time he got to the front door, she was already dressed, with four canvas bags lined up beside her there in the yard, ready to leave just as she had promised. Will saw her and felt ashamed, apologizing for the rough handling of her deceased husband's body. He was forced to admit to her that he was unable to lift the man.

Catherine had watched his struggles and was heartened by the determination this young man had shown in his effort to follow her wishes. In truth, she had given no thought to what an impossible task she had assigned to him. She was not sure that she had ever met a man who could have lifted Rhen Larson off the ground.

She smiled at Will. It was the first time he had ever seen her smile. It was a beautiful smile. Without saying a word, they worked together to get Rhen's body into the house. Will was surprised at the strength this girl could muster. Eventually the two of them got the body onto the bed, with arms folded across his chest. This was a difficult and delicate moment, and yet this girl handled it with a maturity and grace beyond her years. Still, Conger was surprised by her next request.

"Please Sir, bring in as much of the firewood as possible and stack it around the bed. Do hurry." There she was, giving him orders again.

It took four trips to bring in all the firewood which was cut and stacked up against the house. As instructed, Will leaned the wood up on end around the base of the bed, while she went back to the barn and fetched up Rhen's trusty hoe. She lay the hoe across Rhen's massive chest, with the handle resting under his arm.

"Rhen often spoke of the ancient Viking funerals of his people back in Norway. They would lay the fallen chieftain in his ship, with his slaves at his feet, and burn the ship and its contents in tribute." Her face clearly showed the love and respect she had for her fallen husband.

"Rhen built this house. It's the closest thing to a ship he'll ever have. Uncle Jacob would have detested the idea of his being someone's slave, so I believe it is fitting to leave him lying at the foot of the bed, right where he is." There was a gleam in the girl's eye now. Here was a way to bring her past to a close, and with one additional advantage.

"I'm hoping that when the Cheyenne see the smoke from this house, they will assume that others from their tribe have been here already, and bypass this place to go on to the next. That might buy us the time we'll need to get away." Will hadn't thought of that. For a grieving widow, she certainly had a clear head about her.

Catherine had Conger to pour the contents of two large jars of lamp oil onto the bodies, and onto the wood they had stacked around the bed. They quickly exited the house to get away from the potent fumes. The girl then threw a shovelful of hot coals she had pulled from the fireplace back into the house, immediately igniting the oil. Something appropriate probably should have been said right then, but there were no words left. She threw the shovel in as well.

They were forced to back away as the flames caught the dry wood, and black smoke shot through the unrepaired doorway and up into the sky. There were now five columns of smoke drifting across the West Kansas skyline.

Picking up her four canvas bags, they made their way to the barn. Will still saw no horse, and was wondering just how they were going to ride out of there. He wasn't certain the stranger's horse could carry double, at least not for any distance. He could try to ride the mule, but figured that attempt would only meet with disaster, as it had only ever been used as a pack mule and never been ridden before. He could walk, but his foot was still aching from his earlier attempt to kick down the door. To make things worse, his head had started pounding again.

The heavy poles which had mystified Will earlier in the day lay undisturbed across the opening. At her request, Will took them down and set them aside. The girl then spoke softly in a language he did not understand, and a smile once again appeared on her face.

Suddenly, rising up from the stalls, powerful and dark as night, stood the biggest horse Will Conger had ever seen. Now he had seen big horses before, being raised on a horse farm near Lexington he had seen all manner of horses coming and going. Draft horses were bred mostly for plowing, with great power to pull through heavy soil, and possessing the gentle nature preferred for farm work. The army used the big brutes to move supply wagons and field artillery, and occasionally some self-admiring General or some such would ride atop some big old horse to make himself look more important. The enlisted men called those 'ladder horses', as a fellow was going to need a ladder to climb up to the top of such a mount.

But this horse overshadowed any of those. It had to be eighteen hands or more, and its lines spoke of immense power. And it was a mare! Watching it rise from the stall, Will could see how he had missed it. He expected to find horses standing up. They even slept standing up. But with a body this massive, perhaps it was easier for the mare to lay down while at rest, so as not to put undue weight on its legs. Still, those legs looked stout enough to carry a wagon, not just pull it.

The mare came out from the barn and walked right over to the girl. They nuzzled and rubbed one another for a few moments of reunion, and then the horse did something even more astounding. Again speaking words that Conger did not recognize, the girl gave instruction to the horse, which in turn proceeded to kneel down flat on the ground before her. Catherine then hung two thick blankets over the horse's massive back, and over these draped the four canvas bags tied in pairs.

Smoke from the burning house was beginning to shift toward the barn, and Will mentioned that they needed to be getting away from there. The girl seemed indifferent to the effect the fire was having on the contents of the little house she had so recently called home. Catherine simply nodded in agreement, and climbed aboard that big black mare, with no saddle or reins to be seen. Again following only verbal commands, the big horse gracefully stood up, and turning to the left, walked to the back of the barn where the roan horse remained tied.

Will was still shaking his head in disbelief of what he had just seen, as he brought the mule over to where the roan was standing. The horse seemed to welcome the mule's company, and accepted Will's reassuring manner without hesitation. After a brief exchange of neighs and whinnies, the newly formed parade headed down a brief incline toward the river.

The animals drank eagerly, each having been away from water for some time. From the looks of things, it was clear to Conger that the mule had eaten just about everything within reach during his absence, and would most likely suffer a belly-ache for it the next day. Served him right, Conger mused. The girl stayed on her mount as it drank, while Will topped off each of their six canteens upriver from where the livestock were watering.

Knowing the way, the girl then led the party down stream about two hundred feet to a place where it would be easy to ford the river. The horses and the mule seemed grateful to be moving out again, and took to the trail with genuine enthusiasm. Of course, using the word 'trail' would be an overstatement in this case, as their route was more of a direction than a well-worn path. Roads were pretty scarce out that way, and what few there were, often had to be detoured due to high water, drought, prairie fire, buffalo, Indians, or just plain bad luck.

The big black mare took the lead, its rider presumably knowing where they were headed, and how to get there. Will had mentioned Fort Davis, and assumed that was where they were going. He really didn't wish to bring the matter up right then and there, as anywhere had to be safer than back at the farm. Plus, traveling would give them something to do, and hopefully would help the girl forget the events of the day, if only for a while.

Now it's true that a man of Welsh-Irish decent will find it hard to keep still even when there is no one else around to talk to. But in the presence of another person, or even a mule for that matter, he can become downright chatty. Will had been doing his best not to disturb the girl's solitude, but there were a few nagging questions which needed answers.

"Excuse me Ma'am, but it would be helpful for me to know your name, if you'd please. I feel awkward calling you Ma'am all the time." Conger was a little taken aback by the long silence that hung in the air before she replied. He had expected an immediate answer.

"You may call me Catherine. I suppose it would be proper for me to know your name as well." Well, at least they were talking now.

"My name is William Conger. I am from Kentucky. Where do you come from, Catherine?" Conger thought he was doing well here. After all, now that he had asked the girl to marry him, and she had accepted, the least they could do was get acquainted.

"I was born and raised in Western Virginia, near the mountains."

"Tell me about your family." Again, silence, and now Will felt like a fool. If that had really been her uncle, she might not wish to talk about her family, or even be thinking about them for that matter. This wasn't going to be easy. He tried a different approach.

"Your mare is a beautiful horse. Did you name her?" They were obviously close, so maybe the girl would talk about that. He thought that talking might do her good."

" Mr. Conger, I thank you for your interest, and I will be happy to answer any and all questions you might have at another time. At this moment, however, it would serve me best to remain still, and to concentrate on the task at hand. Please do not think me rude. I really do want to visit with you, but not just now."

Right then Will felt very much put in his place, and was. But he liked this girl's spirit, and understood that since women were different than men, that her working things out quietly might be the best thing for her. Truth be known, Catherine would have loved to have sat down with this young man and visited for hours. She had so many questions she wanted to ask him. But this was not the time. She wasn't all that sure that the diversion of the fire at the house would do the trick, be they Cheyenne as she believed, or maybe even Washazhe. She fully expected pursuit. It was important now that she listen to the voices of the grasslands, to the sounds of the wind, the trees, and the birds in the air. She hoped they could get far enough away in time. She knew the danger, for the odds were against them.

Almost nothing was said between them during the next two hours, as neither was inclined to talk. The girl rode cross-legged on the mare, her mind distracted, as one would expect after the day she had already endured. Still, her eyes were busy, constantly looking about, seeing nothing, but aware of another presence, nearby and getting closer.

Conger rode behind her, still hoping she knew the way to Fort Davis, or at least had a good idea. Truth was, she and Rhen had been there twice since coming into the Cimarron basin, and she did have a pretty good idea. Rhen never ever seemed to get lost, so she hadn't much bothered to pay attention to where they were going. She could kick herself now for not watching more closely. Instead she was forced to look for any features on the land which she could recognize. There was no such thing as a road sign in Western Kansas, but thankfully, for their purposes, west was still west.

Suddenly Catherine stopped, and like an acrobat, she quickly stood up atop that big horse and looked back to the east. She had sensed pursuit, and looked to find what she knew in her heart was there. They were close now. The danger was very near.

Will stopped short as well. This little roan handled quite nicely, and showed some breeding. Somehow it didn't seem possible that a brute like McPhearson could own a gentle beast such as this. Of course, Will didn't know that the horse was stolen, or to whom the horse actually belonged.

After a minute or so, the girl sat back down, and remained there in thought for a few seconds. She then turned back to Will with a determined look filled with dead seriousness.

"Mr. Conger, we need to stop right away, and find a place to make camp." She had yet to use his first name.

"Don't you think we should go on a little further? We have at least another hour of sunlight left." Will hated to argue with the girl, but he believed in traveling while the traveling was good, which it was right then, or so he thought.

"We are being followed sir, and have been for the last several miles. I believe them to be Cheyenne. If we continue as we are, we won't be alive in another hour. We must stop and plan a defense." Her face had not changed. Speaking softly, she continued.

"You are obviously new to these grasslands, sir. Out here it is easy not to see that which is in plain sight. We are being surrounded as we speak, and need to get over to that ridge as quickly as possible. But we dare not look like we're in a hurry. There's no time to talk now. Please follow me."

She rode off leaving Will just sitting there in wonderment. He had seen no one following them. Either that bump on her head was affecting her judgment, or she knew something he didn't know. Remembering that he had failed to see the world's biggest horse in a half-finished barn, Will swallowed his pride, and with a deep sigh of resignation, turned the roan and followed after her. He was tired of riding anyway, and would welcome a hot cup of coffee.

It only took a couple of minutes to get to the rocky ridge she had mentioned. It wasn't all that different from many other places Will had seen there along the river. This outcropping of stone butted up to the water for several hundred feet in either direction, and had a stand of cottonwood and some other trees that Conger did not recognize along the riverbank. She had chosen this spot quickly and wisely. Will could immediately see the strategic advantage of this place, as approach from the rear would be difficult, and getting through the underbrush would likely create too much noise.

By the time Will caught up to her she had already dismounted and was making improvements to the campsite. His sore foot had no more than touched the ground than she was giving orders again.

"Mr. Conger, we well need a very large fire, right about here." She marked the spot with a rock. It was some distance from the river, and seemed too far away from where Will figured they should make camp, to be of much use. He started to say something to that effect, but decided against it. If she said they needed a fire, they needed a fire. If she said there were Cheyenne, then there were Cheyenne. He'd never met one himself, but chances were, living out here, she might well know more about them than he did. He commenced to build a fire.

Catherine was busy moving dried branches and such to the perimeter of the camp. Dead, dry branches were difficult to move through without creating a lot of racket. She wanted only one approach to be available. Catherine knew how desperate their situation was, and was wishing she had a better weapon than her shotgun.

The sun was just beginning to set, and Will had the fire up and going with plenty of spare wood ready to add to the flames. Deadfalls were plentiful there, most likely the result of strong winds which had plowed through sometime in the recent past. There were no signs of anyone else having camped there lately, but all in all she had chosen a good site.

"Do you have a rifle, Mr. Conger? We may need one very soon. I only have a shotgun, and it doesn't have much range." It was unusual for Will to hear a woman talking about guns, as it had been uncommon for women to do much, if any, shooting back home. He did recall that his mother had shot a raccoon that was pestering the chickens one night, but that just seemed fitting, as his father was away on business at the time. Still, Will was pleased, as this was finally his time to shine.

"Yes, Ma'am, I have several firearms here." Will began by unpacking the rifles. He then went to the other side of the mule and pulled out some side arms, still in holster. By the time he got back around Catherine was already testing the sights of one of the Colt repeating rifles. Conger was horrified.

"Pardon me Ma'am," he forgot to say her name again, "but I think one of the smaller pistols might suit you better. That's a substantial weapon you're holding there." He moved to take the Colt rifle away.

"Mr. Conger, I am not a novice when it comes to firearms." She pulled the gun away from his outstretched hand. "And you had best be correct when you say that this is a substantial weapon, because at this moment there are five or six Cheyenne within the sound of your voice, and we may need to shoot quickly and accurately at any time. Please save your concerns for someone else, and show me how this thing works." Will stopped arguing, and a few minutes later, she was ready to shoot.

Will had no idea how she knew where the Cheyenne were, or how many there would be, but decided to go along with her assessment. It was near dark, and any plans for defense needed to be finalized right away. Conger had been fighting an enemy in butternut brown for three years, and had become very good at it. But the plains Indians most likely did not wear butternut brown, and would have him at a disadvantage on their home turf.

Conger was as brave as the next man, and skilled in the use of firearms. But out here, knowledge would be as important as weaponry. He would learn quickly, or die.

Catherine had several strips of smoked ham roasting on sticks by the fire, with a pot of coffee nearby. There was more ham cooking than the two of them could possibly eat, and Will made comment.

"That's a lot of ham there. We expecting company?" He felt like a fool as soon as the words had fallen out of his mouth.

"Yes, Mr. Conger, we are. Anything we can do to get them off guard, the better. They have come for my horse, your guns, your horse, your mule, and me, in that order. They will kill you first. After they have all finished with me, they'll most likely kill me as well. We would be dead already had we not stopped here when we did. They almost had us encircled out there. They let us stop here because they are curious to see what we are up to. This only delays the inevitable, but it does give us a better chance in a fight."

The girl made sense. It seemed she always did. He just needed to pay more attention. She certainly wasn't one of those fine little debutants he had known back in Lexington. He was coming to appreciate the difference.

Although it didn't matter all that much at the time, the Indians pursuing them were not Cheyenne, but rather Washazhe, known to most folks as Osage. This small band of renegades had joined in on the Cheyenne raids and collected their share of the bounty. There were in fact five in the party, with one spare horse. Their leader was a fine looking buck who was known as 'Tall Tree', both for his unusual height, and his habit of wearing tree branches in his braided hair. He did not use his real name, and none knew what the tree branches were all about. He was, however, a striking figure.

Tall Tree knew all about the Larson farm, and when hostilities broke out, he was determined to get his hands on the big black mare. When he reached the farm, he found the house already destroyed by flames, but with the barn still intact. Tall Tree was no fool. When a quick inspection showed that the big horse was gone, He wasted no time burning the barn, but instead followed the tracks to see where they led. Tracking the big horse would have been easy for a child. With footfalls so immense, that horse could go nowhere without his knowing. The other two mounts were a little harder to figure. One was a saddle horse, probably being ridden by a white man, but the other tracks were inconsistent in their depth, and indicated a mule carrying heavy packs, or perhaps two smaller riders. In any case, none of the tracks indicated the weight of the huge blond man who had lived there. Tall Tree rightly assumed that he lay dead in the burned out house, and was not among those whom he now pursued.

It was Tall Tree who had led the party which had made off with Larson's oxen earlier that spring. The butchered meat was welcomed by his people, and the feat of stealing the oxen in broad daylight, and right out from under the big man's eyes, was a source of great pride. Tall Tree had watched the farm for days as he planned the theft. He had seen the girl as well, and was impressed by her shooting skills. She somehow did not seem like a white woman in the way she moved, but certainly dressed like one. The big man was slow but very strong. It would require many arrows to bring such a man down.

The Washazhe war party had been forced to travel quickly to catch up with the girl and her big mare, as it took large strides and could cover ground quickly. It seemed no effort was being made to hide their trail, either because they had no fear, or they assumed that burning their own house would keep their pursuers confused.

It was in his rush to catch up with the girl that Tall Tree made his mistake, and came up upon Will and Catherine too quickly. Somehow she had sensed their presence, and standing on the back of the horse, had spotted them as they came up over the rise. The Washazhe had already begun to fan out, giving Catherine the impression of her being encircled. Truth was, they weren't yet that far along in their plans.

Darkness would soon be upon them. The man and woman had stopped sooner than expected, and were casually eating their meal as though they suspected nothing. The Washazhe were already very near the campsite, and could smell the cooked meat. The fire burned high, and provided a clear field of vision far out from where the horses were kept. There was a tent at the back of the site, close to the river, with several packs lying near the tent. The presence of the mule and those packs explained the tracks which had been difficult to read earlier in the day.

There are some tribes who will not do battle at night, for fear that any warrior who dies in battle during the night would wander in darkness for all eternity. Still, certain individuals from those same tribes were unconvinced, and were willing to take their chances, if the prize were rich enough.

Tall Tree had gained his reputation by taking chances, and had done well. The young men following his lead that day were anxious and eager to ride with one as great in battle as Tall Tree. But so far they had been unable to penetrate the reinforced perimeter which Catherine had prepared, and were instead preparing an assault both from the front and from the river. Therefore, they could not have been more surprised when the girl, speaking in Spanish, invited them up to the fire to eat. They understood her words.

"Come and join us by the fire, brave warriors of the Cheyenne. We have food and whiskey here for you."

An invitation to a fire was serious business among the Indian tribes. The fact that she knew where they were was an embarrassment to their skills, but this invitation into the camp, especially from an enemy, was an honor not to be taken lightly. Perhaps there would be an opportunity for a trade. For many tribes, the bartering done in a trade was as much fun as a good fight.

Tall Tree accepted the invitation, and walked boldly into the campsite, bringing two warriors with him. The other two would remain hidden, ready to follow his lead. As they approached the fire, Catherine quickly determined the big man to be their leader, the other warriors being much younger.

She also noticed the scalps hanging from their belts. One of the scalps caught her eye immediately, and caused the bile to rise in her throat. It was a scalp of long red hair, curled and glowing in the firelight. The Cowan family lived about twelve miles to the north, and were known for their bright red hair. The two Cowan boys and their sister Fern had come over to help Rhen with the barn. Fern was bright and pleasant, and nearly as tall as her brothers. She and Catherine were about the same age, and enjoyed their afternoon together as they prepared a meal for the men folk.

It was obvious to Catherine that this group had raided the Cowan farm that day, and that the Cowans had lost the fight. Looking into the eyes of their swaggering leader, the one wearing Fern's hair, she was convinced that he had enjoyed his conquest too much. Fury ran through her veins. Fern Cowan had been her friend.

"We are not Cheyenne. We are Osage, great warriors. I am Tall Tree. We have come to trade for horses." He smiled, pleased to show his knowledge of the words of the Spanish. He had even used the white man's name for his tribe, Osage, instead of Washazhe, a word which the French had so badly mispronounced many years before.

Will stayed back by the tent, whittling a stick as he was often known to do. He looked for all the world to be uncaring of the events up by the fire, or of whatever the woman was doing for that matter. But in truth, from where he was sitting, Conger had a clear line of fire throughout the camp and down the river as well. The tent, while not much use for stopping bullets, would serve well to conceal his movements in a fight.

The plan had been to draw the Cheyenne up to the fire, and for the two of them to stay by the tent, using the river bank for cover. When only three of the Indians came forward, the plan was dealt a serious blow from the beginning. Will did not know where the others were hiding. She had been right again---the Indians were there alright, just like she said they were.

Catherine remained fixated on that bright red scalp, and was now forming a very different plan of action than the one she and Conger had agreed upon. She realized that even if these warriors feared the night and might not fight now, they would attack them in the morning, most likely out on the trail. Whatever was going to be done would need to be done tonight.

"We will trade," she said to Tall Tree. And with that, she turned and walked back to the tent. Pulling her shotgun from the canvas bag, she spoke quietly to Conger.

"Be ready. The shooting will start any second now." Before Will could say a word, she had turned and was walking calmly back toward the fire. Tall Tree was just finishing his brag to the others of what all he was going to do to the young woman, and they were laughing and anticipating the spectacle to come. They had no way of knowing that Catherine understood nearly every word they were saying. Not that it would have mattered. What she would do next had been decided by her anger several minutes before.

She came back to the fire, holding the shotgun clumsily, as though she had no knowledge of its use. Standing about eight feet in front of Tall Tree, she spoke the terms of her trade.

"I will trade this shotgun for the life of the woman whose hair you wear on you belt." She had spoken this time in her native Cherokee tongue, not in Spanish, and the Washazhe were at once on guard. This was no white woman. She spoke the tongue of the Cherokee. The Cherokee were known as wise and powerful with the spirits.

Just then, as if by some orchestrated cue, an owl spoke from a nearby cottonwood. The voice of the owl is the harbinger of death in the lore of many Indian tribes. Catherine heard the owl, and feeling the spirits were with her, leveled the shotgun at Tall Tree's head and fired.

There had been no warning. A shotgun blast at such close range could yield only one deadly result. Tall Tree's face disappeared under the onslaught. His companions held perfectly still, as the second barrel of the shotgun was already pointing directly at them. Will was up and in a flanking position, Colt rifle in hand. He vowed never again to be surprised by anything this girl might do.

Catherine ordered the youngest of the Washazhe to bring the other ones up to the fire or he too would die in the darkness. Soon enough, two more came out of the night, looking stunned and confused. Their leader lay dead, taken at night by dark spirits. The owl had spoken his name. These young men who would have faced a grizzly bear armed only with a knife, were terrified by what they had seen and heard. Catherine saw their fear and made the most of it.

As part of their preparation earlier, Catherine had obtained three cloth cartridges from the Colt magazines, and had wrapped them in wet leaves. These were to be used as a distraction if the need arose. There would be a short lapse of time between her dropping them into the fire and the eventual explosions. She would use them now.

"Tall Tree is dead. The owl called his name, and I delivered him to the darkness as the spirits demanded." By now, Will had worked his way around behind the young men. There would be no escape.

Catherine had assumed that the owl had most likely been frightened by the sound of the shotgun and had flown away, so she secretly dropped the cartridges into the fire to create more "magic." But no sooner had she dropped the cartridges, did that persistent owl give off another hoot for good measure. The Washazhe cringed before her shotgun.

Taking the unexpected cue, Catherine stepped back a few feet, and proceeded to give a great oration in her native tongue. She proclaimed that she now owned the soul of Tall Tree, and would make him her slave.

Furthermore, she informed them that the woman with the red hair had been her servant, and that they had angered her by taking the woman's hair. She warned them that both the great black horse and the man were her servants as well, and therefore were never to be harmed.

"I am on a journey to the far mountains to make sacrifice to the Great Spirit for the People of the earth." By this they understood that she was referring to all the many tribes.

"If I do not complete my journey, all the People will perish beneath the wheels of the white man's wagons. I see by the scalps on your belts that you have killed many of my servants this day. How am I to complete my journey for the sake of the People, when fools like Tall Tree take away my servants on earth? The Spirits are angry!"

Just then the cartridges exploded in rapid succession. Sparks flew from the fire and showered the Washazhe with hot coals. If they weren't convinced before, they certainly were now. This woman was surely who she said she was. They were standing on hallowed ground.

Catherine then walked over to Conger, and handing him her shotgun, took his knife in trade. She walked back over to the faceless body of Tall Tree, and cutting off his belt, proceeded to cast Tall Tree's trophied scalps into the fire. She then ordered the other Washazhe to throw the scalps they carried into the fire as well, along with the clothes they wore, and the weapons they carried. Under the steady aim of Will and his Colt rifle, the young warriors quickly obliged, not wanting to anger this Spirit Woman. They were ordered to throw Tall Tree's clothes and weapons into the fire as well. She had one thing left to say.

"Take Tall Tree's body away from this sacred place, and bury it among your people. It will serve as a curse and shame for the Washazhe, for it will have no soul. Only when I have completed my journey to the mountain, and have made sacrifice, will I release Tall Tree's spirit and allow your people to be whole again."

Without hesitation, the four naked warriors lifted the body of their fallen leader and started for their horses, wide-eyed and frightened. Catherine suddenly got an inspiration and delivered one final warning.

"If you or any other members of your tribe disturb my journey or my sleep again, I will do as the owl has demanded, and turn each of you into coyotes, just as I did the two coyotes you will meet tonight on your journey home. Go now!" Catherine had not even been thinking of coyotes. The story about the two coyotes was just some crazy idea that came into her head, almost like a suggestion.

Call it coincidence, call it fate, or even magic, but those young warriors hadn't ridden two miles before they ran into a pair of coyotes standing in their path under the risen moon. They did not shy away as coyotes are known to do, but instead, stood their ground unwilling to move or give way to the horses.

That did it. These four young men were now terrified of the Cherokee Spirit Woman, and of the spells she cast. The events of that night would grow in the telling at campfires among the many who called the vast plains their home. These young men had a story to tell, and a warning to give, and anyone who saw their faces as they spoke knew the truth of their words.

Catherine stood there, watching the Washazhe ride away under the half moon which had risen above. The bloody knife was still in her hand as she turned to walk slowly to the river. Will stood by as she washed, first cleansing the blade and then her hands. She gave the knife back to Will, handle first. She then walked into the water in a effort to cleanse herself of the blood she had spilled that day. She began to shiver in the cool evening air. Whatever strength she had called upon to get her through that encounter with Tall Tree was now waning away. She undressed, and washed her clothes as well.

Conger did not stare at her this time. He stayed busy instead keeping watch over the campsite, fearing the return of the Washazhe. The stench from the burning scalps and the leather clothing was soon dissipated by the heat of the flames. Conger added more wood to keep the fire high. Catherine accepted the dry clothes that Will offered from his pack, and sat near the fire to get warm. Will wrung out her things and hung them on a nearby branch. They would be dry by morning. He also offered her the use of his cot for the night, but she politely refused. Instead she took a blanket over to her mare, and having the horse lay down, leaned up against her. For all the world it looked like a mother horse sheltering her foal.

"You won't need to stand guard anymore tonight, Mr. Conger. They will not return." She then curled up closer under the blanket, and was soon fast asleep.

Conger was grateful for this. He knew that sleep was what Catherine needed most. He was far more amazed than ever before by the unpredictable ways of this girl, and of the bravery and cunning she showed in the face of danger. At that moment he felt like a fool for having asked her to marry him. He felt unworthy of such a woman, so lovely, so wise, so brave.

Will sipped coffee, and recounted the events of his very busy day. How had he ever ended up in the midst of such a whirlwind there in the middle of nowhere? He thought back to the speech she gave those warriors there by the campfire.

It must have really been something, as they were hanging on every word. Will had not understood any of it, but the sound of those words matched the language she had spoken to her horse, and must be familiar to the Indians around these parts. He would have to ask her about it in the morning, if he lived that long. Still, she didn't seem a bit worried, why should he? It didn't take very long for Will to fall asleep as well. His head was feeling better, but his foot hurt to stand on it. His cot felt like a feather bed that night, as the day had taken its toll. Tonight, the mule would be standing guard.

The sun was already well up over the horizon when Conger awakened under his army issue tent. During the war he had gotten used to sleeping in a tent, away from the rain and snow and such. Furthermore, he used a cot, and therefore enjoyed sleeping without the company of snakes and scorpions and spiders and their like. It seemed that some fellows out this way thought lightly of his tent, even claiming that real men slept out in the open under the stars on the hard ground no matter the weather. Will just let them talk, after all, they seemed good at it. He preferred to keep his powder and himself dry whenever possible.

Long before Conger woke up to meet the day, Catherine had been up and busy making breakfast beside a fire built much closer to the tent than the one from the night before. She had chosen not to cook over coals which had seen the scalps of those who had been butchered by the Washazhe. That fire had been allowed to die away during the night, and only the embers were left.

She had made herself at home among the many items Will had stashed away in the packs which the mule carried. Coffee, smoked ham, and dried fruit would make up a tasty breakfast. But she had also rounded up some eggs from the nests of prairie chickens which lived nearby. The eggs were small, but would provide a nice change of pace.

Conger was surprised to see her wearing one of his cavalry pistols, complete with snap down holster. He was even more surprised to see her wearing a pair of his moccasins which she had found in the packs. She had already changed back into her own clothes which had dried on the tree limb overnight.

"Good morning, Mr. Conger." Her bright smile lit up the morning, and showed no signs of the troubles of the day before. Will would make it a point not to remind her. "Breakfast will be ready soon. You have time to wash up. The stock have already been watered, so you won't need to bother with that. I'll thank you in advance for the use of these moccasins. They fit very nicely, and feel wonderful." She smiled that special "What are you going to do about it?" smile that came standard with every pretty girl Conger had ever known. Some things never changed.

Will just smiled and went off to wash up at the river. At least he still had one extra pair. He had already decided to change back into boots now that he had a horse to ride again. He traded in his moccasins on the way to wash up Returning from the river, Will accepted a cup of strong black coffee and sat down on his cot which was now over by the fire, having been moved there by Catherine while he was washing up. He had never thought of doing that, although he had often sat on the cot and ate in his tent when it was raining. Catherine sat down beside him and got right to it.

"To answer you questions from yesterday, my horse's name is 'Ooh-luh', it is a Cherokee name which means sister. She is very much like a sister to me. The language you have heard me speak is of the Cherokee people. My mother was Cherokee, but was forced to pose as Spanish nobility to fool the snobbish people who lived in our part of Virginia. She called herself Rebecca. My father's name was William, just like yours. I find that very interesting."

She went on and on. For a girl who wouldn't say anything the day before, she was certainly making up for it this morning. She filled Conger up with more talk than he could digest. It seemed as though she hadn't spoken to anyone for quite a while, and was using poor Will to take up the slack.

And he loved it. She was so vibrant and alive! He couldn't imagine that this was the same girl who had shot two men to death the day before, and had wielded that knife with such deadly skill. He wasn't sure whether to feel safe or threatened in her presence. But she sure was pretty.

"How far do you figure we are from Fort Davis?' Conger started moving the conversation in a different direction. This was no time for idle chit chat. They were in a bad spot here if the Washazhe returned in numbers. Still, she didn't seem too concerned.

"I'm really not too sure. It took us most of a day to get there from the farm, and a day to get back. I would guess we are about half way there by now. There will be a stream up ahead, and from there it will be about another two hours. Is there someone waiting for you there?" She suddenly had a look of dread on her face. Conger figured he must have said something wrong, but had no idea what it could be. Maybe he seemed too anxious to get to the fort, although he figured that would be a pretty good place to be right about then. He didn't understand women folk at all.

She had become quiet, and was busy putting things together for their leaving. Will had no idea as to how she felt, or what had caused the sudden change. Having not spent much time in the company of women during the last few years, Will did not yet understand that the best way to figure out a woman was not to try.

Truth be known, Catherine was suddenly feeling very much alone, and was worried that Will might have someone else in his life. She knew in her heart that he had offered to marry her only to get her away from the farm. She wasn't sure how he could have been attracted to her after what she had done to her Uncle Jacob.

She knew it would be best to let Will know the dark details of her past, so that he could understand the way she felt, and why she had done those things. But this just didn't seem like the right time, and she wasn't real sure just when such a time would ever be. So far Will had made no move to be affectionate with her, although he was always very kind and considerate. But then again, he had not had many opportunities to show affection. If he had just wanted her physically, he'd certainly had his chance back at the farm. She remembered the gentle, almost loving way he had looked at her as she lay helpless on the bed. Why had she been so frightened of him?

Catherine realized that she had been rather pushy ever since they first met, and she had lost her mind and done things she would have never dreamed of doing. She had no choice but to take charge of the situation the night before, what with her knowledge of the tribes out here on the plains. But she feared that she had somehow embarrassed this fine young man in the process. She needed to become a part of Will's life, and quickly, if she intended to keep him around. It seemed that she no longer had a life of her own.

Already she had been married twice, both times without so much as an engagement. The first time was to Jacob, as an act of desperation to get herself out of a bad spot. The next time was to Rhen, on a riverboat to St. Louis, once again to get herself out of a bad spot and find somewhere to hide. And now here was Will Conger, who had proposed marriage in order to get her out of yet another bad spot.

The truth of the matter was that, unknown to Conger, he had shot Jacob while he was in the act of doing what he probably had every legal right to do, leather straps or no. Her marriage to Jacob was a sham to be sure, but her signature on the wedding license was legitimate, no matter the circumstances. She had even allowed those vows to be consummated, albeit to aid in her escape.

She had no right to marry Rhen Larson while she was still legally bound to Jacob. In fact, the right court of law would have probably excused Jacob for killing Rhen under the circumstances. If that weren't enough, on the day both of her husbands were shot dead, she had agreed to marriage with another man whose name she did not even know at the time. All in all, she felt like some wanton hussy, and wondered what sort of woman this Conger fellow must think her to be. Catherine labored with these thoughts as she packed up her things.

As they left the campsite, Catherine once again took the lead, and was once again quiet and withdrawn. But this time it wasn't so much for the sake of the Washazhe, but rather because she didn't know what to say to this wonderful young man whom the spirits of heaven had sent to her rescue.

Conger rode behind her in silence as well, not knowing what to say to such a lovely and spirited girl as this.

And so they rode westward, with pistols on their waists, and Colt rifles in their hands, bound to one another by their silence.

chapter 4

AT FIRST GLANCE, Fort Davis was not unlike a dozen or so other outposts which could be found dotted across the Western Kansas countryside at the time. It consisted mainly of a barracks, blacksmith shop, ten or so assorted shacks, houses and storage buildings, a mess hall which doubled as a church on Sundays, and a large barn with adjacent corrals.

In fact, this sorry-looking encampment hardly resembled anything which one would even begin to call a fort. Now, it did have a flag on a pole, and the garrison even sported a cannon, although it hadn't been fired in months. There was guard at the main gate at all times. However, there was no fence or wall surrounding the place, and all in all, Fort Davis appeared to be a sitting duck for any kind of attack the local native population might decide to bring against it.

But on closer inspection, the fort was far more secure than one would think. Stored between those buildings were piles of firewood, bales of straw, stacks of seemingly discarded furniture, and the like. It was all a ruse. The space between each building was heavily reinforced with stone and nearly impenetrable. The outside walls of each and every structure and been lined on the inside with native stone quarried from rocky outcroppings in the area. The houses themselves seemed to be set in an awkward and inconsistent manner, shunning the typical straight rows so common in planned government installations. In truth, each building was set in a specific position to provide an overlapping line of fire completely around the perimeter. Many of the buildings had been shifted from their original foundations to accomplish the desired effect.

The windows on the outside walls of the structures were set higher than usual, allowing defenders to shoot standing up, while the stone in the outer walls would deflect any bullets which penetrated the thin wooden exteriors. Only the mess hall and the barn stood away from the outer perimeter. The mess was built entirely of stone, and would serve as a defense of last resort should the need arise. The barn sported stone walls up to ten feet, with heavy timbers supporting a sod roof. In fact, every roof in the compound was covered with thick blocks of sod, making an attack by fire arrow or torch fairly futile. The grass on the roofs might burn for a time, but the thick layer of sod was virtually fireproof. The corral stood completely away from the outside perimeter, protecting the stock from would be thieves.

The only way in or out of Fort Davis was through the main gate, which had its own special wooden drop-down gate that could be quickly lowered by simply cutting a rope. That gate was quite heavy, and once deployed, required two strong horses and six men to get it back up and into place again. The grassy area on either side of the gateway looked like an easy way in, but in fact was nearly impassable to horse or man due to the hundreds of sharpened spikes sticking up six inches above the ground, and yet well hidden in the tall grasses which were native to Western Kansas. A pole fence was all that stood between any would-be attacker and the pain and agony those four acres of spikes could produce. Reinforced wagons were placed at the perimeter there by the gate, ready to be overturned for additional defense, but carefully maintained as rolling stock should the need arise.

All of this had been produced using the materials the locality provided, and reflected the strategic genius of one Colonel James Peters, U.S. Army, who upon taking over this post, immediately went to work to secure its totally vulnerable position. The garrison consisted of only forty men, and the few settlers who lived there relied on the Army's presence for safety and income as well. Fort Davis was typical of frontier outposts for its time, temporary at best, and never intended as a permanent installation.

Colonel Peters had been badly wounded at the Battle of Gettysburg when a Confederate shell had burst behind him at the beginning of what was to be known as Pickett's charge. He had suffered a lengthy and difficult recovery. Peters still walked with a limp, and on many mornings could be seen using a cane. Just riding a horse was a painful task, and he avoided doing so whenever possible. His wife Bess had come out west with him, and was as active as he was in the day-to-day management of life in this wilderness outpost. Plump and pretty, Bess was known for her engaging smile, and down-to-earth ways. She had volunteered as a nurse at the hospital in Washington City so as to aid in her husband's recovery, and quickly became a favorite among the wounded and staff alike for her bright spirit and uplifting manner.

In these last few days, the Fort Davis parade ground had become a little village unto itself, what with the constant flow of refugee settlers running before the rampaging Cheyenne. Homes had been burned , and livestock stolen, up and down the western prairie. Others had bravely but unwisely stayed to fight, but could not withstand the firepower and lightening tactics these native warriors could unleash.

Fort Davis provided a place of safety and supply, a meeting point in times of danger, and a starting-out point for those who had given up, and decided to try their luck further west on the Santa Fe trail. It had two deep wells for water and a clear field of fire for a quarter of a mile in every direction. This was a land that made seasoned veterans out of raw recruits in record time, and Colonel Peter's men understood the dangers better than most.

It fell to Bess to arrange for these newcomers, organizing the families with their wagons and livestock as they trickled in hungry, tired, and frightened. These were the lucky ones. They had chosen to run, leaving their possessions behind them, and saving their lives, and the lives of their children, for the tomorrows yet to come. The soldiers helped get them settled in and maintained a peaceful order about the place. Bess organized dormitories for the women and children, while the men were obliged to sleep wherever they could, often in or under the very wagons they had ridden in on.

Peters had assigned patrols to cover the surrounding area at a distance not to exceed five miles. Settlers who made it through were escorted to the fort under armed guard, providing a sense of security, and preventing folks unfamiliar with the outpost from wandering around aimlessly in a prairie short on landmarks. This was the best Peters could do with the manpower he had available.

Shortly before noon that day Will and Catherine found themselves in the company of two wagons they had met coming up from the south. Those families had gotten out in time, and moving through hostile lands, took comfort in the formidable firepower this young couple carried with them.

After breaking camp that morning, Will had been obliged once again to follow Catherine's lead as they rode toward Fort Davis. He continued to be amazed by this girl's handling of the situation with the Indians the night before, and wondered to himself what other surprises she had in store for him. There was much more to this girl than he had ever imagined. He had to admit that it was a real comfort to have a traveling companion like her on the trail. Not to mention, she was pretty.

His offer to marry Catherine had been genuine, but now he feared it might have been misguided. The truth was they really didn't know each other at all. Conger also considered the very real possibility that his offer for marriage would be forgotten or dismissed once they got back to civilization. Given the circumstances, it would be wrong for him to demand that she live up to the bargain. In fact, that would be wrong of a gentleman no matter the circumstances. But right then he was even more concerned about the Cheyenne, and the danger they presented while the sun was high in the sky. There would be no room for magic tricks and orations during the day. It would be a matter of marksmanship against heavy odds that would decide the outcome.

It was true that Conger was new to this country, but he had been in new country before, with a formidable enemy gunning for him then as well. The classroom of war offered no make-up tests, and each day added to the body of knowledge needed to stay alive. He already knew how to sniff out an ambush, and to vary the path of travel so as to keep a waiting adversary off balance. He knew to stay to the low ground whenever possible, and to make sure his equipment didn't rattle. Conger had assumed the leadership role now, as he had before, leading their little group west, and hopefully in the direction of Fort Davis.

They had seen no one so far, but Will was taking no chances. His pack mule carried many things that would be needed on his journey, not the least of which was a veritable arsenal of rifles and handguns. Among them were two Colt five shot repeater rifles originally carried by the Iowa cavalry at Vicksburg. He had seen them in action and was amazed by the effect they could have when massed against an oncoming enemy. He made sure he had a pair before he left the field, and had used them for the rest of the campaign. Both he and Catherine carried these now, along with two side arms each, safely tucked away in standard cavalry issue snap down holsters. Conger was pleased to see that she knew her way around weapons, having caught on quickly to their use.

About three miles out, one of the patrols intercepted Will, Catherine, and the others, and made sure they knew how to get to the fort. After seeing the imposing firepower these two carried, along with the rifles brandished by the folks in the wagons, the sergeant in charge determined that an armed guard was not necessary, and almost wished the Cheyenne would give it a try. The surprising image of a lovely young woman in men's garb, perched atop an enormous black horse while sporting a repeating rifle would provide something for the men to talk about for days to come.

Bess Peters was standing in the shade of her porch enjoying a cold drink of some of the best well water she had ever tasted. It had been a long day already, and families were still coming in. Watching the gate, she couldn't help but notice Catherine and her black mare arriving, but was concerned as that big blond husband of hers was nowhere to be seen. They had seemed an unlikely couple, but he was good to her, and the girl was always chatty and friendly when they came around.

The Larsons had stopped by the fort months earlier when they first moved in, and again about a month or so later to have the post blacksmith refit a horseshoe for the big black mare. It took him a while, having never worked on a horse that large before. The blacksmith was known only as Browner, and no one really knew where he came from. But he was good at his work, and did well at a trade desperately needed in a land such as this. Still, Catherine secretly enjoyed his discomfort in dealing with her big horse, as Browner was a mean spirited individual, unclean, and impolite at best.

Catherine could not know that Browner had been the man who had later sold McPhearson the information he needed to locate the Larson farm. Browner had also turned a blind eye to the horse Jacob was riding that day, knowing full well that it belonged to a man named Richard Durbin. This was the same sweet little roan that Will rode into the fort this day. Browner made a quick buck any way he could, and had accumulated quite a stash over the years. He looked forward to the day he could head out to San Francisco and live a life of luxury. Browner had a past, and his real name wasn't Browner. But he had stayed out of trouble at this isolated outpost, and plied the trade practiced by his father and his father's father before him. Browner didn't care much for people, but he knew how they were, and was certain that having a lot of money was the best way to get people to treat him with respect. Sadly, and for the most part, he was right.

Bess set her cup down and walked out to meet Catherine as she came through the gate. She noticed a young man riding beside her leading a pack mule, but wasn't sure they were traveling together, or even knew one another. Bess motioned Catherine over to the Post Commander's residence, and invited her in. The young man rode alongside, suggesting some connection there after all.

"We hadn't seen you yet and were worried you hadn't made it out in time. Come on in to the house where you can freshen up a bit." Bess could see the sadness in Catherine's eyes and feared the worst for Rhen. She was curious to know this other man's role in all of this.

Catherine guided her mare up to the house, and using verbal commands only, balanced herself as the horse once again knelt, allowing the girl to simply step off onto the ground, while Will had to dismount the old fashioned way. The big mare then stood back up, awaiting further instruction. Bess had watched Catherine with her horse before, and was still amazed by the way she was able to control such a huge animal with nothing more than a few gently spoken words.

Catherine came over to Bess and got a motherly hug, just like the one she got the first time she came to the fort. Bess served as acting mother to most everyone she met, and especially to all those young soldiers so far from home.

"I don't believe I've had the pleasure, sir. I am Bess Peters, wife of Colonel Peters, the commanding officer here at Fort Davis." Bess had never been known to beat around any bush. Conger removed his hat when spoken to, and was amused by this woman's straight forward manner.

"The pleasure is mine Ma'am. My name is William Conger, late of Lexington, Kentucky." Catherine was busy handing her weapons over to Will as he spoke.

"Go along inside Catherine and make yourself comfortable. I'll join you in just a minute." The girl went on inside as asked, looking back curiously before closing the door. She wasn't sure she wanted to leave Will Conger's company. She felt safe with him there beside her.

"That's quite some weaponry you have there, young man. I'll expect you to use them in defense of the fort should we be attacked. I see that you are wearing cavalry style holsters. What outfit were you with, and what rank did you hold?" Bess certainly got to the point.

"I served with the Illinois Sixth Cavalry, Ma'am, and attained the rank of Captain before the war's end. I am a civilian now." Will immediately wished he had said corporal instead. His military life was over, and he didn't really want to spend endless hours talking about the old days with some stuffy old Colonel. This woman seemed sweet enough, but way too nosey. He would try to change the subject.

"Tell me Ma'am, could you direct me to the officer in charge of your riding stock here at the fort? There are some things he may be able to help me with." Bess could tell he was being evasive, but wanted to get in to visit with Catherine.

"You will find Lieutenant Whittle down by the corrals, at the far end of the compound. He's the man you need to talk to. But feel free to approach any of the men assigned here to the fort with any needs you may have. Please make yourself at home here, Captain Conger." Somehow her emphasis on the word 'Captain' made Will a little uncomfortable. Now he wished he had said 'Private'.

"Thank you Ma'am." With that, he returned his hat, and with the mule and the roan in tow, made his way over to where the corrals met the barn. He left the big mare standing where she was, figuring it wouldn't move from that spot until the girl told it to. As he approached the corral he could hear considerable shouting and other goings on over that way, and wondered what all the commotion could be about.

Bess watched as Conger headed toward the barn. She was duly impressed with this fellow, and promised herself to find out more about him later. She was certain that the Colonel would want to meet him, and most likely talk about the war for hours on end. But right then she was much more concerned about Catherine, and walking into the house, wished she had come in sooner.

Catherine sat there at the table, looking off into the distance, with tears streaming down her face. Bess sat down beside her and waited. It was only a few seconds until the girl opened up, and the tears which flowed began to release waves of horror and confusion held inside for hours, and days, and years. Her story came out, first in bits and pieces, and then in devastating detail, a story of guilt, torment, betrayal, and fear.

Bess once again played the role of a mother comforting her child. The lurid details of Jacob McPhearson and his ruthless behavior drew a portrait of unspeakable evil, repulsive even to a woman who had seen so much of the horrors of war in her time. This was a story which had to come out, had to be told to begin the process of healing that this girl so desperately needed. It was also was a tale which should never be repeated, far too deep and dark to be trusted to those with busy tongues, and questionable discretion. Catherine's words finally ended with the events of the night before, of their run in with Tall Tree and the Washazhe, and of her fear of losing the wonderful young man who had come to her rescue. At last, the girl sat quietly, exhausted and drained, with no words left to speak. Bess led her over to the bed, and covered her up with a warm blanket. Within minutes Catherine had fallen asleep.

It was only then that Bess saw the wound on the back of Catherine's head, a mute witness to the truth behind the story the girl had told. The blood would ruin the fabric, but no matter. The girl had earned the right not to have her sleep disturbed for the sake of a pillowcase. Bess would just have to make another to replace it.

Bess sat quietly for a time, and considered the dark and troubling story this girl had told. She knew that Catherine was lucky to be alive, and for this she had Captain William Conger to thank. It would take a long time, maybe years before she would be able to put these things behind her. Catherine would need someone close by her for comfort and for protection, perhaps even from herself. Then she began to smile that little smile of hers, known all too well to those who knew her there at the fort. The solution for Catherine was right there for the taking. A deal was a deal, and Bess was not going to let such a chance for this girl slip away.

So, young Mr. Conger had proposed marriage, had he? Well, he was going to get just what he asked for. Colonel Peters would be presiding at the wedding of Will and Catherine that very evening. She couldn't wait to tell him.

Bess wasn't the only one to notice the girl riding the big black horse into the fort that day. Browner knew that horse well, having shoed it just a month or so before. It had been all he could do to deal with the huge beast, and he would have had to admit it was one of the few horses he had ever been afraid of. It wasn't just its size, but also the way it behaved. It somehow didn't act like a normal horse. It was more like a person, and the way it looked at him! And all that gibberish the girl used to speak to the horse seemed scary and unnatural. Browner was glad when that job was done, and charged more than usual, supposedly to cover the cost of the extra metal he needed to make a shoe that large.

Browner also saw the young man who had ridden in on Richard Durbin's horse. It was likely that no one else at the fort had ever seen that roan before the day that McPhearson rode it in looking for directions to the Larson place. Browner had shoed that horse over at Durbin's place some time back. The fact that McPhearson and not Durbin had ridden it in months later was no concern of Browner's. After all, McPhearson could have bought the horse from Durbin. But in truth, Browner knew quite well that Durbin would never sell that horse, not with all the fuss he made over it. But with the money he got from McPhearson for information, Browner kept quiet.

The girl's big blond husband had not come in with the rest, and Browner had a pretty good idea why, things being as they were in southwest Kansas those days. No matter. He'd just keep his head down and his mouth shut, and if there came a chance to make a dollar or two with what he knew, so be it.

Will Conger made it to the barn and went looking for Whittle. It didn't take long for him to find the lieutenant, busy directing traffic at the overly-crowded corral. With all the livestock the settlers were bringing in, this facility, which was barely adequate for their needs before, now looked more like Noah's ark than an army cavalry post.

There were horses aplenty, as was to be expected. But there were also mules, donkeys, ponies, oxen, cows, dogs, barn cats, chickens, geese, and even pigs! Whittle's men were doing the best they could, but it was a losing battle. Some of the stock were not overly pleased to be in one another's company, and skirmishes between the donkeys and the dogs were ongoing. Donkeys don't like coyotes, and apparently some of the dogs seemed all too closely related to their wild cousins for the donkeys' comfort. In addition, some of the dogs were of the herding variety, and pigs do not take to herding as enthusiastically as do sheep. The barn cats were far too interested in the chickens. It was bedlam.

Former Captain Conger of the Illinois Sixth was briefly tempted to step in and take charge of this madness, but remembering his place, he instead simply tried to be sympathetic to the helplessly outnumbered Whittle.

Conger would have had to honestly admit that he probably couldn't have done any better under the circumstances anyway. Still, this whole mess couldn't help being amusing to watch, as long as he wasn't the one in charge.

"Would you be Lieutenant Whittle, sir?" Conger was working hard to keep a straight face.

"I would be if I had a company of regulars at my disposal. As it is, I'm little more than a baby sitter running a four-legged nursery school. I have half a notion to turn this lot loose onto the parade ground and let their masters deal with them." Conger had an immediate liking for this man, and knew for a fact Whittle would do nothing of the sort. He was too stubborn to give in, and too much a soldier to be derelict in his duties. Will introduced himself as a former Union cavalry officer, this time without specifying rank. He had come to swap horses and possibly saddles for something far more standard issue, and preferably on the well used side of things.

Whittle looked over the roan, and saw good lines on a healthy animal. Conger explained that the horse's owner had been killed out on the prairie, and he had gotten away on the man's horse just in time. All of this was true of course, and as Conger did not feel free to give up the details of his encounter with Jacob McPhearson, especially where Catherine was concerned. This would have to be the story of record.

Conger knew horses, and he knew how to trade horses. His father had taught him well. In this case he was making it a point to trade down in return for familiarity. Whittle knew horses too, and wasn't buying any of it. This man wanted to be rid of this horse and its outfit, and he was happy to oblige. The roan was of fine riding stock, and he knew he had just the horse Conger was looking for.

They called her 'Pumpkin', due mostly to the slightly reddish hue of her coat. She was also one of the sweetest saddle horses a man could ever find. Pumpkin was well up in years now, and while still in excellent shape, she no longer had the flat-out galloping speed needed for cavalry operations. She had languished there in the barn, overlooked more and more often as the troops chose their mounts and went out on patrol without her.

Conger liked her at once. Her eyes had wisdom, with the ready look of a traveler. This was a horse built for the trail, and it would not do for her to spend her last years cooped up in some barn. The deal was made. Amazingly enough, picking out a used saddle was a bit more of a challenge than choosing a horse. Using Pumpkin as his model, Will strapped three different saddles onto her back, each time mounting the mare to try them out. The horse thought he was daft, but having dealt with numerous riders over the years, she was not surprised by much of anything a human might do. That was exactly the kind of horse Conger needed.

Whittle wrote out a bill of sale and both men signed the document. Importantly, it was made mention in the agreement that Conger held ownership of the roan by found only, with no knowledge of the identity of the previous owner. Will hedged a little on that matter, but wanted to keep as much distance between Catherine and the events of the previous day as possible, and therefore did not want to mention McPhearson by name. It seemed the best thing to do at the time. That would turn out to be a terrible mistake.

While he was at it, Will made a deal for a second mule. He figured that now with Catherine along he might well be packing a whole lot more than he had originally planned. He bought the mule from one of the settlers who had made it in safely from the Cheyenne threat. But the man was throwing in the towel on Kansas, and was determined to head back to Ohio. He was leaving his wagon behind and didn't need his mules any longer. Conger paid a fair price, not taking advantage of a man who had just lost everything. The mule was a mare as well, a good match for the jack, Conger figured.

He made arrangements for their care until morning, and satisfied with his dealings, sought out a barber to shave his week-old stubble and trim his hair up a might. It didn't take long to find an Italian fellow with a wagon full of kids who was well-practiced in the art of barbering, and had the tools to prove it. They agreed on a price, and Conger, removing his hat, sat down in the chair the man provided.

Seeing the wound on Conger's head from his earlier encounter with the rock, the barber went into action with an assortment of salts and salves to clean and treat the swollen flesh. He talked calmly and quietly during the shave, mostly in his native Italian tongue, but strangely enough making perfect sense to Will in the general sense of it all.

The barber had just finished the shave and was re-examining the wound when his oldest daughter ran up to the wagon with exciting news---there was going to be a wedding that night! It seemed the girl who rode that big horse was getting married to that nice young man who had ridden in with her today. She looked over at Will, still seated in the chair, and realizing who he was, congratulated him on his good fortune with all the exuberance a young teenage girl could muster.

Within seconds a crowd had gathered around Conger, wishing him all the best, with plenty of hand shakes and backslaps to go around. Conger was stunned and a little bit

numbed by it all. Obviously, Catherine must have said something to someone, the Colonel's wife no doubt, and the whole
thing had gotten cooked up while he was busy trading horses.

When Will had proposed to Catherine, he had been sincere and genuine in not wanting anything to happen to her,
but hadn't really figured it would actually ever come to this,
her being so pretty and wise and independent and all. He
assumed they would at least have some time to get acquainted
first, and then maybe make a final decision on the matter at
a later time. And after the events of that morning, he wasn't
even sure she still wanted him with her anyway." He needed
to go see that girl, and sit down and talk with her. He needed
to get the straight of it all, and soon.

That wasn't going to happen. Within minutes an armed
guard, consisting of a corporal and two privates, came by to
escort Will to the Post Commander's office. The well-wishers
all thought this was part of the ceremony to come, and eagerly
applauded. Will wasn't so sure. Maybe there was some question regarding Catherine's late husband, and the circumstances
surrounding his death. Or maybe he hadn't paid enough for
that extra cot he'd bought along with the horse. Knowing the
army as he did, it could be just about anything.

Whatever it was, he was soon to find out, as they had
already covered the distance to the Colonel's office.

Bess Peters had been a busy girl. Leaving Catherine to
her much needed sleep, she had taken it upon herself to put
together as nice a wedding as possible in the few hours she had
available. By now the men and women of Fort Davis were as
used to taking orders, referred to as 'official requests', from the
Colonel's wife as they were from the Colonel himself. Truth was,
most would have followed the woman into battle if the situation demanded. Bess wasted no time in getting things rolling.

First off, a dress had to be found. She gave that task
to Mrs. Tanner, the best seamstress at the fort. It was joked
that she could turn a private into a general with only a spool
of thread and four copper coins. Bess determined that the

Spencer girl was about the right size to serve for fit. A pretty light blue dress was scrounged from Mrs. Lassiter, who reluctantly admitted that after four children she was never going to squeeze into that dress again. Leaving Mrs. Tanner in charge, Bess went on to her next objective.

Sergeant Richards ran the mess hall like a well-tuned organ, with his finger on every key, and not a note to be missed. He had been busy these last few days feeding not only the troops, but the refugees as well. Enormous pots of soup and gallons of hot coffee were always at the ready, with bread baking around the clock. He was equal to the task.

When Bess came into the kitchen with that look on her face he knew he was in for it. But he, like all the other men at Fort Davis, loved this woman like a sister, and was anxious to hear what devilment she was up to this time.

"We're going to have a wedding in the mess hall at seven o'clock tonight." She certainly didn't waste the Sergeant's time with chit chat. He liked that about her, as though he could refuse her anyway. Richards didn't even bother to question her words, knowing that if she said there was going to be a wedding, there was going to be a wedding, even if a bride and groom had yet to be found.

"We need the place swept out and scrubbed down. I'll arrange for some pine boughs and flowers for decorations. Have everyone fed and out by six o'clock sharp. There'll be some girls here to help with the setup. We'll need some kind of cake or pudding or such to celebrate the occasion. Plan on about twenty people in all, and break out that keg of cider for a toast." How did she know he had a keg of cider stashed away? No matter, she had it all planned out, and it must be a special case for her to get all worked up like this.

"Yes Ma'am. We'll have everything ready by seven o'clock sharp. Might I ask who's getting hitched?"

"Be there and see for yourself, you're invited, you know. And be sure to wear your best bib and tucker!" With that she scampered out the door and on to her next objective. Richards laughed out loud, having always enjoyed the banter between them. He promised himself that if he ever met a woman like that he'd marry her on the spot. With that thought, he started rummaging through his pantry in search of raisins.

Soon after, a heavily armed detachment, protecting a wagon full of giggling girls, was sent out to gather pine boughs and wildflowers for the décor. The entire sortie took less than fifteen minutes, under the watchful eye of Bess herself, who came along to see things done right. A stand of pine grew near the fort, and the only such within forty miles. These were no doubt the remains of what had been a much larger pine forest in times long forgotten. The fragrance of the freshly-cut pine would add a nice touch as the mess hall was transformed into a wedding chapel.

It had fallen upon Corporal Dugger to locate Conger and escort him to Colonel Peters' office. The Post Commander wanted to have a word in private with the bridegroom before the happy event. Peters was also inclined to assign an armed guard to prevent the young man from making a run for it. Bess had not yet even told her husband about the wedding, or the role he was to play in it. But word gets around quickly at a place like Fort Davis, and Bess's plans were already common knowledge to the Colonel. Besides, he knew his wife well.

Conger knocked first, then walked in to the Colonel's office, standing at attention, and saluting a superior officer by force of habit. Will still wasn't thinking clearly, having yet to absorb the news of his impending wedding. Peters returned the salute as though nothing was out of order. The Colonel quickly sized up the young man, wearing eastern style clothing with unpolished boots and a blocked grey hat. This man looked tired, but ready to go into battle if need be. Peters knew at once that this man was solid.

"I understand that you were in the army. I will remind you that as a civilian, you are no longer required to salute me, sir, but I appreciate the respect you show the uniform. Please have a seat." Conger felt like an idiot. It had been over a year since he had worn a uniform. He wasn't thinking clearly at all. Maybe he had hit his head harder than he thought.

"Thank you, sir. It is a pleasure to meet you. How may I be of assistance to you this evening?" Conger almost said 'sir' again. He wasn't sure how to act. And Peters was enjoying his discomfort.

"I understand that you are to be wed to Catherine Larson this evening. Tell me, what of that big blond husband of hers? Does he have anything to say about it?" The Colonel had already guessed the worst, but needed to hear it straight out.

" He is dead, sir. When I arrived at their farm yesterday I came across his body out behind the barn. He had been dragged there from where he had been killed. I found his killer inside the house making things very difficult for Mrs. Larson. I shot the man and he is dead. My horse had gotten spooked and ran off the day before, and I had been on foot. It was that man's horse and outfit that I rode in with today."

A good clear report. This man had held rank, Peters could tell. He had taken charge of the moment yesterday, just as he had taken charge of this conversation this evening. Peters was duly impressed.

"So then tell me, Conger is it? What does all this have to do with a wedding?" He needed to know the facts if he were to officiate at this ceremony. He had the authority to do so, but needed to be clear as to the goings on here.

"The young lady was unwilling to leave the farm in the face of the Cheyenne attacks, preferring to die there along side of her late husband. I believed her to be hysterical at the time sir, and unable to think clearly. After coaxing proved futile, I proposed marriage as a way to get her to safety. She accepted my offer, and here we are."

Peters was sure there was more to the story, but could sense that Conger was holding something back in deference to the young woman. There are certain things that gentlemen simply do no discuss.

"I understand, and I congratulate you on your quick thinking. However, do you feel it proper for you to hold the girl to your offer of marriage, when your purposes were merely to make good an escape in the face of hostile action?

"I will stand by the offer I made, if she will have me. She was too good a woman to be left behind then, and too good a woman to let get away now, sir." Somehow the "sir" seemed fitting. Conger sat still, looking down at his hands. He was worn out, and he had just about run out of words.

"What rank did you hold soldier, and with what unit." A smile had found its way onto the Colonel's face, as he already knew the answer. For the next two hours the two men drank coffee and exchanged stories of the war, comparing the names of the men they had known, and the friends they had lost. Satisfied as to Conger's character, Peters got on to the duty he knew would be his when Bess showed up to tell him all about the wedding.

"Captain Conger, the clothes you are wearing are not suitable for you to be wed in, and we do not have adequate time before the wedding to do much with them. I can, however, supply you with a nicely tailored uniform, and with your former rank, if you would care to wear it. It should fit you reasonably well from the looks of you, and I would take it as a personal favor, if you were to accept my offer."

Conger really didn't have anything better to wear in his mule's packs. He felt a little funny about wearing a uniform he figured he no longer had a right to be in. But the offer was genuine, and the man had said it would be a personal favor. As he didn't have any quick alternatives, Will accepted.

"Well done sir. Mrs. Peters will be pleased. Have you had the chance to make acquaintance with my wife, Mr. Conger?" Walls have ears. Peters knew all about Will's previous introduction to Bess, the weapons he carried, and the horse he rode in on. Peters knew what went on at his fort.

"Yes sir, although only briefly. When we first arrived she met us at the gate. She took Catherine into your home, and told me to be sure to use my guns in defense of the fort if we were attacked."

Peters smiled. "Sounds just like her. Tell me, what kind of weapon were you carrying at the time?"

"It was a Colt five shot repeater. I picked two of them up after engagements at Vicksburg. I had intended to use them to greet the Cheyenne had they come a-calling on our way in."

"I've never seen one of those, only heard about them. Be sure to bring one by in the morning and we'll try it out. I look forward to it. But right now we need to get you dressed and put a shine on those boots of yours. You're getting married in half an hour."

Bess had outdone herself this time. The wedding preparations had gone off without a hitch. The women of the post, along with some of the settlers, had all pitched in to make the evening a success. Flowers were placed in whatever containers could be used for vases. The pine boughs hanging from the rafters filled the mess hall with their lovely scent. Sergeant Richards had made quick work of the cleaning, recruiting a squad of 'volunteers' to clean the place out and scrub it down in record time. Those men who showed up after six o'clock for their evening meal were forced to eat outside. Complainers were obliged to take their place among the volunteers. The complaining quickly ended.

For Bess, this wedding was important for two equally important reasons. It was first and foremost a chance to give young Catherine a proper wedding, which she had never had, and to put her in the hands of a man who cared deeply for her, and could protect and provide for her. Secondly, it gave the settlers something to do, something else to talk about besides the Indian menace. Spirits were lifted by the busyness of it all, and Bess was thankful. There had been too much sadness as of late.

Catherine was allowed to sleep for about two hours before her ladies in waiting arrived in force. Water was drawn for a bath, and herbs and special soaps were gathered up for her hair. The wound on her head was still seeping a bit, so Ma Tucker, who was arguably the best doctor at the fort, the army surgeon notwithstanding, went to work on it with a mixture of ground sugar and flour that did the trick. Catherine's long dark hair was pulled up and above the wound so as to hide any sign of a problem. A light blue ribbon was added to complete the effect.

The dress was finished in plenty of time, and fit rather nicely, albeit a little tight in the arms. Catherine's time on the farm had hardened her up a bit, and the fabric strained against the strength of her upper arms. There was nothing to be done abut it at this late hour, so Mrs. Tanner simply cautioned Catherine about lifting heavy objects with that dress on. This little gaggle of women was having a wonderful time of it all, but Catherine was having some doubts.

Earlier that day, she had mentioned Conger's proposal of marriage to Bess, and shared her misgivings as to whether he really had meant it. Catherine truly feared being marooned by this fine young man after he had a chance to think things over. As she was riding through the gate that afternoon, she certainly had not expected to be wed that same night. She asked to speak to Bess alone.

Always in charge, Bess shooed the other women out to go make themselves presentable as well. It was nigh to six o'clock, and the wedding ceremony was little more than an hour away. Now that they were alone, Catherine made her concerns known, fearful that she might be doing the wrong thing. Older and wiser, Bess got right to the point.

"Catherine, you are to be wed tonight to a very fine young man of excellent breeding and with good prospects. Your past is behind you and you can do nothing to change it. The Good Lord kept you alive for a reason, and that reason may well be to help that young man through life. Don't try to defy the plans providence has set out for your time here on earth."

Catherine was stunned. This was not at all the response she had figured on. Bess was right. It was a gift of Heaven that she was still alive. She had screamed for help in her darkest moment, and this man suddenly burst through her door as though dropped from the sky. Whatever forces of luck, coincidence, or Heaven above were at work here, who was she to turn her back on them?

"Is he still here? I mean, has he gone on?" Catherine's question amused Bess, which made the answer even more fun.

"At this moment he is trying on one of my husband's old uniforms. It's the one he wore at our wedding all those years ago. Captain Peters was much thinner then, so was I." Bess smiled and patted her tummy and sighed. Time takes its toll. Catherine looked puzzled, and asked about the uniform.

"Your young man was a Captain in the Union army during the war. He has the right to wear that rank if my husband says so. Besides, the Colonel is doing it as a surprise for me. I promise to be totally amazed and delighted by his thoughtfulness, which I am." That brought out a giggle from both of them.

"Catherine, I have taken the liberty of writing out a very brief set of vows. Under the circumstances, I feel that many of the traditional words and phrases which are often included in wedding vows may not be all that appropriate for this occasion." Bess handed the paper to Catherine for her to read the words she had written down. It would be from this paper that Colonel Peters would read the ceremony.

It was brief and to the point. There would be nothing said about the sanctity of marriage, or the wedding in Canaan. There would be nothing said about death and parting. Catherine read the words twice through, understanding what Bess was trying to do, and seeing the sense of it all.

"There is one change that needs to be made." Catherine was certain in her words, and her voice was filled with conviction and purpose on this matter.

"My name is Dawn Flower O'Dell. That is how I wish to be known from here on. Catherine was the name my mother gave me to use in the white man's world so no one would speak against me. She was Cherokee, and pretended to be Spanish royalty to protect her true identity. She gave me two names, knowing the difficulties my Cherokee name would cause me in white society. But I am Dawn Flower down in my soul, and my future husband has heard me speak the words of my people. If he later puts me aside because of who I am, I will accept my fate. Catherine Larson died yesterday along with her husband. Today I will start my new life as myself, who I truly am. Please have the Colonel call me 'Dawn O'Dell' as the vows are read. I can answer as Catherine no longer."

Bess took a deep breath. This was not the whimpering young girl she had taken under her wing that morning. Before her sat a beautiful, strong, self-reliant Indian maiden, one with the earth and with the spirits which dwelled there. Catherine had indeed died, she could see that now. Dawn was someone very special, with a power and a presence Bess had not seen in her before.

"I will change the name to read as you wish. He will address you only as 'Dawn O'Dell'. And what would you have us call your groom?"

"Since he'll be in uniform we'll address him as 'Captain William Conger'. If I am to marry a Yankee blue coat, we might as well say so."

The sun was well along on its journey westward as the wedding guests gathered outside the mess hall. The tables had been cleared away to the walls, permitting chairs to be placed two abreast, with an aisle running down the middle. The pine boughs were a very nice touch, mixing their special fragrance with that of the wildflowers which were to be found in a wide assortment of cups and glasses which served as vases for the occasion.

Army posts often boasted several men whose abilities ranged far beyond the daily requirements of soldiering. One such fellow was a private named Phelps who played the fiddle as well as anyone could remember. Bess had pressed him into service by promising a special breakfast of griddle cakes in return for his services. He would have done it for free, but this was the way Bess worked. After all, she liked griddle cakes, too. The Colonel was never jealous of the attentions Bess showed the men at the fort so long as things went smoothly and there was no mischief involved. There never was.

The fiddler started playing at five minutes 'til seven, signaling the time for the guests to file in. The music was lovely and appropriate to the occasion, with some of those assembled humming along to the familiar tunes. The guest list completed, an armed guard stood at the door to make sure that no one disturbed the proceedings.

Conger stood in the kitchen along with the Colonel, nervously waiting to make his entrance. He would have been calmer facing a firing squad. At least with a firing squad a fellow knows just how things are going to turn out. Will assumed, and rightly so, that marriage offered no such certainties. He remembered being told that "married men didn't really live longer, it just felt that way." Well, it wasn't as though he hadn't asked for it. Him and his big mouth.

Suddenly the fiddler switched tunes to something far more stately and majestic, pulling hard on the bow to make his little music box speak with as much authority and grandeur as possible. Conger didn't recognize the tune, and while it was important sounding enough, it was no toe-tapper.

The crowd was seated, and mostly in uniform, with a few ladies sprinkled in for effect. Will entered the mess hall through the kitchen door, following Colonel Peters who led the way. The Colonel's old uniform was a bit tight in the chest, but otherwise fit Conger rather nicely. He had certainly never worn such a nice garment while serving as Captain with the Illinois sixth.

Will still didn't feel quite right wearing a uniform with a rank he no longer had any right to call his own, but felt it was not wise to argue with a full Colonel, and at his own post to boot. There was no guardhouse that he had seen, but there was a barn overflowing with horses, and the mess they made would be worse than any KP duty a man could ask for. Plus, one never knew what they might decide to charge for boarding a horse and two mules overnight if they took a bad feeling toward the fellow who had insulted their Post Commander.

Talk about shotgun weddings! This girl had an entire garrison at her disposal should he try to cut and run. Conger figured that was why there was an armed guard at the door. All things considered, his best option was to stay put and like it.

Will had only been there a matter of seconds when Lieutenant Whittle came through the doorway exclaiming a hearty "Ten-hut!" With that, the crowd lifted itself as one, and turned back to get a glimpse of the blushing bride.

Truth was, she wasn't blushing at all, in fact, she was white as a sheet. The crowd didn't know it, but while this girl had been married twice before, this was the first time she had actually walked down an aisle toward her husband-to-be. She was overwhelmed with appreciation for all the things these total strangers had done for her, not fully realizing how much this wedding was doing to help all of them as well, as it gave them something meaningful to do. Being able to take their minds off of the many tragedies they had each suffered in the recent days, even for a little while, was tonic for the soul.

The duty of escorting Dawn to the front of the room fell to Whittle, and a better man could not have been found for the task. The Lieutenant looked splendid in his dress blues, which went nicely with the bride's light blue attire with matching ribbon. A good stiff drink of bourbon had helped Dawn to deal with the pain in her head, but did little toward harnessing the butterflies dancing in her stomach. She walked slowly in, fingers digging into Whittle's arm.

Conger hadn't really looked at any of the faces in the crowd, worrying instead about the words he was going to say, and praying he would not foul the whole thing up. But his focus at once became clear as his bride to be started up the aisle on Whittle's arm. Will no longer heard the fiddle, and the gathered crowd seemed to disappear. Suddenly all was right with the world, Catherine was there.

Dawn saw Will at the end of the room, and the color quickly returned to her face. It wasn't a dream after all. He looked so handsome in uniform. And to imagine, her marrying a Yankee of all things! And he said he was from Kentucky! This Southern girl would have a talk with him about that later.

She saw the flowers and smelled the pine boughs, and her bouquet no longer felt heavy in her hands. Suddenly Whittle came to an abrupt halt, and placed her hand into the waiting hand of her husband-to-be. She seemed vaguely aware that the music had stopped, but wasn't really listening. The Colonel was asking the crowd to be seated. This was the first time she and Will had ever held hands. He had strong hands. She felt safe in those hands. It was as though she had finally come home. Her father's name had been William. It would be good to have that name nearby again.

Having successfully delivered the lovely lady in blue to her appointment with destiny, Bess remained in the doorway to watch the ceremony. She knew at once they had done the right thing. Seeing the two of them together seemed as natural as a pleasant spring rain. The sight of Conger wearing her husband's old uniform was far more moving than she had imagined it would be. She was incredibly proud to be married to the Colonel, and prayed daily that her zany antics never caused him too much trouble.

The Colonel stuck to the script Bess had provided him. He never had been much of a public speaker, but as Camp Commander, he couldn't pass this duty off to some other officer. Fortunately this ceremony would be short and involve very few words. In fact, he had already come to the only part that really mattered.

"Dawn O'Dell, will you take this man to be your husband?" Dawn? Conger had been listening very carefully to what was being said so as not to miss his cue. But she had told him her name was Catherine! Had he missed something somewhere? Now he was more confused than ever.

"I will." Well, she had said it, and now it was his turn.

"Captain William Conger, will you take this woman to be your wife?" Conger wasn't sure what the 'Captain' part was all about, excepting it must have been thrown in to justify his wearing the Colonel's old uniform. He would remember to carefully check the small print on the marriage certificate before he signed, just to make sure he didn't accidentally re-up, and start drawing army pay again the next morning.

He was still wondering about 'Dawn.' He thought he was marrying Catherine! Well, she had answered to it, and this was not the time to start asking a lot of questions. Besides, the Colonel had already asked him a question that he had best get to answering, and quickly.

"I will."

"Whereas you both have agreed to this union, by the power vested in me by the Government of the United States of America, I now pronounce you man and wife." At once the crowd, both inside the mess hall and out on the parade ground, raised their voices as one, with loud shouts of approval and whoops of joy. They had all remained quiet for about as long as they could anyway.

Customs vary from place to place, especially for things as important as weddings. Immediately the chairs were passed out through the door to make room, and the fiddler took up a festive little tune for the bride and groom, to have their first dance together as a married couple. Until a few minutes before, Will had not so much as held the girl's hand, and now here they were to have their first dance!

The thing was, dancing was something they both excelled at. Will held out his hand and took her by the waist and away they went. It was fun, and a fellow could have sworn they'd been dancing together all their lives. They were both smiling ear to ear, as much from relief as from the joy of it all. There was no past now, only that moment, as their eyes met and a bond was formed. Other couples were dancing around them but they didn't notice. This was their beginning, a dance that would go on for the rest of their lives.

The celebration quickly spread out into the parade ground where couples started dancing in a dozen different ways to the lively music. Soon a mandolin, a banjo, and a mouth harp had been added to the orchestra, along with folks clapping and pounding on all sorts of things to keep the beat. Before long there was a full-fledged hoe down in the works.

Inside the mess hall, Sergeant Richards was serving up a raisin pudding made up especially for the wedding party. This was accompanied, as ordered, by a hearty cup of strong cider for a toast to the health and long life of the newlyweds. Bess knew how fragile Dawn would be at this moment, and how badly things could go if the wrong things were said by well-meaning guests. She pulled the newlyweds out of the party, and moved them on to their next destination. The Colonel was there beside her, wondering what his wife was up to now, and preparing himself for whatever the love of his life had cooked up this time.

Will and Dawn were led over to the Colonel's quarters, where an armed guard stood watch by the door. Peters had not ordered any such guard, and knew that Bess had been busy giving orders to the troops again, and on his own post of all things! But of course he had become used to it by now, and enjoyed giving Private Jackson, who was standing at guard, a good stern look for his unauthorized participation, knowing full well the fellow had no doubt been bribed with some of Bess's delicious biscuits.

"You two will be staying here tonight. Consider it our wedding gift to you both, as you don't have a place of your own here at the fort. Your first night together should not be subject to interruptions by the common folk. If you should need anything at all, Private Jackson will be happy to take care of it. Isn't that right, Private Jackson?"

"Yes Ma'am!" He could say nothing else to this woman, even though he knew he could be in deep trouble for following orders given by a civilian. Of course, no one thought of Bess as a civilian, she was all army.

Colonel Peters simply rolled his eyes at the absurdity of it all. And reminded himself to chastise his wife firmly for her insubordination, at the proper time of course. But for the moment, he was wondering where he would be spending the night, as the wedding couple would be sleeping in his bed. Conger spoke to the Colonel.

"Thank you for your generosity. This is where I am supposed to try to refuse your hospitality, but instead, I will humbly accept this gift on behalf of my wife and myself, as I know it has come from the heart." It was a fine speech, but little did Conger know that the Colonel had found out about these arrangements the same time he had.

Bess gave both Will and Dawn a big hug, and Conger shook hands with the Colonel. The couple started to go on in, and Private Jackson took his place on the porch in front of the door. He would be relieved during the course of the night, Whittle would see to that. The night guard at Fort Davis left nothing to chance.

"You seem to have been busy today ordering my men around." Peters tried to sound stern, but he knew it wouldn't work. Bess just smiled, and taking her husband by the arm, led him back across the parade ground. It seemed as though the music and dancing could go on for hours. So be it. These people needed an excuse to be happy, if only for a little while.

As if on cue, Lieutenant Whittle appeared with a large basket, its contents covered by a red and white checkered napkin.

"Thank you for all you have done this evening, Lieutenant. You have made this day very special for us all." Bess's tone convinced the Colonel that she was up to something. He also knew it was in his best interests to go along with whatever she had planned. Whittle saluted the Colonel, and with a smile, took his leave back toward the mess hall. Peters recognized the basket, and knew that whatever was under that napkin was Bess's doing.

"I'll take that, dear." Peters took hold of the basket's handle and was amazed at how heavy it was. They seemed to be walking straight for the livery barn. Peters was wondering if she were planning a midnight ride, complete with a picnic lunch, or snack, or whatever one would call eating in the middle of the night. He might be forced to draw the line here, as riding outside the fort at night in these times would be a down right foolish thing to do. He just couldn't allow it, even at the risk of disappointing her.

Bess led him right up to the barn door, where Private Thomlin was standing guard. This was not a regular guard post either, and Peters was at once intrigued by what his wife was up to this time. They passed through the door, and heard it close behind them. The interior of the barn was lit by four lanterns, and the horsy smell seemed to have been replaced by that of fresh hay. A squad of soldiers must have been busy cleaning the place out all day. That was surely the work of Whittle.

"Do you remember when we were courting, and you and I would sneak off to my Grandfather's hayloft?" She didn't need to say any more. He remembered those times vividly, and the big grin on Bess's face told him everything he needed to know. They would not need their bed that night, and armed guards would see to it that they were not disturbed. Peters followed her up the ladder, and found blankets and pillows already laid out. Uncovering the basket, she produced biscuits and honey, along with a bottle of wine she had purchased from the Italian family which had arrived the day before. Peters felt like the luckiest man in the world.

"By the way, I never told you this, but Grandpa knew what we were doing up there the whole time. He and I had worked it out between us. In fact, it was his idea. He really liked you." Peters took his lovely wife into his arms and held her close to him there in that hay loft. It would be nearer to morning than midnight before they finally fell asleep.

The newlyweds opened the door to the Colonel's house, not quite knowing what to do next. The room was lit by a single oil lamp, and all four windows were draped to discourage prying eyes. Conger felt the need to take charge.

"Would you like to be carried over the threshold?" Well, he had to say something. Dawn looked at him for a second, and then a smile came to her face.

"If it's all the same to you, I'd like to wait on that until we have a place of our own. I'll try not to gain too much weight between now and then."

They both laughed at that, with neither one of them knowing how to act at the moment. After all, just the day before they had been complete strangers, and now they were husband and wife.

There was a bottle of wine already opened, standing along side some tumblers there on the table. Bess had obviously purchased more than one bottle from the Italians. Will wasn't much of a drinker, but offered a glass to Dawn. Her thoughts went back to that night back in Virginia where a bottle of drugged wine had played a major role in her escape. She had often found herself recalling the events of that night when she was with Rhen. Now, here she was with Will, and she had told neither man about her dark past, and about that night in particular.

But that was Catherine, and she was now Dawn Flower. If she really intended to start a new life, this was her chance.

"Just half a glass, a final toast for our wedding night." Conger poured the wine, and they tapped glasses, drinking to their marriage. The wine was clear in color, very unlike the dark red vintages they had both become familiar with growing up. And it was really good! They each had a refill.

Will looked around the room, getting familiar with the setting. Dawn had already slept on that bed earlier in the day, and knew her way around the place. She could tell that Will was stalling for time, and might be feeling awkward or even reluctant around her in this situation.

Bess had arranged for their packs to be brought in from Will's mule and from Dawn's big black horse. They were lying there alongside the door. Dawn had an idea.

"They seem to have brought our packs in for us. To tell you the truth, they smell a lot like the dear creatures that have been wearing them. I'm certain you don't intend to sleep in that uniform tonight. Would you be willing to take out the things you'll be needing, so we can set the packs outside for the evening?" They really did smell bad.

"Of course, that's a great idea. They are pretty gamey." The two of them rummaged through their packs, pulling out the few items they knew they would need.

"Private!" Still dressed as Captain, Conger opened the door and gave an order the likes of which he hadn't spoken for nearly a year. "The lady needs these foul smelling bags taken out of here at once. Line them up along the side of the house here."

Private Jackson stacked his rifle and made quick work of the packs. The Captain's uniform spoke louder than anything this man said. Besides, if he didn't get it right, he'd have to answer to Bess. God forbid.

Conger complimented the young man for his quick work, and promised to give a positive report to Whittle concerning his top notch conduct. Private Jackson would like to have smiled, but knew that such a thing would not be in keeping with tradition. Instead, he smiled after Conger wasn't looking. Dawn motioned for Will to join her.

"I have something I want to show you." Dawn had a very large book in front of her at the table. As Will walked over to sit down, he could tell it was a Bible, and an old one from the looks of it.

"This is my family's Bible. In it are the names of the births and deaths, marriages and other important entries of my family's past. This is the book of the O'Dells. My mother's family also kept such records, but in a very different way." Dawn opened the book, revealing a long list of names and dates. Will was genuinely interested, as his family had such a book, kept safely now in the hands of his older brother James back in Kentucky.

Looking down at the list of names, he saw the most recent entry showing the date of her marriage to Rhen Larson. Will had no idea it had been that recently. Directly above that entry was a reference to the death of on Rebecca O'Dell, and before that, William O'Dell. Will assumed these were Dawn's parents. Dawn had not listed her forced marriage to Jacob McPhearson, or given any mention of him at all for that matter. He had not even been listed as an adopted child. It was as though he never existed.

Of course, Conger was not aware that anything was missing from the list, being unaware of the sham ceremony her Uncle Jacob had forced upon her, or that they had actually been married at all.

Next up was where Dawn first appeared. There were two entries with girl's names, Catherine, and Dawn Flower. Each was born on the same day and date. Dawn went on to explain.

"As I told you yesterday, my mother was of the Cherokee people. In order to avoid prejudice from the white society there in Virginia, she went by the name of Rebecca, and pretended to be of Spanish royalty. Her dark features were thus explained away, and she did in fact speak Spanish rather well. When I was born, she gave me two names. It made things easier for me growing up. I have used the name of Catherine until today. From now on I wish only to be known as Dawn Conger."

A child could have knocked Will off his chair with a feather. At least this explained the name switch at the wedding. Oh well, a rose by any other name...

"I am proud to have you as my wife. I never figured this all would happen so quickly, and to tell the truth, I really didn't know if it was going to happen at all. I tried to talk to you before the wedding, to be sure this was something you really wanted to do. But I didn't have the chance. I just know that when I saw you coming down the aisle, my whole world came together again. You are so beautiful tonight."

Dawn blushed, and a warm glow ran all through her. The buds of romance were ready to blossom between them. But there was something bothering her, and it was important. She didn't know if Will would understand, and she didn't want to ruin their first night together. But it had to be said.

"Mr. Conger, I am the luckiest girl in the world tonight. I am very proud to be your wife, and I know we'll have many wonderful years together. Funny as it might seem, I can't wait to get to know you." They both laughed at that. She was holding his hand to keep herself from shaking. She had something important to say.

"You know what happened to me yesterday. I'm not sure just how far along Jacob got, but you must understand how unclean I feel after what he did. You also need to know that Rhen and I had been together only a few nights before that. He was my husband then, and his advances were welcomed as part of out lives together. I hope you can understand what I am saying."

Conger remained still. Some of these things had crossed his mind as well. He had wondered how she would feel about all of this, but never dreamed they would be married this quickly. He had already decided to leave it up to her discretion, if and when, and on her timetable. But as pretty as she was, keeping to himself would be a challenge.

Dawn sat there, squeezing his hand, hoping she had said the right thing in the right way. This man had every right to do whatever he wished with her, and she was determined not to deny him anything this night. It was just that she wanted a new beginning in that way as well. Will calmed her fears.

"I sincerely hope and pray that I will never do anything to you, or with you, that makes you feel uncomfortable in any way whatsoever. If all we do this night is hold hands as we're doing right now, I will be a privileged man indeed." That was no speech. Those words had come out as easy as breathing, and he meant every word of it.

Talk came easy after that. They shared their childhoods. They talked about their parents, and about growing up. They finished that delicious wine and giggled like children for hours. Somewhere in the night Dawn lay down on the bed and Will lay beside her and kissed her. Within minutes they were both fast asleep, still wearing the borrowed clothes they were wed in.

Sometime before sunrise the changing of the guard woke Conger up. The lamp was still burning softly, and he realized he had fallen asleep still wearing Colonel Peter's uniform. Dawn was sleeping soundly, and being careful not to wake her, he changed out of the uniform and into his nightshirt. He hung the uniform out over a chair, doing his best not to wrinkle the garment any more than he already had.

He glanced down at the table, and noticed that the Bible was still open to the long list of names and dates going back several hundred years, obviously predating that particular book's printing. He looked again at the entry for Dawn, and noticed a name there he had somehow overlooked before. Marybeth O'Dell—could that be the famous Betty O'Dell? Stories were still told about that woman. Now that would really be something! He'd have to ask Dawn about that later.

Not being sleepy at all, Conger proceeded to pull out the papers he had found in Jacob McPhearson's saddle bags the day before. This would be the first time he had the chance to look them over since they left the farm. It took well over an hour for him to finish reading them all, as much of the handwriting was little more than careless scrawl. There were personal letters from those he apparently did illicit business with, and contracts for the movement and sale of what were referred to as 'casket wares,' along with marriage and death certificates as well. There was some very troubling information hidden in these papers. Will would need to consider them very carefully.

Will Conger learned some very important things about his new bride that night as well. He learned why this marriage was very important to her. He learned she couldn't hold her wine. He learned that she snored. He learned that she had been married twice before, and just who those men had been.

And more important to him than all those other things together, he learned that the day he had found her, tied to a bed, with her life in peril, had been his new bride's seventeenth birthday.

chapter 5

COLONEL PETERS WAS finally one step ahead of his wife this time. There at Fort Davis, each and every morning was announced by the bugler sounding reveille, the raising of the flag, and a nifty three gun salute in honor of the country they so proudly served. Peters had stopped shooting off the cannon months ago to save on powder.

Knowing full well that any party following the wedding would most likely go well into the night, Peters had already ordered Whittle to dispense with the rifle salute that morning, and to just raise the flag on the quiet side. And no bugles. Colonel Peters knew that flags can't hear, and that such salutes were far more ceremonial than useful, but nevertheless important and needed in an environment where duty often replaced personal safety. Today would be an exception. Colonel Peters was determined to spare those poor souls who had been forced to run for their lives in the past few days. Having to wake up to the sound of gunfire, possibly fearing they were under attack, just didn't seem like the best use of gunpowder that day. A rifle salute at noon seemed just as effective. Those folks had been through enough already. He'd let them sleep in.

Flag ceremonies and traditions were very important to Peters. Anyone who knew the man understood that right off. But people came first. His duty was to protect the people first, and the traditions after that. Leadership wears many hats.

The mess hall had already seen the comings and goings of enlisted men, officers, and civilians alike that morning. The Colonel and his wife came in to the mess shortly after sunup. They had been awakened as gently as possible by Whittle, and were allowed ample time to get back down the ladder and out of the barn before the morning cleaning crew descended on the place. By now the overcrowded barn had begun to smell like horses again, quite unlike the pleasant aroma of fresh hay from the night before. Once outside, the Peters remembered that they had nowhere to go, what with Will and Dawn having been given use of their quarters.

So, taking Bess by the arm, the Colonel led her over to the mess hall. At least he could have breakfast. They pulled up some chairs at an empty table and waited for something to happen. Sergeant Richards was surprised by the presence of such illustrious guests, as they seldom ever came to his mess hall to eat. It was Bess's preference to make breakfast for her husband at home each morning.

Richards decided to have a little fun, and draping a towel over his arm, strolled out to the dining area, doing his very best French waiter imitation. He had seen this act done in a play back in Philadelphia years back.

"Good Morning, and welcome to Café Chateau Davis." His French accent was actually pretty good.

The Colonel wanted coffee and was tolerant of Richards' nonsense only because the Sergeant already had the coffee pot in his other hand. Bess was loving every minute of it.

"Just pour the coffee, Sergeant." The order from the Colonel had to be obeyed at once, of course. But the playful gleam in Richards' eye did not diminish. He, like everyone else at the fort knew precisely where those two had been all night, and figured correctly just what they had been up to. He gave Bess a knowing wink, and strolled back into the kitchen to whip up some eggs. The chickens were doing much better in their egg production now that they had stopped shooting off that fool cannon every morning.

Bess was still smiling when Richards returned with plates of fried eggs and smoked bacon, along with a bowl of potatoes, onions, and beans, with dried sage sprinkled on top. Peters was still suffering the effects of last night's Italian wine, while Bess wasn't feeling much of anything at all, except hungry.

She wasn't worried that her escapade with the Colonel in the barn loft would be the talk of the fort for days to come. She didn't mind one bit being known as the Colonel's hot little vixen. Bess was honored to play that role in this wonderful man's life, and besides, it helped to keep the competition at bay.

A few minutes later, the newlyweds came dragging in, looking tired and hungry and not quite fully awake. Dawn had slept like a rock, and Will had gone back to bed for a couple more hours of sleep after he had finished with the papers from McPhearson's saddle bags. Having read their contents, he felt luckier than ever to have this girl as his bride, and was now in possession of additional information which needed to be thought over carefully before being acted upon.

Richards greeted the young couple with a warm welcome, and at Bess's insistence, they were seated there at the Colonel's table.

"Good morning, Sir, Ma'am." Conger hoped he had done that in the right order, as the Colonel was still the presiding officer at the fort, whether Bess ran things around there or not. Bess greeted Dawn with hugs, and Will somehow remembered not to salute this time. Within minutes, Richards had two more plates filled just like the others, and had poured coffee for Conger. Dawn had other ideas.

"Would you have any tea, Sergeant?" Will was a bit surprised by Dawn's boldness in asking for tea at a wilderness outpost such as this. But Richards was equal to the moment.

"Why yes of course, Ma'am. In fact, we have a fine assortment of imported English blends. I'll bring some right out. Would Mrs. Peters care for tea as well?" Richards was having too much fun now. He knew Bess hated tea.

"Echoing the words of a famous Colonel, just pour the coffee, Sergeant." Richards scampered off to fetch the tea, pleased that he had managed to get the best of her for once. The Colonel wisely ignored the whole exchange.

They made the usual useless small talk for a few minutes, and then Will reminded the colonel that he had wanted to see the Colt rifle. The two of them got to talking weapons while the ladies went on and on about dresses and such.

"I folded the blue dress and left it on your bed. Please thank the woman who loaned it to me. It was so very pretty the way Mrs. Tanner finished it up."

"That dress is yours to keep, Dawn. The woman who owned it before will never fit into it again. That's why she gave it up. Furthermore, she was paid in trade with two dresses that I too will never be able to wear again."

"Life is short out here, Dawn. Even in the best of circumstances, life seems to get pressed together even shorter. You wear that dress anytime you have a mind to. Chances are, and not too awfully long from now, you won't be able to fit into it either. Enjoy your youth while you're still young. Don't wait 'til tomorrow to enjoy what you can do today. Tomorrow won't always be there for us."

Dawn heard every word, and for a moment there she would have sworn it had been her own mother talking to her. She was beginning to understand that the difference between an older woman and a younger one was the years, and the experiences, not the woman herself. While she had not really changed much at all since she was a little girl, her experiences, good, bad, and awful, had really only made her wiser, and more realistic about her prospects.

"So what now, Conger?" The Colonel was curious as to what the newlyweds had planned next. He could use a man like Will around the fort. He might even be able to get him a commission of some sort, although not likely as Captain.

"To tell the truth, sir, my wife and I have had very little opportunity to talk that over. I came west to see what all was out here, and I feel as though I have barely begun my journey.

Now that I have Dawn with me, I want to be sure that the plans I make include her wishes as well."

The women had stopped talking, and were looking at Will as he finished speaking. They both wore smiles of appreciation for the words they had heard. Amazing how women can talk and listen at the same time. Looking back at Dawn, Bess said it all.

"Dawn Conger, you are one lucky girl." Will blushed, and started to say something stupid, when the Colonel jumped in to rescue him.

"Let's go look at that rifle of yours." Will eagerly agreed. The men excused themselves and headed outside, and just in time. Seeing Bess and Dawn through the open doorway, three women from the wedding party rushed in like a gaggle of noisy geese, all hugging and smiling and talking at the same time.

Sergeant Richards threw up his hands in defeat. Once upon a time, this had been a highly disciplined mess hall, for military types only. He wondered if he would ever get things back to normal. Flowers and pine boughs, indeed!

Conger and Peters found their way over to the Colonel's porch, where Will's packs were still stacked against the wall. On the way over, Will once again had thanked Peters for the use of the uniform, and told him where he had left it.

"It is I who should thank you, Conger. It made the evening very special for my wife. In fact, she cried when I made Major, as I would no longer be wearing that uniform when we went out. It meant so much to her, that she wouldn't even let me put my new rank on the coat. She made me buy a whole new outfit instead! I made Colonel just two weeks before Gettysburg. I had hoped for General some day, but after my wounds, I knew it wasn't meant to be. But at least I'm still alive. I have Bess to thank for that. A lot of would-be Generals were buried back there that day." Peters went on to talk about his time in the hospital, and the way Bess had been on hand to help him along. He really loved that woman, Conger could tell.

"Colonel, the biggest problem with these rifles is the danger of a backfire. I've seen some pretty ugly burns on men who hadn't been real careful how they used their wax when loading the cylinders." Conger showed the Colonel the loading process, and the extra cylinders he kept ready. He also showed him the leather baffle sleeve he had made to protect his hand and arm should a misfire occur.

By now they had walked on through the main gate and out a ways for a little target practice. Will fired first, demonstrating the action for Peters. The Colonel then proceeded to empty the chambers, taking shots at visible targets at different ranges. He was pleased with the results. "I'll send a letter to the War Department, and see if we can maybe get a few of these out here to Fort Davis. It seems well-balanced. How is it in a fight?" Peters could use the firepower.

"When massed together, they can stop a charge in its tracks. It's as easy to use as a pistol on horseback, but with added effective range. Of course, up close it has its limits due to the added length of the barrel." They were still comparing notes on the weapon and the best tactics for its use, when Dawn met them at the gate on their way back in.

"Mr. Conger, there is a group of six wagons, all loaded up and getting ready to head on toward Santa Fe. We've been invited to tag along. They are leaving right away, but I'm sure we would be able to catch up in just a few miles. I'm not real sure just what we're going to do if we stay here." She always called him 'Mr. Conger.' He'd have to talk to her about that, but not now. The girl made sense. There was safety in numbers, and Will figured they had probably already out-stayed their welcome there anyway.

"Tell them we'll catch up in a few hours. We'll need some time to get our things together first." Dawn reached up and planted a kiss on his cheek, and then trotted off to let those folks know they'd be coming along later. Will smiled. He would have gone along just for the kiss.

It was a full hour later before Conger finally got every-thing in order and all the goodbyes had been said. They had met some very good people there at Fort Davis, and would not soon forget them. More importantly, this young couple had left something very important behind as well, that being a good impression.

Will led the way this time, astride a proud horse named Pumpkin, eager to be on the trail again. The two mules trailed behind, with Dawn temporarily bringing up the rear. She turned back and waved at Bess, who stood next to the Colonel on their porch, waving a white handkerchief, as tears ran down her face. It wasn't long until Will and Dawn were out of sight.

The Colonel gave his wife a tender kiss on the forehead, and excusing himself, went back to his office. Bess blew her nose as ladylike as possible, and headed over to the infirmary to check on a man who had been brought in several days before. He was suffering from a gunshot wound to the chest, and had been found lying in a deadfall near the road. A limp-ing dapple gray horse had been brought in with him. The man was alive, barely, and so far had not regained consciousness. It did not look good for him.

Interestingly enough, the surgeon claimed that the man had been shot with a large caliber pistol at short range, but that the powder had apparently not discharged properly, and the bullet had failed to pierce the man's heart. He had seen something like this only twice before. Richard Durbin was very lucky to be alive.

Many miles to the east, another band of travelers were riding westward as well, but with a very different purpose in mind. They rode with only one goal---to overtake the Cherokee Spirit Woman and her great horse.

The prayers of the Washazhe people rode with them as their undertaking was of the utmost importance. The story of this woman and her encounter with Tall Tree had spread like lightning through the many tribal encampments scattered throughout the Kansas Plains. Her quest to make sacrifice in the far away western mountains, and to then release the spirit of Tall Tree was now of great importance. Her words had not fallen on deaf ears.

At first light four Washazhe warriors, chosen for their courage and cunning on the trail had begun their journey west, charged with the task of overtaking the Spirit Woman, and fulfilling the wishes of the tribal elders. The loss of Tall Tree, and the humiliation of the warriors who had accompanied him, had caused a great outpouring of sorrow and outrage among the people, and fear as well, knowing that his soul wandered in the darkness alone and lost. Something had to be done.

To succeed, these four riders would have to move swiftly and carefully, as the woman riding the great horse already had a substantial lead. Once the Washazhe had passed through the lands of the Sioux tribes, they would not likely find welcome among the other nations whose lands they might cross.

They were charged with a task of which they must not fail. The future of the people hung in the balance. And so they rode, like ghosts on the plains, like wind in the grass.

"Does your horse have a name, Mr. Conger?" Dawn was lively and playful today. It was obvious she loved to travel, as did her new husband. They had much to talk about as they rode out from the fort that day, very much unlike the day before. Still, they were vigilant, with eyes searching and heads turning constantly as they traveled. The Cheyenne could be around anywhere.

"Lieutenant Whittle told me they called her 'Pumpkin'. It's because of her color, and also because she is known to be a really sweet little horse. He said that she isn't as fast as she used to be, but loves the trail. I think she'll be perfect for my needs." Pumpkin certainly was a pretty little mare.

"How about your mules? Do they have names too?" Conger had to think about that.

"Well, a boy mule is called a John, and the nick name for John is Jack, and I guess I've just always thought of the mule as Jack. I don't remember actually ever calling him that to his face, but I guess it would have to be Jack."

"Is the other mule a boy too?" She was being playful now, and Will was having a good time with it as well. This was a part of Dawn he hadn't seen before, and he loved it.

"No, that one is a girl mule. Girl mules are known as Mollies. The man who sold me that mule didn't mention her having a name. I guess we could call her Molly."

"Oh no, Mr. Conger, that just won't do. I knew a girl back in Lynchburg named Molly, and she was very disagreeable. We will call her 'Jill' instead, you know, like from the song." Dawn proceeded to sing about Jack and Jill and the hill and all the rest of it. Conger didn't know the tune, but the words seemed vaguely familiar. If Dawn wanted to call the mule Jill, who was he to argue. Jill, it would be.

The thing was, Jill the mule wasn't very happy pulling up the rear behind Jack. She kept trying to get over to Jack's left, but was held back by the positioning of the lead rope. From where she was riding, Dawn could see Jill's frustration growing, and asked Conger to stop for a minute.

"Mr. Conger, Jill is having a problem back here. I think I know what's the matter." Dawn once again stepped down from her mare, and speaking softly to the mules, led Jill over to the left side of Jack and tied her off again. Jill at once quieted down, and Dawn satisfied with her handiwork, stepped back up onto Ooh-luh and signaled Conger that they were ready to go again.

Conger was baffled. He heard quite clearly every word that Dawn had spoken to those mules. Did every four legged animal in Kansas understand Cherokee? It was something to ponder on. And why did she insist on calling him "Mr. Conger"?

The ongoing battle for position ceased, and Jill fell in next to Jack just as happy as could be. Dawn had it figured right. Jill had been part of a two mule team previous to this, and had always pulled in double harness with another mule to her right. She was not used to having another mule in front of her. Truth is, having a mule in front of you is never the best place to be walking at any time. This is where Jill knew she was supposed to be. Dawn would fill Conger in on Jill's situation later on, but for now, and much to Will's relief, the uneven tugging on the lead rope had come to an end. The ride would be much easier from then on. Dawn nudged Ooh-luh up beside Pumpkin, and now everyone was traveling in twos.

They had only been on the trail for about an hour when they caught up to the wagon train. Following their trail had not been difficult, as the wagon wheels were digging deeply into the prairie grass. As they got closer, the canvas covers were easily visible in the open plain. Those canvases had once been white, but now appeared to be more a shade of gray, as rain and dust had taken their toll. The livestock seemed to be pulling strong, having benefited from a few days' rest at Fort Davis. There were now ten wagons in all, as four more families had decided to tag along. Will and Dawn took up a flanking position beside the little wagon train, and waved to the folks they saw.

Rose Spencer had served as Mrs. Tanner's model for the pretty blue dress as it was altered to become Dawn's wedding gown. She saw Dawn and ran right over to greet her, having felt so excited and proud to have played such an important role in Dawn's wedding. Conger was not surprised when Dawn stopped her mare, and having her kneel down, pulled Rose up on the horse's back. The packs the horse had earlier carried were now on Jill, but truth be told, that enormous mare could have probably carried a dozen more girls that size, with room left over.

As it was, Dawn and Rose both sat cross-legged and facing one another while talking and giggling like a couple of schoolgirls, which Rose was and Dawn acted like.

Will loved it. Seeing his lovely young bride having such a good time was tonic to his soul. She had such a beautiful smile. It was wonderful to see her giggling and happy.

They had only ridden for about another hour and a half when the lead wagon came to a stop, and all the others halted behind it. Folks came pouring out of the wagons, and a couple of the men started to build a fire. Will was curious as to what this was all about, and rode over to find out.

"We're stopping for lunch." At least that's the answer one of the men gave him. Sure enough, it was about noon, but it was pretty hot to be standing out there in the sun, and there wasn't any water around for the livestock, who were apparently expected to stand in harness in the heat, while these folks stopped for a leisurely meal.

Will shared his thoughts on the matter.

"And just who do you think you are, telling us our business?" That came from a thin, hawk-nosed man, who had just climbed down from the lead wagon. Jed Dooley was the leader of this group of travelers, and wasn't going to stand for any insubordination in his outfit. What he said was law, just ask him.

Will didn't know the man's name, nor was he impressed by the man's self importance. But he did know livestock, and these animals were suffering. First off, the wagons were loaded up much too heavy. Second, the livestock needed water whenever possible, and provision needed to be made for them.

On top of that, whoever heard of stopping and building a fire for lunch when the object is to get as far a possible each and every day? A fellow could always fix something ahead of time and eat it on the way if need be.

And they certainly weren't making very good time. In fact, at this rate they might reach Santa Fe by the New Year, if they ever got there at all. Will got down from Pumpkin and decided to oblige this Dooley fellow and his desire to talk. But Dooley wouldn't talk. Instead he turned his back and walked away from Conger as if he weren't there. Will decided to let it slide for now, and walked Pumpkin over to where Ooh-luh was lying down, drinking the water Dawn was providing from a canteen. Jack and Jill would be next, along with Pumpkin. Dry horses don't go very far.

It was over an hour before the wagon train seemed ready to go again. About that time, Dooley, along with a couple of tough looking gentlemen, strutted over to where Dawn and Will were resting. It was obvious these men meant business. Dooley let Will know how it was going to be.

"Now that we've allowed you to travel along with us, you are bound to follow the orders that I give. That's the way it is here, and I'll take no more of your back talk. Right now we need that big black horse up front pulling my wagon, and your mules helping out with Bauer's team. You can keep your horse if you have a mind to, but we expect you to ride out and shoot a deer or such for our evening meal. The girl can walk with the others."

Dooley hadn't said more than ten words or so of this pompous self-serving speech, before Conger had his response ready. He'd considered talking it over, but decided it was all going to come down to one thing in the end, and all that talk would be a waste of breath and time.

Conger hit him. This wasn't some friendly little Sunday punch, or even a harsh slap, such as would be given before a duel. Rather, this was the same left-handed haymaker that many a soldier had become so familiar with when challenging their Captain's authority. The punch came from nowhere, and had a far more positive effect on the situation than it had on the man who received it.

Dooley flew backwards, feet leaving the ground, and was out cold before his backside felt the grass beneath him. The other two men stood there in disbelief as their fallen leader lay motionless, no longer in charge of much of anything.

Will stood there as well, and looked them both in the eye. If they wanted some too, he was more than able to oblige. Conger had not lost his touch in this form of communication. A man doesn't make Captain in times of war just because he looks good in a uniform. The older fellow spoke first.

"I wish I'd done that a long time ago. I guess I never had the guts. The man's a fool, and a bully. He'll get us all killed out here. Thank you, mister, you did us all a favor." The man turned and walked back to his wagon, leaving Dooley in the dust. The other fellow grabbed Dooley's arm, and flinging him over his shoulder, carried him back to the lead wagon, where he deposited the unconscious Dooley not so gently into the back. Dawn had not expected this from her husband, but was not surprised by his courage under fire, as she had seen him in action before. She herself had been ready to pull a pistol on anyone who tried to take her mare away from her. If that horse was going to pull any wagon, it would be hers. And she didn't have a wagon.

Will figured they needed to go on ahead by themselves now, having surely outstayed their welcome there. They were just about mount up, when pretty much the whole company of travelers came walking up toward them, men, women, children and all. It looked like trouble.

"Captain Conger, could we have a word please?" This was Rose Spencer's mother. The man standing beside her was the fellow who had hauled Jed Dooley's useless carcass back to the lead wagon. Mr. Spencer looked a little sheepish at the moment, but he was brave enough to come forward, and that said something for him being a man. The group gathered around Will and Dawn. Will was concerned by their sudden appearance, but they didn't act like a mob and weren't brandishing any weapons. He would listen.

"Well, Carl, tell him what you came to say." It seemed like Carl Spencer had somehow gotten himself appointed spokesman for this meeting. The words were getting caught in his throat as he spoke.

"Mr. Conger, or I mean Captain Conger, sir, we feel like we're maybe in a heap of trouble here. None of us has ever traveled this far from home before, and we've been listening to this Dooley fellow, and putting up with his nonsense way too long. I guess it never dawned on us just to tell him 'no'. We apologize for the way he acted toward you and your wife here, and for whatever part we had in letting that happen." A chorus of agreement sprung up from the crowd. But now

Mrs. Spencer took matters into her own hands, and got to the point.

"Captain Conger, we're all going to die here on this trail if we don't get some help soon. We're not moving fast enough, and if things don't change we'll find ourselves caught knee deep in snow with no food or shelter. We're in trouble, and we know it. We have our children to think of." Conger was forced to agree with what she was saying, based solely on what he had seen so far. The wagon wheels were digging in far too deep. That meant that the wagons were loaded much too heavily for the journey. Painful choices would have to be made. It seemed up to him to tell them.

"Turn back. You aren't going to make it. She's right, you are going to die out here." Conger stared them straight in the eye as he spoke. They didn't believe what they were hearing.

"You don't even know where you are going. You're all heading west, on what is basically know as the Santa Fe trail. But you have no destination, no crops, and no way to support yourself when you get there, wherever there is."

"But we hoped you might help us, by leading us through." Well, there it was. They had decided to appoint him wagon master, or guide, or something. Glancing over towards Dawn was a big mistake. She stood there smiling, with her "Well, what are you waiting for?" look on her face. Conger knew he was doomed. That's what he got for clobbering their leader, useless as he was.

Will looked across that sea of faces, tired and worried and knew that fate had found him again. Will was a born leader, and things like this always seemed to gravitate toward him, just when he would prefer to be left alone. But the look on the face of his new bride had sealed the deal. It was a thing he would have to do.

"I'm not really qualified for the task you have set before me. Like you, I have never been in this country before either. I do know a great deal about livestock, and military tactics and such, and I will do my best for you. But I can't promise success." Well, he had at least warned them, anyway.

"Tell us what we need to do." Carl had found his voice, and at that instant Will Conger became Wagon Master. Will took a deep breath, and grasping the situation as it stood, asked everyone to sit down in the shade the nearby trees provided. Then he commenced to preaching.

"Your wagons are too heavy. The stock are being forced to work too hard to move your goods. The wagons themselves are heavy enough already. You're all going to have to leave things behind that you really don't want to, and it's going to hurt. You saw the faces of those folks who came into the fort the last few days, having lost everything. But they had left everything behind to save their lives. That's where you are right now. Each and every one of you must remove one half of the weight in your wagons right here, right now, if you are to have any hope of surviving. There's the truth of it.

If Conger had told them they would all have to turn themselves into rabbits, the response would have been the same. They mumbled and grumbled to themselves. They didn't like it much at all. Will's popularity had shrunk considerably in the last few seconds. Carl Spencer spoke up first.

"These things are ours, and we brought them with us to help build our new lives out here in the west. Who are you telling us what to do?

Conger was livid. It had been a whole lot easier to deal with the troops in the Illinois sixth---they did as they were told. Now Conger was ready to move on without them.

"He's right." The crowd turned as one toward the familiar voice. Jed Dooley had come to, and seeing the meeting in progress, had come quietly over to see what it was about.

"This is all my fault." Jed continued. "Clear back at Independence I told several of you to lighten your load, and you just laughed at me. So I've been trying to move you on the way that I have, to somehow make it all work. I've been short of temper as of late because I realize the mess we're in. I just haven't had the courage to face you down. I'm sorry. I guess I wasn't cut out for this." The crowd sat silent, stunned by the realization of what Jed had said to them. It all made sense now. The short days, the noon breaks---it was all designed to help save the livestock. Jed had done better for them than they knew, but for all the wrong reasons.

"Mrs. Spencer, what is the heaviest piece of furniture in your wagon?" Conger had jumped back in now. There was a chance of turning this thing around. Mrs. Spencer thought for a second, not because she didn't know, but because she knew that her words would doom her plans. It was a hard pill to swallow.

"We have an old dresser, it was my Grandmother's. I had always hoped to leave it to Rose as a wedding gift." She looked down, reluctant to deal with the unthinkable.

"If we don't lighten your wagon by half, and soon, chances are she won't live long enough to be a bride. However, there is a town about twenty miles west of here. If you're so married to your things that you just won't live without them, stay there, and go no further, for you won't make it. I will do my best to help you to get that far. If you wish to go on, maybe you can unload your things there to others who might need them. And then you can join up with some other outfit headed on the Santa Fe. The bigger the outfit, the better your chances of getting through. If you had listened to this man from the start, you might have already been long past there by now."

Four days later the little ten wagon outfit was safely on the outskirts of the town Conger had seen labeled on his map. The canvas tops of dozens of wagons were scattered about, as many groups of travelers and freighters alike had stopped here for trade, re-supply, and some of the amusements which always seemed to find their way to temporary places such as this.

It was evening, and Will and Dawn had already split off from the main group and made camp in a lightly wooded area near a creek about a mile from town. They had decided to stay the night and go into town the next morning.

The last few days with the wagon train had proved to be a useful lesson in human nature. Not one family had lightened their load, but Conger had overheard talk among them as to what they would be willing to leave behind. Conger had the opportunity to ride with Dooley once or twice, and talk over his situation. It seems Dooley had been out this way before to scout out the territory on his own, and had been appointed Wagon Master for that reason only. He really wasn't cut out for the job, and had tried to accomplish the task the best way he knew how. All in all, he was a pretty good man, once you got to know him. Still, Conger did not apologize for hitting him.

Whatever these folks did next was their own business. Will had helped to get them in safely, and they knew their options. Each night Conger had held council with the men and the women alike, talking about defense, and water, and the handling of livestock. The noon breaks had ceased, replaced by a water break for the livestock every two hours for five minutes at a time. It was a patchwork plan at best, but it got them in. Dooley led them on down to the town, a better man for what all had happened, and wise enough now to leave that job to someone more qualified from there on out.

Will and Dawn slept dry and comfortable under the canvas tent that night, as a gentle rain poured down upon the plains. Dawn had become used to the Army cot by now, and saw the wisdom of it. She looked forward to bathing in the creek the next morning, and planned to fix up and go into town before noon. It would be fun to walk beside her new husband, and she would wear that new blue dress of hers. Bess had been right---the time would come that it would no longer fit her.

It was quiet on the prairie that night.

The trail town of Mullit was not much to look at and chances were it never would be. It seems that before the war, some fellow named Mullit from places unknown broke down here on his way to Santa Fe. Apparently Mullit was an extremely disagreeable sort, and the other families traveling with the wagon train agreed to give him food and supplies if he promised not to come along with them any further. As no one would make any effort to help him fix his wagon, Mullit accepted the offer and just stayed where he was.

It wasn't long before other wagons came through, and this Mullit fellow managed to do a good business trading and selling the supplies he had been given, all at a handsome profit. Seeing the opportunity, others stopped and set up shop as well, supplying the needs of settlers traveling to Santa Fe and other places out that way. Over the course of a few years the town of Mullit became a regular watering hole for wagon trains and cattlemen alike. No one knows what ever happened to old Mullit.

Dawn was up early that next morning, down at the creek with her horse, the both of them playing like children in the cool, fresh water. Will had heard Dawn splashing and giggling like a little girl, and stripping down, jumped right in with them. Of course, his weapons were very close by all the same. A man just never knew about such things out here.

Dawn needed some supplies, women's things and such, and felt an urge to fancy up a bit and go in to town proper like. Will thought it all a lot of nonsense as Mullit wasn't much of a town, and certainly didn't rate getting gussied up for. Still, he had no real reason to challenge his new bride on the matter, and just kept his mouth shut. His father had taught him never to argue with a woman, for even if the man wins the argument, she'll always make him pay dearly for his victory in one way or another for days to come. Truer words were never spoken.

They rode in to Mullit around ten o'clock that morning, and turned more than a few heads as they arrived. Will and Pumpkin took the lead, with the two pack mules trotting behind almost in lock step. To see those two mules together, a fellow could have thought they had been together all their lives.

But no one noticed Conger, or Pumpkin, or the mules all that much either. All eyes were on the lovely girl wearing a light blue dress, with her dark hair pulled back into a bun, and sitting atop an enormous black mare. She looked like a royal princess entering her realm, or maybe rather like a circus acrobat, sitting cross-legged atop that huge horse, with only a blanket beneath her, and using no bridle or reins to guide the beast.

There were three dry goods stores in town, along with a barber, bath house, hotel, and three saloons, which also served as the local eateries. A livery was set up further down the road. This may all sound like a lot, but in truth, the whole shebang could have fit within the modest confines of Fort Davis with room to spare.

Will determined that the first store would most likely be the most expensive, as it was on the right, and furthest east in town. Most folks will turn in at the first place available after a long trip, and finding what they need, not bother to compare prices elsewhere. This would not be the place the locals would trade at. Instead, he went to the left side of the street, if you could call it a street, and stopped in front of a neat little shop with a sign overhead which simply read 'Smith's'. Dawn, having captured the attention of just about everyone in town, especially the men folk, rode up beside Will, and with a quick set of instructions to the mare, stepped right down to the street with ease.

They more than likely were in Smith's shop no more than fifteen or twenty minutes, but it seemed like an hour to Will. Before long she had several packages bundled and ready to go. Mrs. Smith, a sprightly woman only a few years older than Dawn, delighted in helping her try on some of the dresses she had in stock. They giggled and carried on like school girls behind the curtain, and eventually came out with three more bundles to add to the pile.

For his part, Will chose some extra cartridges, two new bandanas, four shirts, two pair of trousers and a selection of medicines and ointments. Mr. Smith was especially helpful with the munitions, having served in the war as well. Unlike Dawn, Will managed to select his purchases without giggling.

The Smiths had a good selection, and as Will had guessed correctly, were not overly pricey. Still, he was forced to get into his money belt for the first time on his journey to ante up. The Smiths didn't have everything the couple needed, and politely directed their patrons to the 'Prairie Mercantile' a few doors down, to finish up their shopping list.

Between Smith's store and the Mercantile, were the barber shop and a saloon. Will eyed the red and white pole with some interest, wondering just how long it might be until he would see another barber. The saloon was more of a cantina, built low in the traditional adobe manner, with seats and tables right out on the street. While Will studied a wooden Indian in the barber shop window, Dawn was making her way down the street, heading for the mercantile.

Will watched her go, and got busy loading all those supplies onto the pack mules, figuring that he needed to hurry and catch up with Dawn before she spent all his money. A light breeze was bringing delicious aromas up from the cantina, and Conger was determined to make a case to his new bride for stopping in that day for a bite to eat.

While the great trail herds were not yet traveling up from Texas, cattle were already moving this way to fill the needs of ranchers staking their claim on this part of the West. With cattle come drovers, and about a dozen or so had taken up station at the tables at the front of the cantina. They had already had too much to drink, and it was not even noon yet. Looking as lovely as a spring flower, Dawn passed near to one of those tables, and received a proper slap on her behind from one of the men.

Smith had just come out carrying the last of the bundles and saw the whole thing, so did Conger. Smith, fearful of the trouble that could come of this, became alarmed as he saw the look on Conger's face, fully expecting a brawl, if not a shooting, then and there.

Jake Bellows was the drover who had glad-handed Dawn, and this community was frightened to death of him. Many a man had suffered terribly from the power of his fists, and he had made it his game to take liberties with just about every woman he came across. His gun skills were even more deadly than his punches. An impertinent slap on the behind was just his style.

Dawn stopped in her tracks, and just stood there. The laughter of the men at the tables was already dying down, in eager anticipation of what would happen next. Dawn surprised everyone watching by turning slowly around, and with a wonderful smile on her face, and with that butter thick Southern Belle accent of hers, addressed Bellows in the most ladylike manner.

"I do declare, sir, why forever would you do such a thing as that? Perhaps it is a local custom to which I am not yet acquainted. Do tell me if it is, as I wouldn't want to seem rude among strangers, seeing how I'm new in these parts." The men laughed at her apparent naiveté. Much to Smith's surprise, Will's face broke into a soft grin, which changed to a gentle laugh. Smith was astounded.

"Sir, are you going to permit this? That's Jake Bellows! He is a known killer, and molester of women. You'd best get your wife out of there before it's too late!" The rise in Smith's voice showed his fear of the man. Several people had gathered around, waiting for the drama to unfold. The looks on their faces showed that they were all afraid, for the girl, and for themselves.

"If I interfere," Will calmly responded, "it will be to save this Bellows fellow from having his hide tanned and nailed to the side of that barn over there." Smith was certain that Conger was daft, but Will had good reason to be concerned about just how far his new bride might go in a situation like this. Bellows sat there in his chair, feet spread apart, with a big greasy grin filling his face. He proceeded to look Dawn up and down like she was first prize in a raffle, and made the fool's mistake of opening his mouth.

"My, my, fellows, a lady of the South, I do declare!" The laughter roared as he mimicked her accent. Big Jake was in his element here.

"Why missy, that's what's known around these parts as a Kansas hello! Anyone with such a fine looking backside as yours is welcomed to our fair land with a proper smack on the behind just to show how appreciative we are of the view. It's a long-standing custom around here---isn't that right boys?" The raucous laughter got going again, as things were starting to get ugly. Conger, watching Dawn closely, unsnapped his holster and readied his pistol, fearing what was about to happen.

"Why sir," Dawn replied, still sporting that Virginia accent, "I must thank you then for thinking so highly of me and this old blue dress I am wearing. How very nice of you to notice." The townspeople were taken aback, not quite knowing what to make of this girl who would so easily accept this affront to her privacy. Will moved in closer.

"You must allow me to return the favor, sir." Her playful manner gave no hint as to what was to come. "Please sir, do stand up and let me look at your back side as well. Such a big strong man as yourself must have a backside far superior to most others. Surely you would allow me the opportunity to return the greeting."

Jake Bellows was full of whiskey and full of himself. That, along with a lifelong dose of stupidity led him to stand up, and turn his backside to Dawn, playing the joke for all it was worth. He had visions of other games he might be playing with this little Southern girl before the night was over. He stood there, very pleased with himself.

"My, my, sir," Dawn spoke, echoing his earlier words. "What a fine backside you have indeed. Had you not been sitting as I passed by, I surely would have noticed it before now. Please sir, could you bend over the table a bit more, so I might have an even better view?" Bellows looked around at his compatriots with a sly grin, enjoying himself immensely, and hearing their bawdy encouragement, bent far over the table, to give the whole world a fine view of his ample bottom.

Now under that lovely blue dress, Dawn was wearing Eastern style riding boots, made especially for her of excellent leather, and sharply pointed so as to allow for easy access in to the stirrups which were common to most saddles. She did not use a saddle on her mare, but these were the only boots she owned, and she had not wanted to get Will's fine moccasins dirty in the streets of Mullit, much to Bellows' misfortune.

Bellows bent further over and the raucous laughter increased even more. Dawn wasted no time, and immediately kicked the unfortunate fool square between the legs with those pointed boots of hers. Her kick was strong and sure, and she actually left the ground in the effort. Truth be told, her aim was a little further in than the man's bottom, and the effect was all that she could have hoped for.

Bellows' ample bottom took the full force of the kick, and screaming like the pig he was, he fell forward, collapsing the table, and causing a chain reaction of tables, chairs and bottles, which sent drovers and whiskey flying across the room. The resulting mayhem was punctuated with curses, crashes, and the breaking of glass. It was now the turn of the townspeople to enjoy their laughter at the expense of these ill-mannered loafers. Bellows meanwhile remained on the ground in abject agony, while others jumped up, ready to teach this girl a lesson. How dare she show such a lack of respect?!

Instead, they froze still in their tracks. In clear sight for all to see, the little lady in the blue dress held a large caliber, double-chambered derringer. The look on her face could have melted iron, and every man there knew he had only to act the fool to invite a slug from her widow maker.

"You men have insulted me and every woman in town by behaving this way." The Southern belle accent was gone. "What would your mothers say if they saw you acting like this? Is this the way you were taught to treat a lady? You should be ashamed, how dare you?!" The men looked down and around at the ground at the suggestion, being a long way from home, and knowing that she was right.

"Listen to me very carefully. I'm going to finish my shopping, and then I intend to return to this place and enjoy the delicious food that I can smell cooking in there. You men will now clean up this dining area, and I mean swept clean, so that it will be presentable on my return." Then she got them where they lived.

"I would be pleased if those among you who are truly gentlemen would see fit to dine along with my husband and myself when we return. We have much to learn about this new country, and I am certain each of you could be very helpful in telling us of the terrain, the Indians, and the trails ahead."

"You are fools to follow the lead of a man such as this." She pointed down at the whimpering Bellows with her left hand, her right still holding the derringer dangerously steady. "You men need to ride your own trails and make your own path in life. Work beside men, not for them. Call down bullies such as this, and deal with them however you must, or their stench will cling to your boots, as you blindly follow them, walking in their filth."

Immediately the men spoke words of sincere regret and apology, removing their hats, and scraping their feet like a bunch of little school boys dressed down by their teacher. Dawn, ever in control, thanked them for their time, and putting the derringer back into the folds of her dress, turned abruptly around and renewed her walk toward the 'Prairie Mercantile.' The crowd was breaking up, laughing and retelling what they had seen and heard that day. Some of the women decided they might do better to go armed themselves. Smith turned to Conger and shared his astonishment at what he had just witnessed.

"I don't believe it! She took on the whole lot and made them take water, every one!" While Smith went on and on, others came up to congratulate Will on his wife's courage. It was Mrs. Smith who asked Conger if he was surprised by his wife's behavior.

"I suppose I am," Will replied, calmly. "I didn't know she had a derringer."

About twenty minutes later, Will and Dawn were returning from the store with another load of packages. There was a skip in Conger's step, knowing that they would be lunching at the cantina after all, and he hadn't even had to talk her into it. It sure smelled good.

Their stock had been standing quite a while in the hot sun, as they had remained in Mullit longer than planned. Taking charge of the horses himself, he paid two boys to help him move the mules down to the livery, where they would have some shade and possibly a bait of oats or some such if any were to be found. Dawn insisted on going ahead to find a table at the cantina.

It pleased Dawn to no end that Will had complete faith in her ability to take care of herself. There are women in this world who want their men around all the time, like a handbag, to make all the decisions, and handle things while she just stands around looking pretty. Such a woman is never all that pretty.

Dawn was not that way. For her part, she had come to truly like this young Welshman, and was certain that in time they would grow very close. It was the respect he showed her at all times that meant so much to her. It was a new and wonderful feeling. As Dawn returned to the cantina, she wondered what awaited her there. She had made her speech, and laid down the law. She was amazed at what she found.

The place was absolutely spotless, with tables and chairs neatly arranged, a cloth across each table, and flowers in glasses all around. They sorry carcass of Jake Bellows was nowhere to be seen. As if on cue, about a half dozen drovers stood up, hats in hand, like schoolboys at their first dance.

Will had not been nearly as trusting as he let on. While Dawn shopped, he looked in on the progress being made at the cantina, and had spoken with the proprietor. The man's name was Rivas, fine looking Mexican fellow, up in years, but strong and full of life. He had been losing business while this cattle crew had infested his cantina, as the regular decent folk were afraid to come near. He had hired girls from the town to help with cooking and serving the food, but would not allow them to go near this group of ruffians, especially when Bellows was nearby. Will advised Rivas that some of the men might choose to stay to eat as Dawn had offered, and promised to provide security as needed if things started to get out of hand.

Will also put in a good word for any of the men who chose to stay and clean up.

Rivas greeted Dawn and showed her to a table in the shade provided by an outcropping of the roof. Will excused himself to check on the mules. In truth, he thought this might be a good time to disappear while his bride took charge of the festivities. He wasn't the least bit worried now about his wife, or for her safety. After all, she still had that derringer.

Dawn, being the solid Southern lady that she was, immediately stood back away from her chair, and asked the men if they would care to dine with her and her husband. She was genuinely delighted when they said yes, to a man, and she instructed them to reset the tables into one long family style table. They hopped to it, and the smiles on their faces showed how much they were enjoying the company of this lovely girl. One of the men started to sit down, but was immediately chided by the others, as the lady still remained standing. Dawn took charge again, expecting the best from these young men.

"Gentlemen, I will not dine with anyone who has not washed before coming to the table. Your hands are filthy! I fully understand that you must sometimes eat that way out on the trail, but this is a table, and these are chairs, and they require clean hands."

The rugged cowhands of the 'Slash M' brand nearly knocked each other over as they rushed to the rain barrel out back to wash up. It was very fitting that these fellows who had taunted her so recently now showed their hands to Dawn for inspection before they returned to the dining area. Dawn moved now to the middle of the long table the men had put together, and one of the men, not forgetting his manners, held the chair for her. Will had quietly returned, and sizing up the situation, sat at the end of the table where he could easily keep an eye on the cowhands, and on the street beyond. He fully expected Bellows and his die hard cronies to return to even things up. But that didn't happen, and the afternoon meal went without a hitch. Still, Conger would need to keep a sharp look out, knowing the kind of man Bellows was.

The dinner went well, and the men helped clean up after themselves when it was over. As Will and Dawn were about set to leave to go back to their campsite, Mr. Rivas hurried up to them with a special request.

"Please, may I have a word with you? Already others from town are here to enjoy our food and hospitality. This is because of what you have done here today. Please allow me to do something for you as well. Come for breakfast in the morning. I will have something special for you. Please say that you will." Conger was about to decline, wanting to get back on the trail again yet that day. But Dawn was already accepting the invitation.

"Why thank you sir. What a wonderful idea. We would love to come by in the morning." Will just hoped the man knew how to make coffee.

chapter6

THE RIDE BACK to the campsite didn't take all that long. Will had already decided to move upwind a hundred yards or so, away from the droppings the stock had left the day before. It was against his better judgment to camp in the same area two nights in a row, but since Dawn had accepted Mr. Rivas' invitation for breakfast in the morning, they would have to stay the night around town somewhere. This location offered about as good a place as they would find on short notice anywhere near Mullit, and in truth, anyone who was looking for them would find them sooner or later anyway. Still, Conger took extra time looking around the area while Dawn was putting something together for dinner.

The welcomed breeze of the morning had died off, leaving the air hot and damp. Sleeping under the canvas tent was not nearly as comfortable as the night before. Even the stock seemed restless. Conger got up and listened to the night sounds more than once. He was uneasy. Something just didn't feel right. Right then he wished they had moved on down the trail after their luncheon. He just didn't figure that a man like Bellows was going to be put off that easily. Conger's sixth sense told him of danger. His family name was Irish in origin, but that family had lived in Wales for over four hundred years, and had intermarried with several of the local inhabitants over the generations. Some of the Welsh were known for having what was called 'the sight' a mystical ability to see the future before it occurs. He was told that his father's mother had the sight, and had used it to save her own life and the life of others more than once. Will didn't have it, at least not so he could tell, but possessed a kind of sixth sense that had saved his skin on battlefields in the South more than once. It was talking to him now. He slept with one gun across his chest, and another strapped to his waist.

The morning remained on the hot and sticky side, and Dawn was anxious to get down to the creek to wash off the night's sweat. The big black horse came along as expected. They played in the water together, but not for quite as long as the day before. Dawn sensed the concern in her husband's manner, and got ready quickly, but with none of her usual playfulness. Besides, as their breakfast was waiting for them in Mullit, there was little to do except break camp and ride into town.

It was about an hour after sunrise, and Mullit was already busy with the sounds of the day. Folks waved as Will and Dawn rode in, her exchange with Bellows and his gang having been the talk of the town ever since. Following Dawn's example, many of the women in town were now armed, and a peace keeping council of men at arms had been formed to patrol the streets. "Ask once, and then shoot," would be the order of the day from here on out. It was a start.

Conger and wife rode up to Mr. Rivas' cantina and tied the stock off at the rail nearby. There was no reason to board the animals, as they planned to hit the trail right after breakfast. There seemed to be no sign of the drovers who had bothered Dawn the day before, and the bright morning sunshinehelped to lighten Will's worried mood.

Mr. Rivas beamed as the young couple arrived, and led them to a table he had prepared for them, tablecloth and all. Dawn was delighted and Conger equally impressed. Coffee, tea, milk, and cold water were served along with bowls of fresh fruit and bread with honey. Real silver service accompanied the wooden plates at the table. It was all very nicely presented.

Then came two young dark haired girls, each carrying two platters of food. There was ham with gravy, more freshly baked bread, a delicious looking mess of eggs, slices of cheese, and at last came Mr. Rivas himself, with a large bowl in hand, and a huge smile from ear to ear.

Grits! He had no more put the bowl down than those two Southern kids were reaching for their spoons to see who could get there first. Grits of all things!

"I couldn't help but hear the Southern accent in both of your voices yesterday, and I knew that this is a favorite in the South." Rivas went on to explain that he had worked at a restaurant in New Orleans for two years before heading out west, and had learned to make the dish from scratch from a special recipe supplied by a fellow from Richmond. Conger stopped eating long enough to stand up and shake Rivas's hand.

"Thank you sir, thank you very much. This is really a wonderful surprise and a delicious breakfast. You keep cooking like this, and keep the troublemakers away, and you will need a much bigger place to serve all the customers." Indeed, word had spread quickly, and already many of the tables were filling up with townsfolk and passers-by alike. Rivas sent one of the girls home to fetch her sisters---he would need extra help this day.

Rivas would not accept any of Conger's money for the meal, claiming that the boldness he and his wife had shown had made it possible for him to do business again. Conger laughed to himself at that, knowing full well that Dawn had carried the day, not him. But he still wondered where she got the derringer.

As the Congers rode out of town that morning, Will couldn't help but notice that now most of the men, and many of the women, were wearing side arms now, unlike the day before. Anyone causing trouble around there was liable to get a belly full of lead as a result. But Will knew that wasn't always such a good thing, as more than one man had died needlessly due to an unintended slight, or a misunderstanding of intentions. This kind of thing went both ways, as the other fellow most likely had a gun, too.

It looked as though the town of Mullit was expecting the return of Bellows and his bunch of hoodlums at any moment, coming back to even the score from last night's humiliation. Mullit was ready and waiting. But what they needed to understand was that even if Bellows was done away with, there would always be some other fellow out there to take his place---always had been, and always would be. That's just the way things are.

As they rode out, the trail west was clearly marked by the ruts of wagon wheels, until the grasses slowly took over again. It was a beautiful morning, and a slight breeze had picked up. Full bellies and good weather promised for a wonderful day. Amazingly, there had been no talk of any recent Indian trouble out this way. Conger figured they were nearly into New Mexico via the nation, and that tribal boundaries could shift a traveler's priorities and expectations. He had talked to some freighters who had just been over the trail as they headed back east, and with their help had made up some maps locating water and landmarks. The distances these fellows were mentioning seemed a bit on the long side, but Conger decided to go with what they said unless he learned otherwise. After all, they had been there, and he hadn't.

Suddenly Dawn stopped, and reminiscent of their escape from the farm, she stood up on the back of her horse and looked off to the north. Will didn't say a word, nor did he bother her. She would say anything she had to say soon enough. As it was, he knew already that she had better eyes than his for distance, and he also knew she could feel and sense things that he wasn't aware of. He would wait, and listen.

"Someone is near us. I noticed something this morning back at camp, but I thought it must be some deer. Now, I'm not so sure. I can't really see anything, it's just something that I feel."

"I believe you. A lot of people are out traveling this way nowadays. Some might not be friendly. Do you want a rifle?" Conger was carrying one of the Colt repeaters along with his pistol. Dawn was only wearing a side arm.

"Not just yet, maybe later. It gets awfully heavy after a while. Just keep one handy."

They rode on, seeing no one, and hearing nothing out of the ordinary. And then, out from the south came a lone rider, moving right along but not in any sort of fast panic or anything. It was clear that it was a white man, and that he was headed straight for them. Whatever he wanted, they would find out soon enough. Conger lined up his rifle with the rider's mid section. No sense taking chances.

They were now about four miles west of Mullit when the rider finally caught up with them. Will had stopped when the man was about a hundred yards off and let him come on in. The stranger raised his hand in greeting.

"Hey there, wait up!" He waved his hat and rode on in. Will and Dawn were wondering what someone was doing all the way out here. The Colt rifle stayed at the ready, just in case a disagreement broke out.

"Howdy!" The rider finished closing the gap to within a few feet. A big smile filled his face, and he took off his hat so as to wipe the sweat off his brow. Will noticed that the rider's horse on the other hand showed no sign of being hot and tired at all.

"I kinda figured it was you folks, what with that big black horse of yours. I wanted to apologize for all the trouble we caused you yesterday , Ma'am." Once again he removed his hat, but this time to show respect to go along with his words.

"I don't recall seeing you at the dinner, sir." A little bit of Virginia twang had returned to Dawn's voice. Will caught the significance at once, and slowly guided his mount to a more strategic position around to the other side of the rider, thus getting Dawn out of the line of fire. If the rider noticed Will's movement, he didn't let on.

"No Ma'am, I'm sorry to say you didn't. After you left, and after all the things you said, the most of us decided we needed to do better and all, and so we set to putting things right by you. They left it to me to get Bellows out of there and back to the outfit. It took three of us to get him on a horse, beings where you had kicked him and all, not that he didn't have it coming, mind you. Anyway, by the time I got back, the dinner was over and I'd missed out on the whole thing." Conger studied the man carefully as he spoke. There was something nervous and unnatural about his voice, something that didn't quite fit right. The fellow's accent certainly sounded like Texas to him. He'd heard plenty of that lingo the day before at the cantina. Yet his words sounded almost memorized, somehow. Will started to speak, but Dawn jumped in first, taking charge of the conversation.

"Why, I thank you sir for all that you did on our behalf." The Virginia sorghum was still flowing. "Won't you ride along with us for a while so we might get to know you better? Please ride along side of me here, won't you?" Clever girl, Conger decided. With this fellow riding along side of Dawn, Will could easily keep an eye on him from behind. If he was up to any mischief, she would flush it out of him in no time. Still, he seemed sincere enough, and if he had wished them harm, he could have easily shot from ambush instead of riding up to them. Will figured that maybe he was getting a might bit too suspicious nowadays. Having Dawn with him made things different.

The three of them rode together for another mile or so, when the rider, who had since given his name as Rusty, mentioned that his horse was in need of water, and that there was a good clear stream up ahead just off the path to the north. Sure enough, there was a stand of healthy looking cottonwoods there, and knowing that it could be awhile 'til the next good water, Will and Dawn followed Rusty though some undergrowth to where the cottonwood cast a heavy shadow in the early morning sun. True to his word, there was the stream, clear and crisp and running free.

Rusty moved toward the water, but then suddenly turned his horse around and had Conger pinned under the sights of his pistol. Those cow ponies could turn on a dime and Rusty showed this Kentucky boy just how it was done. Conger had his rifle out, but it was pointed in the wrong direction now. Even though the Colt had a relatively short barrel as rifles go, he would never get the weapon into action before Rusty mowed him down. The fact that he hadn't shot Will already, meant that there was something else at stake here, something very distasteful, Will was sure.

Dawn sat very still, holding her horse's mane, and speaking softly in words Conger could only assume were Cherokee. She was looking around as she spoke, as though she saw something there in the trees. Only seconds passed until more riders came up to encircle them, with Rusty moving to the back behind the mules. Then came Bellows riding out of the trees, with a sinister look of pure meanness about him. The horse he rode seemed small for his huge frame, and tobacco juice flowed down the side of his face. For awhile he just sat there, looking the girl over, and paying no attention to Conger at all.

"Well there, little lady, seems like you've ridden a long way just to see me again." He chuckled to himself, and a familiar chorus joined in. These were the men who had preferred not to stay for the meal the day before. They had other appetites.

Dawn continued to speak to the mare, almost in a whisper. She had uncrossed her legs, and was sitting close up on the horse's neck. Will had never seen her sit on the horse like that before, and paid close attention.

"Alright mister," Bellows had suddenly turned his attention to Will, "shuck that fancy rifle of yours. You wouldn't want to see the little girl here get hurt would you? We figure you're carrying quite a bit of cash on you, and being neighborly, we intend to ease your burden a bit by taking it off your hands."

There was no laughter this time, and Conger knew this was no robbery. Something far more sinister was involved here, and he was certain it had to do with Dawn. His Irish was starting to rise, but his Welsh had to think him through it if they were going to get out alive. He laid the rifle down as carefully as he could from the saddle. Throwing it could have easily caused it to discharge, which could spell disaster in any number of ways.

"There, that's better." Bellows felt triumphant. "And don't you go trying for those pistols of yours, or Rusty here will drill you faster than you can say 'boo'." There was laughter that time, and Will knew whatever was going to happen would happen soon. He was working on some way to break this up and get Dawn out of there, but from where he sat he saw no chance to make any move that would not put her at terrible risk. They had laid the trap very nicely.

Had Dawn not been there, Conger would have opened up already and taken his chances. But having the girl along made for a very different set of rules. He rightfully figured that she was the one they had come to see. He was just in the way.

"We all plan to spend some time getting to know you a lot better, little lady. You know, you were rather rude to me yesterday, and I felt badly that you didn't invite me to stay and have dinner with you like you did the other boys. So we're going to start off by getting a much better look at that cute little behind of yours. We'll just let your boyfriend here watch and see how a grown man handles a spirited little filly like you."

Their laughter resounded through the trees. Conger knew he must do something now, even if it meant his death. Still, Will had noticed a subtle movement on Dawn's part. She was now gripping the mare's mane with two hands, and leaning over the horse's massive neck. She had tightened her legs against the mare's body, and turned her head away, eyes shut tight. Will watched as the mare's ears, which had been standing high and straight, suddenly pulled back as its hindquarters tensed.

The stream was no more than six feet across at this point. Bellows sat on his horse on the far side along with one other rider, with the other two on the same side as Conger. The laughter had begun to die down as Bellows, full of himself started to speak again, but his words were cut off short, as suddenly all hell broke loose.

While Bellows had sat there talking his brag, Dawn had been busy whispering instruction to her mount, telling of the danger of the moment, and commanding her faithful friend to overcome these men, and to lash out against them. Her words became more and more intense, until the sound became like a chant, calling upon the powers of nature to intercede against the evil which stood there before her.

Conger had heard the building intensity of Dawn's incantation, and temporarily abandoned his desperate plans, waiting instead for the move which he was certain would come. He readied himself to leap into action, and planned his attack. He would not have long to wait.

Dawn gave a signal that only Ooh-luh understood, and the speed and fury of what happened next was beyond the mettle of these men who had spent most of their lives riding horses chosen only for their ability to work cattle. They had no experience with a horse such as this. Dawn's great black mare was the end product of hundreds of years of perfecting the breed. This was a Percheron mare, eighteen hands, the descendant of those mighty war horses which had led the Crusaders into battle in times long before. This was the fury Dawn unleashed upon her enemies.

The black tensed, and then lunged forward, clearing the small creek in a single leap, and crashed headlong into Bellows and his lighter cow pony. There had been no warning, no preparation, only the horrified look of terror on the face of the braggart as Dawn's war horse descended upon him, clamping its teeth down on his outstretched arm, and dragging him from his saddle. His gelding fell backwards in a heap of flailing legs, as Bellows, his arm still caught in the mare's powerful jaws, became trapped under those enormous hooves and disappeared below.

Then, with only a gentle nudge, Dawn redirected her deadly charge toward the rider to her right, who while trying to draw his pistol, suddenly stopped in mid motion just before the giant black nightmare drove headlong into his smaller pony as well, sending them both tumbling. The horse landed its full weight on the body of the helpless man, as he seemed unable to jump free of his falling mount.

Will had been ready, but he didn't know for what. Her move was so sudden that he was caught totally off guard, as were the men surrounding him. But here Conger had the advantage. He was the veteran of years of deadly cavalry engagements, where split second decisions and close quarter maneuvers meant the difference between victory or an early grave. The horse beneath him was cavalry trained, and used to the sound of gun fire. Pumpkin was skilled in the type of riding Conger demanded of her now, quick and agile, responding instantly to the wishes of her rider.

Will had watched as Dawn's mare suddenly burst into action, flying over the creek as though it were a puddle. He did not wait to see any more. These men had come to kill them both, and there would be no quarter given. With a well-practiced move, known to both man and horse, Conger ducked down and turned his union mount clockwise, while cross-drawing his pistol in one continuous motion.

Within seconds both of the men on his side of the creek were down, each leveled by a shot to the head, victims of Conger's practiced marksmanship on horseback. He had learned his trade in some of the most brutal and unforgiving classrooms the war could provide. These men, however, untrained and unprepared, were no match for Captain Conger's tactics and experience. He gave them no chance, no opportunity to react. Despite having pistols drawn, neither man had gotten off a shot.

Conger spun his mount again, ready to join battle with the other two, praying that Dawn had somehow survived her reckless attack. But he was too late. The mare's momentum had taken Dawn far away from the fighting, and she had finally turned, ready to charge back into the fray. Conger saw Bellows lying on the ground, with his face crushed from the weight of an enormous hoof. The other fellow seemed trapped beneath his horse, and neither the man nor the horse was moving. Will dismounted, walking up to the fallen drover with gun drawn, ready to respond to any threat or challenge this man might make.

There was no need. The man was dead, and the horse seemed unable to move, wild eyed in its helplessness. There was no question as to what needed to be done here. Conger's pistol spoke again, and the horse was freed from its misery. It was Conger's job to do, and he hated having to do it.

It had all begun so incredibly fast, and it had all ended the same way. Four men were dead who just a few minutes before had been alive and strong. They had threatened two people who had done them no harm, except maybe to their pride, and paid a terrible price for their mistake.

Dawn was back again standing beside Will, calming her mare, and looking down upon the ruined lives surrounding her. Conger could see that she had somehow come through unharmed. Thankful for that, and the pure joy he felt for having this woman in his life, Will put his arms around his wife and held her close to him. He could have lost her today. He knew he must never allow this sort of thing to happen again, ever.

Conger knew that there were matters here to be dealt with. He considered tying the men off to their horses and letting them find their way home. But one horse was dead, and another limping as the result of the power of the great mare. It made more sense in the end just to bury the men where they were and to let the horses find their own way home. Will pulled his shovel from the jack mule's pack, and commenced to digging. The soil was moist and sandy there by the creek, and it wasn't very long before the first grave was ready.

Dawn had been busy caring for the livestock, theirs and those of their attackers. Conger decided it would be best to bury the fellow trapped under the horse first. It would take some doing to free him, and figuring that the longer he worked the tireder he'd get, Will chose to do the hardest work first. Working together they managed to free the body in just a few minutes. But as Will pulled the man out, his hand came away wet. It was blood! This man had been shot in the back! The bullet hole was right on the backbone, and might well explain why the man had been unable to kick free of his horse as it went down.

But Dawn's pistol was still in its holster, and had not been removed. Conger had fired two shots, and both had found their mark. To the best of Will's knowledge, none of Bellows' men had gotten off a shot. A further inspection of their guns proved this to be so.

Then who? Looking off into the small stand of trees, there was little enough cover for another rider to be in hiding. But then, they hadn't noticed Bellows and his men when they first arrived either. Had another gunman tried to shoot Dawn and hit the other fellow by mistake? There were too many questions.

Together they lifted up the body, and then Will slung the man over his shoulder to carry him to the gravesite on the other side of the creek. This fellow didn't weigh all that much, and Will made quick work of it. Hauling Bellows' massive frame was going to require much more effort.

Conger had just begun covering the body when a rifle shot splattered high on a tree behind him. He was yelling for Dawn to get down when the second shot hit right near the first. This burial party was over. Conger knew that these were warning shots, but from whom, and for what purpose? The unseen marksman was obviously a dead shot, and could have easily dropped them both, had he a mind to. Will had no desire to challenge the shooter, and taking the wiser course, lifted his arm high in acknowledgement. Mounting up, they rode quickly away from that place, heading due west. They didn't slow down for a mile or so. Finally catching her breath, Dawn shared her thoughts.

"I was right after all. There was someone else to the north of us just before we met Rusty. But I don't think they were with Bellows and his men. That might have been the one who shot that man in the back." Conger agreed.

"I was thinking the same thing. For some reason or other someone wanted us out of there. I can't for the life of me guess who or why. Whoever it was, I think we had better get out of this part of the country as soon as possible." There was no disagreement from Dawn as they picked up the pace and continued west, making no effort to hide their trail. At least the stock had been watered, after all.

A few miles back a cluster of about a dozen horses were thundering toward that same watering hole. They wore the Slash M brand, and carried riders who were heavily armed, and racing to prevent the unthinkable. Word had found its way to those men who had stayed behind to dine with that feisty young lady from the South, of the treachery planned by Bellows and his gang. They rode their horses to lather trying to close the distance, and prevent the kind of carnage and awfulness that they all knew Bellows to be capable of.

But they arrived too late. Death had already made its mark. But the victims of this slaughter were not the ones they expected to find. Familiar horses milled around, cropping the rich green grass to be had there in the shade of the cotton-wood grove. One horse was limping, while another lay prone, obviously dead.

Bellows lay in a heap, his face a bloody pulp, as though someone had crushed the life out of him with a huge boulder. The two bodies on the near side of the creek had been shot in the head, and at close range. It took only a few minutes for these seasoned riders to read the signs the ground had to offer. The big horse had been here, and unbelievably had somehow leaped across the creek right to the spot where Bellows had fallen, and then on to, and beyond, the place where the dead horse lay.

More importantly was the grave, and in it the body of Dave Stoner, a quiet young man who was known to use poor judgment on occasion, like hanging out with Bellows and his bunch. This time it got him killed. But who had dug the grave, and why didn't they finish? And where were they now?

The Slash M riders had dismounted, and were standing around arguing with one another as to what they had found, when a shot hit a tree, then another, and another. A dozen cowboys lunged for cover, as two more shots hit the same tree.

They blindly returned fire, but with no visible targets to aim at. Then it got quiet. Soon a few foolishly brave souls formed a skirmish line and slowly moved up through the scant foliage using every scrap of cover they could find. Had they taken the time to notice, each and every shot had hit harmlessly on the same nearby tree, and had they been the target of those shots, they would most likely be dead by now. Had they noticed, they too might have high-tailed it out of there by now. They hadn't noticed.

And they found no one. The last shots having been fired minutes earlier, their unknown tree shooter had made a fast and deliberate retreat and was already long gone. His task there was finished, with the Spirit Woman and her companion safely away. He rejoined his companions and continued to follow the path of the great black horse.

Back on the trail, Dawn was riding in quiet thought, considering the events of the morning, and all the terrible things that had happened. She was beginning to wonder just how many men her new husband had gunned down in his lifetime. And yet, had she not done the same? It was confusing to know where to draw the line in these things. His ability to fire his weapon was both comforting and frightening somehow. But her concerns went deeper than that. Breaking her silence, she shared her mind.

"Mr. Conger," she had yet to address him by his first name, "why do men do things like that? I'm not that pretty, and I don't have the kind of full, round body like some women have, that men seem to go crazy over. Why did these men set up this trap just so they could get to me? Why did Uncle Jacob act the way he did? There are women all around who would do those things just for the asking. Why am I being singled out? What am I doing wrong? Why did those men have to die because of me?"

"It's not your fault, and all men aren't like that." Conger was talking now to his friend, not just to his wife. He was going to tell it the way he saw it.

"There are men, and women as well, in this world who prosper by taking things from other people. They want the things they see, just because they are there, not because they need them. You are a very lovely woman, and that makes you very desirable to any man who sees you. But you are not the only lovely woman in this world, and I guarantee you there are others who have had to deal with the same kind of nonsense that you have. I think it has probably always been that way."

"I served with the Union army during the war. I saw where men in both Union and Confederate uniforms had done terrible things to women, and children as well. They were vicious men who used the cloak of war to hide their actions. But I know for certain that most of the men I served with, and fought against as well, would never have done such things, and would step in to stop it when they could."

"This fellow Bellows slapped you because he had gotten by with doing such things before, and would keep on doing it until someone stopped him. The men of that town hoped that if you ignore men like him, they will go away. Those men should have banded together and driven him out a long time ago. Instead, their own wives were being violated, with no one to turn to."

"He followed you because you shamed him. I'm sure he felt small in front of his friends, and believed he had to get back at you to regain their respect. But they didn't really respect him for being a man, they only respected his cruelty, and the danger he represented to them as well. Such men are cowards, following fools on fool's errands." Conger figured he was talking too much, but it needed said, so he went on talking.

"Most of the folks we've run into have been decent and respectful. But this is rough country, and there will be a lot of rough people out this way that we're going to have to deal with. It might be best to stay out of their way whenever possible, and deal with them directly only when necessary. I regret having to shoot those men the way I did, but shoot them I did, and on purpose. They intended to hurt someone I care deeply for. They chose to do what they did, and they have paid the price for their choosing."

Conger's words rang true. All men are victims of the choices they make, or the choices others make for them. Those men had chosen to ruin two lives that day, for foolish pride, lust, and the meanness that ran through them. Dawn chose to fight back with what she had. Will had done the same. It should never have happened in the first place. Now it was over and done with. Nothing was gained, and no good had come of it.

The pair rode on for a few more hours before making camp. There was good grass and ample water there, and the sun would be setting soon. They shared a simple meal, and made small talk about the wonderful breakfast they had enjoyed that morning in Mullit. It seemed so long ago now. No more mention was made of the troubles with Bellows and his men. Nothing more needed to be said.

The livestock were secured for the night, and the young couple sat close together, watching the beautiful sunset as it slid slowly over the horizon. There was a closeness between them now that had not been there before. Perhaps it was an understanding of how fragile life can be, or it could have been the bonding that brings people together after surviving a terrible ordeal. Somehow, the events of that day solidified Will and Dawn as a couple. They were no longer two strangers who just happened to have gotten married after knowing one another for just one day. Nor was it like her relationship with Rhen, formed as much out of necessity as for convenience. She had picked him out among a crowd on a riverboat. He had represented stability and safety, when she was running scared with nowhere to go. Rhen's talk of his farm in far off Kansas seemed a perfect chance to live in peace and put all the troubles of Virginia behind her.

But here with Will she had found something else, something new and wonderful. She was in love with William Conger, not just for what he had done, but for who he was. She finally felt she belonged somewhere, and that was wherever his somewhere happened to be.

Will did not set the cots up in the tent that night. Instead they shared a blanket on a thick carpet of grass, curled up warmly together and comfortable in each other's arms.

A million stars filled the sky, and the evening cooled the air, and in the course of the hours that followed, the two newlyweds at long last completed their wedding vows, and joined together as man and wife.

chapter 7

It was two weeks past the day that Will and Dawn had ridden back through the gates of Fort Davis and joined the wagon train, that Richard Durbin was sufficiently healed from his wounds to get up and out a bit. He walked slowly, using a strong stick someone had found for a cane. His steps were understandably unsteady and hesitant, but there was no denying how good he felt just being up and out of bed. He decided to head over toward the corrals, hoping to catch the morning exercises the soldiers put their mounts through each day. Until now, he'd only been able to watch from a distance.

Durbin loved horses, and was tender in their care. He knew he couldn't stay long, as he would surely run out of strength soon enough. It was just that he needed something to do, and lying around in the Fort Davis infirmary was the same as doing nothing.

Finally making it over to the corral, he was greeted by the Private on duty there. They made small talk, and Durbin commented on the progress of his recovery. It must have been the sound of Durbin's voice that did it, for soon enough, out from the barn came Durbin's roan, the very horse Conger had ridden in on only a week or two earlier. The roan ran right up to the amazed Durbin, eager to be reunited with its master.

The horse stuck its big snout over the corral rails, nudging its long lost friend and nearly knocking the man over in its eagerness. Durbin was nearly in tears as the two enjoyed the moment, overjoyed to see his favorite mount which had been stolen from him at gunpoint over two weeks before. The Private knew full well that this roan horse had been taken in trade from that Conger fellow several days before, but there was no denying the bond between this man and this horse. The story of the stranger who had stolen Durbin's horse and left him for dead was well-known throughout Fort Davis, as being a talkative man, Durbin had told his story more than once to whoever would take the time to listen. But as no one from the fort had seen Durbin with that roan horse before, no one excepting Browner that is, and he wasn't talking, the connection between man and horse had not been made, not until now.

Leaving Durbin and the roan to enjoy their reunion, the Private wisely drifted off to find the Lieutenant. Something was wrong here. This could well mean serious trouble for someone. He would leave it to people smarter than him to sort it all out.

On that same day, and at about the same time of day, a two mule wagon pulled up under the big cottonwoods near the unfinished barn at what remained of the Larson farmstead. The wagon was small, and the mules on the thin side, but it was the best Josiah Washington could afford, and while not top of the line, both the wagon and the mules were obviously well cared for.

Josiah had at one time been a slave, rescued like so many others by the courage and generosity of those who ran what became known as the Underground Railroad. Josiah was a strong black man of unquestioned faith in his Lord and Savior, who had come west for the promise of new lands and opportunity, for those who would work hard to bring the soil to life. He brought with him his wife, and a son and daughter, both under the age of ten. There was no place for them back in Michigan, and being a man of the soil, Josiah gathered up what little he had been able to set aside, and gambled it all on the west, just as so many others had done before him.

He had seen the farm from a distance as he drove his team over a gentle rise, having skirted a marshy field as he headed westward. The big unfinished barn rose like a monument there in the grassland, and was easy to see from a distance. The nearby house, or what had been a house, told a different story. It was burned almost to the ground, from a fire that appeared to have been very hot and all-consuming. Faded clothes still hung on the wash line, and the crops, while neat and green, seemed to be overwhelmed with weeds and grasses growing in amongst impossibly straight rows. Something terrible had happened here, and Josiah knew that the answers more than likely lay buried under the rubble of that burned out house.

He drove his team down to the barn, as it seemed a likely place to stop. The family was already out and walking, but on Josiah's orders, were not allowed to stray far from the wagon. Things might not be the way they looked, and having youngsters poking their noses into other people's property was not a good idea at any time. Taking up his shotgun, Josiah walked slowly into the barn, wary of what he might find there. What he found was not at all what he expected.

In one of the stalls was a flock of chickens, complete with several young ones, in nests made up in the hay. Even more surprising, there stood a chestnut horse, wearing a saddle under its belly, and standing guard over the chickens. Josiah naturally assumed that the horse belonged to the folks who owned the farm. In truth, it was Will Conger's runaway mount that had followed the mule's scent across the prairie to this very place.

Josiah turned back out of the barn, deciding to deal with the horse and its saddle later on. His focus now was on those burned ruins, and what all he would likely find inside. One look told the story.

Only a few boards remained of what had been a bed, with a badly burned body lying atop the partially burned mattress. One of the bedposts seemed not to have burned at all, and it appeared that some kind of leather strap hung from it. It was too narrow to be a belt, and Josiah couldn't figure out its purpose for being there. The stench from the bodies was strong, and recent rains gave the burned wood a musty odor all its own. The rubble on the floor was deep, and little could be made of what might lay buried below.

Josiah saw the need for Christian burial here, and would see to it that this man was taken care of. As he turned to leave, his foot struck what looked like a boot, sticking up from the floor near what would have been the foot of the bed. Clearing some of the darkened timbers aside, he looked down upon a second badly burned body. This one was apparently a woman, who had most likely suffered an assault, as her pants had been pulled down to her ankles. The top of her torso was burned nearly away, and the place between her legs seemed to have been mutilated somehow. A knife hilt lay nearby. He had heard of savages doing such things, as was sad for this couple who had died so terribly in their own home. Josiah would do right by them.

With his wife's help, they buried the two bodies up on the little hill that overlooked the farm, tenderly and with dignity. He smiled as he came upon some cigar butts there, weathered but still visible behind the little row of scrubby trees that grew along the top of the hill. Josiah figured this man must have had to hide up there to smoke them as the wife probably didn't approve.

He did not know these people's names, but was determined to make some sort of marker for them later on. A crude cross was placed at the head of each grave, and words from the Good Book were spoken. Thus, through the kindly and caring act of a complete stranger, Jacob McPhearson and Rhen Larson, whose only connection was to have been married to the same girl, and at the same time, would await eternity together on that hill, side by side, mistakenly buried as husband and wife.

Late that same evening, a lone rider wearing well-worn buckskins, and astride a fast looking horse with three white stockings, passed through the gate at Fort Davis. His long dark hair matched his cropped beard and moustache. The expression on his face was fearsome, as though he would be capable of eating a buffalo, uncooked, horns and all. The guard at the gate gave this man a wide berth, not wanting anything to do with this dark stranger, and the potential for trouble that he represented.

Surprisingly, the rider saluted the guard as he passed through the gate, and carried himself in an upright and altogether military manner. He reined in there, and with a strong Southern drawl, very respectfully asked directions to the Post Commander's office.

The guard couldn't have been more surprised, or relieved. Recovering his senses, he directed this frightening stranger to his destination.

The man in buckskins carefully made his way across the parade ground, and finding the office, knocked on the Colonel's door, waiting for a response before entering. He removed his riding gloves and stood silently inside the doorway, waiting to be addressed before speaking.

Sitting inside that room were Colonel Peters, Lieutenant Whittle, and Richard Durbin, who was still going on and on about the man who stole his horse and left him for dead, not to mention the hanging that would be too good for such a wanton killer.

Peters had heard Durbin's tale several times over by now, each time growing in vivid detail and intensity, and didn't hesitate to interrupt this latest rendition to ask the business of the rough looking man who had just entered his office.

"Good evening, sir. I am Colonels Peters. Please state your name and the nature of your business at this late hour." The stranger was a rough looking individual, indeed.

The man came to attention, and saluting the Colonel, spoke with a drawl as thick as molasses. "I am Brigadier General

Henry James Stronton, late of the Army of Virginia, sir. And I've come looking for a murdering horse thief."

Colonel Peters looked deep into the eyes of the former officer who stood before him. Somehow this man's long untamed hair seemed to accent the look of strength which appeared in those piercing eyes. This was a man who would not allow himself to be taken lightly. Standing now, Peters returned the man's salute, and at once turned to Whittle.

"Lieutenant, the hour is late, and Mr. Durbin needs to return to his quarters to continue his recovery. Please escort him there at once. You may then resume your inspection of the night watch. Thank you Lieutenant."

"Yes sir." There was nothing else Whittle could say, and nothing else he could do. Orders are orders. It was obvious that Durbin wanted to stick around and hear all that this man had to say, convinced already that it would be about that Conger fellow who had ridden Durbin's horse in that day and traded it off as if it were his own. Men like Durbin were known to take a small amount of information and build it into a mountain of absolutes. Such men were the type to lead lynch mobs, not feeling the need to rely on courts and trials when a rope was handy. They were convinced that their wisdom was sufficient for all, and that their verdict was the right one. It seems that those who think they know everything can never learn anything. Whittle took the disgruntled Durbin by the arm and led him out, still complaining as the door closed behind them.

"Please have a seat, Mr. Stronton. Can I offer you some refreshment? I have a pot of day old coffee in the next room?

"Thank you for your kindness, Colonel, but this is not a social call. The man I am seeking is said to have come this way a few days back."

Peters knew he needed to be careful here. The folks who found Durbin near dead, and brought him into the fort, also brought in a limping dappled horse that most everyone had figured to be his. The mystery of the horse grew when Durbin identified the roan that Conger had traded in for Pumpkin to be his instead. Yet, the saddle that came with the roan was not

Durbin's. The overall description of a man wearing city or east-ern clothes fit what Conger had been wearing that day here in Peter's office, but there was no way that Will Conger could be mistaken for a man in his forties, as Durbin had reported. Things just didn't add up.

"What is your purpose for seeking out this man?" Peters was going to be very careful with his words.

"It is a personal matter, sir. I believe he is involved in the disappearance of my daughter, shortly before the end of the war in the east. I have been on this man's trail for quite some time, and I am determined to find the whereabouts of my daughter, be she alive or dead." Stronton had spoken slowly, but with an edge to his voice that could not hide his frustra-tion. He did not know why this Yankee Colonel was being coy in this matter, and did not appreciate the lack of cooperation he sensed here.

"Can you describe your daughter? Many people pass through here, and someone may have seen her."

"Ginny is a beautiful young woman of slender build with long dark hair. She'll turn seventeen years next month. She's friendly and outgoing, with a smile that could light up the day. But I do not believe her to be out this way, sir. It is the fellow who took her that I seek. He himself has been on the hunt as well, looking for a man by the name of Larson."

Peters nearly jumped out of his skin. What did he really know about Catherine Larson, now to be known as Dawn Conger? She certainly fit the description of the girl Stronton was looking for. But was Stronton telling the truth? He didn't know this man any better than he had known Conger, and Conger had slept in his bed!

" Mr. Stronton, the hour is late. Please understand that I respect your former rank, as well as your request. I will speak to some of my people in the morning. If we have any informa-tion that pertains to your search it will be made available to you at that time." Peters saw the look in Stronton's eyes and knew he had said the right thing but in the wrong way. He tried again.

"Brigadier General Stronton, I apologize for being evasive. I do have some information of which I am aware, which could aid in your search. At the same time, there are clearly overlapping coincidences, which if not sorted out properly, could get some innocent people hurt. You of all people will understand the burden of command that I face here. I will convene a meeting early tomorrow morning here in my office to gather the facts. I invite you to attend. Nothing will be done behind your back. But remember, I reserve the right to speak privately with any of my men when matters of military sensitivity arise." Stronton's eyes softened. He was grateful for the Colonel's discretion and concern for the truth.

"I thank you for your kindness sir. I hope I have not behaved rudely. It's just that, well it's my daughter, sir. She's all I have left. I don't sleep nights anymore. I am certain in my heart that Ginny's out there, somewhere. I must find her."

" Please accept the hospitality of Fort Davis for the night. I must ask you not to speak of this matter with anyone. I believe the truth will best be served if the men involved have no knowledge of our intent, and that their words be candid and unrehearsed. May I have your word on this, sir?" Peters wasn't going to put this man under guard. He was convinced his word would be sufficient.

"I am honored, sir. You have my word. You and I were enemies once. In some ways maybe we always will be. But the respect you have shown me this night is more than I expected. I'm just a father looking for his child. I am grateful for any and all the help you can give me." Peters stood, and hesitated before calling the orderly to escort Stronton and see to his needs.

"Before you go, sir, tell me, what is the name of the man you are looking for?" Peters felt foolish for not having asked before this.

"His name is Jacob McPhearson."

Peters spent the better part of the next day interviewing and questioning dozens of the individuals who resided at Fort Davis, military and civilian alike. He purposely took no notes, and did not have a scribe on hand. This was not a criminal matter, at least not yet, and he had no intention of making it seem as such.

However, after each individual was dismissed, the Colonel took a few minutes to write down specific points from the conversation, should follow-up be needed. For the most part, the conversations were general in nature, with very little information to be gained. But Durbin had made mention of something a day or two earlier that Peters recalled while speaking with one of the stable hands. When he got to questioning Browner, he seemed to hit pay dirt.

"Durbin tells me you shoed that roan of his out at his place late last year, any truth in that?" Peters was far more likely to believe Durbin than Browner, but he wanted to give the blacksmith every opportunity to tell his side of things.

"Maybe I did, maybe I didn't. Am I supposed to remember every horse I shoe?" Browner was obviously uncomfortable being questioned about the roan.

"The two hind shoes on the roan bear your mark, so we know it was your work. Bauer says he had seen a man ride that horse in a few weeks ago, and that the fellow riding it had come over to where you work to talk to you. Do you remember the man's name, or what you talked about?" Peters knew more than he told.

"Lots of people talk to me in a day's time. How am I supposed to remember who they are and what they want? What are you picking on me for? I ain't done nothin."

General Stronton had sat quietly off to the side in the Colonel's office, only occasionally offering comment or fielding a question. Peters had already come to appreciate this Confederate's ability to size up a man and the relative quality of their statements. It was with this increased confidence between the two men that Stronton felt free to ask Browner a question of his own.

"Mr. Browner, we do truly appreciate your willingness to assist us in this matter. I can understand how a man as busy as you must be, and in such a difficult and important trade as you practice, would not waste time in idle chatter and socializing when there was so much work to be done." Browner was obviously pleased by the complimentary manner of this Southerner, with his heavy accent and slow and careful way of speaking.

"To get to the point, Mr. Browner, the man who rode that roan in that day, the one who spoke to you, is a known killer, and a reward had been made available to any man who can help in leading to his capture. In fact, as he is wanted dead or alive, even information as to his final resting place could be worth quite a bit of money. We had been hoping that you might recall something that could help lead us to this man, as his trail seems to have gone cold right here at Fort Davis."

Peters decided then and there never to play poker with Stronton. That man was as smooth as molasses, and had managed to say every single word with a straight face. Reward indeed. The Colonel saw the immediate change in Browner's manner.

"You know, I might be able to recall a thing or two, if I take the time to put my mind to it. A reward means this fellow must be mighty important to the Army. It would be my patriotic duty to help in any way possible. Would that reward be payable in gold?"

"Gold coin, right here and now." Stronton was looking Browner straight in the eye. There was no bluffing here. The General then pulled a five dollar gold piece from his pocket and laid it on the corner of Peters' desk.

"Tell us what he wanted to know, and what you told him, and that coin is yours. There's more where that came from." Browner suddenly got real talkative. It was about a half hour later when he left the office, three gold coins rattling in his pockets as he walked.

"That was pretty expensive information my friend." Peters spoke to Stronton with respect, but also with concern.

Chances were Browner was still holding back information in hopes of more coins. Stronton set it all straight.

"I took those coins, and several others like them from the pockets of a fool who tried to rob me back in Missouri. I didn't kill the man, but decided to relieve him of his misbegotten gains. I have lost no sleep over the matter." Peters grinned to himself, definitely, no poker with this fellow. "So, General, what do we know for certain?"

"Nothing really. I am convinced that the man Browner spoke with was Jacob McPhearson. But I would need proof that he is dead to believe it. The man is a monster, and as slippery as a snake. I've been trying to put the pieces together since Virginia, but this story just doesn't hold water. There's something missing here."

"I feel the same way. It appears that something happened out at the Larson farm, and your man McPhearson and these horses all seem connected somehow. I wish I could accept the story the way I want to believe it, but you and I know that wishing doesn't make it so."

"With all due respect, Colonel, I believe a ride out to the Larson farm is called for here. The longer we wait, the colder the trail becomes. Your man Conger said the man who owned the roan horse was dead. Yet the man who owns that same horse said he was left for dead by a man wearing Eastern style clothes, which is what you told me that Conger was wearing when he first arrived here at the fort. Conger said that the man was killed by hostiles before he escaped. If so, then the body would still be out there in the open, and we could confirm what he said."

"Colonel Peters, the truth is that this whole story might be a cover up. Those two got married as soon as they came to the fort. This Larson fellow is reported to be dead, which I believe he is. But it could all be a convenient story made up for covering the man's murder while those two ran off together. If that's the case, I'm wasting my time here on the trail of the wrong man. I need to know. My daughter's life is at stake."

Peters sat in silence. Stronton was a wise and experienced man, and his advice was sound. Nothing the Colonel had heard this day was conclusive in any way whatsoever, excepting maybe to confirm that Browner was a gold grubbing weasel. Peters would need to deal with that problem at a later time.

"General Stronton, it's getting late. We need to stop and get our dinner, and hopefully a good night's sleep. I will decide by morning what course of action needs to be taken here. In the meantime, I must ask you to be our guest here one more night, and to make no attempt to leave the fort. It is unsafe beyond our walls day or night. If additional information comes forward, I will want to confer with you."

"Thank you for your concern for my safety. I will stay the night, and with my thanks. But I intend to head for that farm at first light, and I will travel at a rapid pace. I fear what I might find there."

"What do you mean, General?

"If Jacob McPhearson is indeed dead, then I'm afraid the only link to my daughter is dead as well." Stronton walked slowly out of the Colonel's office. Salutes and formalities were no longer needed between these two former enemies. Their war was in the past. The solution to the problem they now shared would most likely bring sadness and disappointment to one of them. Peters sat alone, and stared into the flame of the smoky candle he had lit a few minutes earlier. Something about all this just didn't add up. But why?

The name of the man Stronton was seeking meant nothing to Peters. However, the matter of a girl with long dark hair was all too familiar. The mystery of the horses did not mesh at all with the facts that he had been told. The combined stories of the men he had interviewed that day seemed strangely consistent, but the conclusions he was drawing from all this did not fit the character of the young man he had loaned his uniform to. Something was missing. He had always suspected that Conger was holding back something, not willing to tell the whole story. But he also felt certain that it was more to protect the girl, and not so much himself.

Suddenly, and without thinking it completely through, Peters decided to tap into the most knowledgeable source of information that Fort Davis could boast. Walking out the door, the Colonel located the sentry and gave an order he had never given before.

"Guard! Please send Mrs. Peters my compliments, and escort her to my office at once." Every now and then he got to order his own men around, just like she did. It was about ten minutes later that Bess found her way to the Colonel's office, wearing her nightshirt covered only by a heavy blanket. She was bare footed, with a towel wrapped around her head to complete the ensemble. She was not pleased.

"What is so important that you had me dragged out of a perfectly warm tub of water in the middle of the night when you could just as easily have come home to the dinner that's been getting cold and talked to me there?" He had never done such a thing to her before, and in truth she was more concerned about his reasons than of her inconvenience. The look on his face answered her questions.

"Tell me everything you know about Catherine Larson, and this Conger fellow she rode in with. Every word, leave nothing out. Their lives may hang in the balance here. Tell me everything." Bess was now being addressed by the Commanding officer of Fort Davis, not just her husband, and she understood by his manner the gravity of the situation. Her reply was both warm and submissive.

"Could we go home first? Walls have ears, and it is important that no one but you hear what I am going to tell you. No one else can know what this girl has gone through." The look on her face convinced the Colonel of the seriousness of her request.

Now Peters felt like an idiot for dragging her out like this, and loved her even more for her coming over when asked. They walked back home together in silence. Back inside, Bess wiped off her dirty feet, and handing Peters her nightshirt, climbed back into the tub. Catherine's story had been etched into her mind, and while the telling of it would be difficult, the recollections were clear and precise. A story never to be forgotten.

The Colonel's interrogation of his wife went well into the wee hours. The story she retold was detailed and accurate, just as she knew he would expect it to be. Peters listened carefully, and did not interrupt. It was apparent the telling of the tale was difficult for Bess. It would have been difficult for anyone.

Following the first telling, Bess stepped out of her now lukewarm tub and got dressed in her night clothes. The Colonel now had questions, searching for detail or things Bess might have left out. The missing pieces which had troubled him from his first meeting with Conger were now mostly in place. He had been right, Conger had been protecting the girl and laid responsibility on himself.

In fact, everything in the story fit together, if he wanted to believe it, and he very much did want to. But he needed proof. There was still the possibility, although slim, that this whole thing had been made up to cover a double murder. It fell to him to decide. There still remained too many unknowns. He needed to sleep on it, if he could sleep at all.

chapter 8

A THREE GUN salute awakened the Colonel the next morning, marking a time much later than he would typically be up and going each day. He had renewed the morning rifle salute to the flag the week before, what with most of the settlers gone now from the fort, and with the need to get the regular daily routine up and going again. Bess didn't budge. He'd have to get his coffee at the mess hall this day.

His orderly met him at the door to his office, and right off he sent for Whittle. Things needed to move quickly that morning, and the sooner he got things started, the better. Peters also sent word for Mr. Stronton, who was bunked at the barn.

Whittle was a man who never seemed to sleep, and was predictably at the Colonel's door within minutes.

"Lieutenant, come in and be seated please. A patrol will be departing within the hour on a fact-finding mission to the Larson farm due east of here. The patrol will consist of twelve men in all. You will be in total command of the fort while I'm away. Conduct yourself in a manner as though I would not be coming back. Make your decisions solely on your assessment of the situation, and the facts at hand. I have here written orders giving temporary transfer of command to you, along with written instructions verifying the orders I have just given."

"Am I to understand that you will be leading this patrol Colonel?" The concern in Whittle's voice could easily be heard. He knew quite well that the wounds Peters suffered at Gettysburg made horse riding difficult and painful for the Colonel, and that he typically took a wagon or buckboard whenever possible.

"You are correct, Lieutenant, and I will hear no more of your concerns about it. That's an order." Whittle was not one bit happy about this, but an order was an order was an order…. He would simply have to shut up about it and do as he was told. The Colonel was a proud man.

Stronton was just coming in as Whittle was leaving with a list of supplies and men he was required to assemble for the patrol. The two men passed each other with little recognition given by either one. The memories of war can be slow to fade for some.

"General Stronton, I will be leading a patrol out to the Larson farm within the hour. As a civilian, you are not required to follow my request to join us, but given your concerns both for your daughter and this man McPhearson, I strongly believe it would be in your best interests to come along for the ride. I will remind you that as part of this patrol, even as a civilian, you will be required to follow any order that I give, and act only in an advisory role as I see fit. Are there any questions?"

"Thank you, Colonel. I accept your terms, and I thank you for your kind consideration. I'll be ready."

Next, Peters had to face the toughest test of all---Bess. He knew she would be up and scurrying about the house by now. She couldn't lay still in bed for long. He also knew that the news of his taking out the patrol would sit very hard with her. She was very protective of her husband, always insisting that there were plenty of highly qualified younger men available to do the job.

And she was right. Whittle, who was more than likely fuming over his Colonel's abruptness, was ready for command, and Peters knew he couldn't leave a better man in charge. But the story Bess conveyed during the night was one that could not be retold to Whittle or any on else for that matter. It had been two weeks, but chances were that the results of what had happened at the Larson farm were still there, waiting to serve as evidence of the truth or falsehood of Catherine's story. He checked himself, her name was Dawn now. Even more reason to be suspicious.

Bess saw the look on her husband's face as he came through the door. The speech she had prepared would not be spoken. She already knew of the patrol, and of her husband's role in it. Word traveled fast at Fort Davis. She had laid out the uniform she knew he would be wearing. A bundle of her fresh biscuits were tied off in a napkin, and a cup of coffee awaited him at the table. Bess was a good woman, a good wife, and most of all, a good friend to her husband.

True to his word, Peters led the patrol out through the main gate less than an hour from the time he had given his first order. Counting Stronton and the Colonel, there were twelve men in all---roughly one fourth of the garrison. They hoped to be near the farm by nightfall, and then descend upon it at first light. At least that was the plan.

Bess didn't wave as he left this time. She just stood there next to Whittle and wept. She had a very bad feeling about this trip.

There was no trail to the Larson farm only a direction. Bauer had been out this way before, and took the point as guide. The men rode carefully in twos, with roughly a two-horse gap between each pair. Peters felt that this was the best way to ride through hostile territory, leaving plenty of room between them to maneuver if attacked.

If Peters was in pain, it didn't show. The men knew of his wounds, and he rode with a pillow under his backside. Only a fool would have said anything in jest concerning that pillow, and the men who had served with Peters for any length of time would have never done so, out of genuine respect.

It was late afternoon when the patrol reached the place where Dawn and Will had encountered Tall Tree and his warriors. One of the men noticed the cleared out brush at the campsite, as well as a pile of charred timbers where a large fire had burned. A smaller fire pit was found closer to the river. There had been rains in the last two weeks, and most of whatever tracks and such that had once been there were wiped out. But two tracks were found nearby of an unusually large horse, which had dug in deeper than the others. Peters saw the hoof prints, and remembering the account Bess had shared with him, saw how this place fit the story. Things were looking up for the Congers.

The men took advantage of the river and watered their horses. In less than ten minutes the patrol was traveling again, a long ride still ahead of them.

Will and Dawn rode slowly past the charred timbers that stood as silent witnesses to the tragedy that had happened in this place, just weeks before. The pleasant sounds of the prairie birds seemed somehow misspoken in this place of death. The scent of decay and ruin filled the morning breeze, ruining the view of pastoral beauty all around.

There had been five wagons in the party. Only a few remaining spoked wheels identified those piles of burnt timbers as wagons, but they didn't begin to tell the stories of the people who had come west in those wagons, the men, the women, and their children, whose lives had ended so abruptly, so savagely, their dreams of a new life in a new land having died with them. Already the grasses had begun their timeless work, turning lifeless bodies back into the dust from which they had been molded. Years later, others would pass by this spot, unaware of the tragedy that had taken place here, or of the names and the faces of those who would go no further.

Will knew better than to stop to provide burial for the fallen. Disease and pestilence were present here. He had seen enough of that during the war, and knew full well the dangers the dead could still present to the living. All he could do was say a prayer for their souls, and for the comfort of those who would never know what had become of these, their loved ones.

Conger thought of the Spencer girl, and her family, and the little Italian fellow who had cut his hair back at the fort. It unnerved him to think of them possibly lying dead and mutilated somewhere out there, just as these folks were. These were good people, the kind of people who were brave and strong and hopeful for the future. It was all such a senseless waste.

Will then recalled his brother James, and his wish that Will would write back to Kentucky from time to time and let folks know of his travels and that he was still alright. Will had never been much of a letter writer, and had not improved in the calling since he left home. He certainly had a story to tell, but realized that much of what he had seen and done in the last few weeks would be unfit to include in a friendly letter back home.

Of course, he could let them know he was married now. Will wondered to himself if James and his wife, Abigail would ever get the chance to meet Dawn. Kentucky seemed very, very far away right about then, both in distance and in time.

Dawn saw the burnt out wagons and immediately recalled the Washazhe warriors who had stood by the fire, proudly brandishing the scalps of their victims. She knew full well that not all tribes took scalps, and more often than not, captives were kept as slaves and not murdered or otherwise harmed. But that had not happened here.

The cruelty of the white man was matched by the cruelty of the Indian. Ironically, she realized that she was from both worlds, but didn't really wish to be exclusively identified as being from either one. She wasn't a category, she was a person. The air freshened as they rode beyond the charred ruins, and the westerly breeze carried the scent of death behind them toward the eastern sky. Conger did not have to be told that whoever had burned those wagons could come through this way again, and at any time. Their chances for survival would be no better than those folks who lay dead behind them, if the surprise were too sudden, or the numbers too overwhelming.

Once again they were carrying the Colt rifles. Will had taken the time to allow Dawn to actually fire the weapon a few days before. She had felled a deer in full flight. Even with an unfamiliar weapon, her marksmanship was amazing, bringing down the running deer with a shot to the heart at some distance. She acted as though she fully expected to hit her target and made no mention of the shot. Many of the men Conger had known over the years would have been beating their chests in triumph, and celebrating as though they had just invented water. Conger appreciated the difference.

Watching her skill with a rifle, Will recalled an old story about a woman who had fought off a band of wild Indians back when the colonies were young. Seems she was working as an indentured servant to a family back in New Jersey or such, and when the man of the house was blinded in the attack, she took up his musket and proceeded to nearly wipe out that band of attackers with her amazing marksmanship. She later married that man, and lived to a ripe old age. Her name was Betty O'Dell! That's the name that caught his eye in Dawn's family Bible. Could it be the same Betty O'Dell? Watching Dawn with a rifle, he certainly could be convinced. He'd have to ask her about it.

As amazed as Will was at Dawn's marksmanship, he was even more amazed while watching her skin out the deer. She took the best cuts and wrapped them in the hide. This she tied to a travois she rigged behind Jill, and then surprisingly covered the rolled up hide with a heavy layer of soil and sod. Will had never seen such a thing done before, and was genuinely curious.

Dawn explained that the soil would both help to keep flies out of the meat, and catch any blood that might drip from the bundle. A bloody trail could bring wolves right to their campsite. Again Will was impressed---the girl had wisdom.

They would be stopping soon enough, as it was nearing midday, and the sun was growing hotter. They had agreed to rest during the heat of the day, and travel on in the early evening. Conger laughed to himself when he realized that this was exactly what Jed Dooley had done with the wagon train, for which Conger had been so critical. The only difference here was that Conger took care of his livestock during that time. Still, the irony of it all was not lost on him.

Hours passed, and the sun continued its journey westward. It was just as the couple were repacking the mules that the wind suddenly turned. There wasn't a cloud in the sky, but the wind, coming from the northwest, marked an abrupt change from the southern winds they had encountered for days. This wind was cooler, with a hint of moisture to it. But the sky showed nothing. They agreed to write it off as another of the many strange things they had already encountered in their journey west that had no explanation.

The patrol made good time getting over to Larson's farm. It was early evening when Peters sighted the half-finished barn, clearly visible against the flat grasslands which surrounded it. The day had been hot, and the promising shade of the cottonwoods down by the river looked like a Godsend. The plan was to hole up there for the night, and return to the fort in the morning. This was a fact-finding mission only, and a few hours work should do the trick.

Based on the information Bess had given him, Peters was looking for a burned out shack with two bodies inside. This alone would be confirmation enough to support Catherine Larson's story. Anything else that could be found which would support her words would be welcomed, of course.

The patrol stopped at the edge of a field of corn, with rows planted straight as a gunshot. A chimney could be seen in the distance, but with no house attached. The barn stood nearby. Private Spencer broke the silence.

"Beg your pardon, sir, but there's somebody moving down there by the barn." The men had been briefed as to what they might find there at the Larson place, and were under orders to report any activity they saw or heard at once.

Peters didn't believe in ghosts, but he did believe in the misgivings he felt as to the accuracy of the girl's story. By all accounts, this place should be abandoned. He would have to assume that anyone on the premises would be hostile, and to behave accordingly. Fearing a trap, Peters divided his patrol, leaving half there by the edge of the cornfield, while he and Stronton went on in with the rest. Weapons were held at the ready. Any gunfire would signal the need for reinforcements.

Skirting the corn, Peters led his horse at a walk, eyes open and alert. Getting closer to the chimney, he could see a pile of charred wood nearby, as though it had been stacked there on purpose. A wagon was parked by the barn, and there stood a horse and two mules in the corral. Hearing a scraping sound, Peters looked to his left, and was stunned by what he saw there.

Leaning against a shade tree down by the barn stood a man, tall and powerfully built, calmly sharpening the blade of a garden hoe.

It was becoming obvious now that this place was inhabited. The livestock in the corral was enough to prove that out, but a man standing down near the barn wasn't at all what the Colonel was expecting to find. Maybe the patrol was at the wrong farm. While there couldn't be all that many out this way, many such places looked very much alike, as buildings at farms filled very specific functions, and followed similar patterns. Peters took a deep breath and rode on in.

Josiah Washington kept on with the sharpening of the hoe, making no effort to stop his task. He could tell they were Yankee soldiers, and he knew very well that a black man squatting on someone else's property might not be well accepted. He'd been worried more about Indians out this way and had not considered problems with the army. But he was considering that right about now.

Peters rode past the burned out house, and motioned for his patrol to spread out and secure the area. He would leave his reserves right where they were. This was no time to be taking chances. He rode up to where Washington was standing but did not dismount.

"Good afternoon, sir. I am Colonel Peters from Fort Davis. Tell me, would this be the Larson farm?" He addressed this man with customary courtesy, although his wariness could not be disguised.

"And a very good afternoon to you, Colonel Peters. I do not know anyone by the name of Larson, sir. I did however find who I believe to be Mr. and Mrs. William Conger lying dead in the burned out house over yonder. There was nothing here that said the lady's name for sure." If Washington was nervous, it didn't show.

"You say there was a man and a woman in the house? Are you certain?" Peters was more confused than ever now. Could there have actually been a man and a woman in the house, instead of two men?---and by the name of Conger?!

" Yes sir, at least as far as I could tell. They were burned up almighty bad, and the lady---well, they had cut her up something awful, you know, down below. The wife and I buried them up on the hill over yonder. We put up some crosses but I haven't had the time to make them a marker yet, on account of all the other things we've been doing these past several days.

Peters was beginning to put the pieces together here. Dawn had been very detailed in the account she shared with Bess. The wounds McPhearson would have suffered by that knife-wielding girl's hand could very easily cause him to be mistaken for a woman, especially if the body had been heavily burned. A hot enough fire could have certainly done such a thing. And yet, other things were still unraveling. Could Conger have really been McPhearson in disguise? And was Dawn really who she said she was, or was she in fact the daughter Stronton was looking for? And what led this man to think their name was Conger? Peters dismounted.

While Peters was busy talking to Washington, Stronton walked over to what was left of the burned out shack. The few timbers that still looked usable had been stacked in a neat pile a few feet away. A larger pile, including what appeared to have been a bed, lay further off, downwind from the dwelling. The hearth and chimney seemed to still be intact, and the place had been swept out to the bare dirt floor, perhaps in readiness for rebuilding. It was apparent that this was the work of a caring and diligent man.

Although this man had mentioned a wife, she had yet to make an appearance. Suspicious, Peters would remain on alert. Stronton came over to where the two men were standing.

"Excuse me sir, did you find any personal items inside the house, like tools, guns or a Bible or such?" Stronton had forgotten himself for a moment, and addressed Washington directly without deferring to Peters.

Washington's heart caught in his throat. He had seen the rough looking man in buckskins as they rode up, and was already wary of him. But the sound of his deep voice, with its deep Southern drawl, sent chills down his spine. This was the voice of a past he and his family has escaped from long ago.

"Colonel Peters sir, I am a free man. I have done nothing wrong here. I found those folks here a few days back on my way west, and I proceeded to bury them as the Good Lord would have me do. I figured I'd stay out the fall and winter on this place and bring this poor man's crop in, so his labors would not go wasted. Just look at those fields! Have you ever seen such straight rows in your life? If I've done wrong here, I'll move on. But I'll not be turned over to that man. He has no claim on me or my family."

It hadn't occurred to Peters just what the presence of someone like Stronton could represent to a man like Washington. Of course, coming out to the Larson farm, the Colonel had no idea that he would find anyone here on the property to begin with. It was Stronton who spoke first.

"Forgive me, sir, but I heard what you said, and I assure you, I have not come for you, nor would I ever do such a thing. I am from Virginia, and proud to be as such, but my family has never held slaves, and I do not approve of the practice. I am here today looking for my daughter who I believe to have been kidnapped by a fellow who might have come through this way. I was hoping to find clues to his where-a-bouts here."

Stronton then went up to Washington and held out his hand in a gesture of friendship. Washington hesitated, and looked Stronton straight in the eye. He recalled the Lord's admonition to turn the other cheek. All he was being asked for here was to shake a hand. And so he did.

Peters stood aside as the two men walked together over to the burned out cabin. Amazingly, these two strangers seemed to have much in common, and soon joined in to a cordial and thoughtful exchange.

"Over at the barn I have a very few things that I thought I might be able to salvage from the house. Mostly it's kitchen things and the like. But there is something there that might interest you." While the men were talking together, Peters went ahead and ordered the rest of the troop to join them. He instructed the Sergeant to make camp and set up a perimeter. He then joined the other two men as they went to the barn, where the other pieces finally fell into place.

There in the corral was the chestnut horse Conger had spoken of. The saddle and saddlebags were neatly stacked by the door, and Washington showed the Colonel the papers he had found in the saddlebags. These papers bore the name of William Conger, explaining why Washington had figured that to be the name of the man he found inside the house lying on the bed. For the time being, Peters would not correct him.

Washington then produced a hand gun, charred from the fire, but still lethal in a beautiful sort of way. Peters had never seen one like it before, but Stronton knew it right away.

"It's a LeMat, newer model from the looks of it. This one is made to take a standard forty-five cartridge. Notice the lower barrel. It is made to hold buckshot. This was the weapon of choice for Southern officers and gentlemen. It is quite lethal in the right hands. I would say that the man who owned this gun would certainly be a man of the South."

"Can you be sure, it may be the only piece of corroborating evidence we'll find here." Peters had a gut feeling now that things were just as Dawn had said they were.

Without hesitation, Stronton pulled his pistol from its heavy leather cavalry style holster, and showed it in comparison. Except for some minor differences in tooling, the pistols were basically the same.

"Mine is an earlier model. His was made in Europe and smuggled in during the war. It's a fine weapon, built way before its time." Stronton's eyes clouded over as he recalled holding that very same weapon in anger so often during years past---the memory of distant battles kindling anew.

The last item to be brought out was a deadly look-ing knife, still razor sharp, but with its once fine ivory handle badly damaged from the fire. Peters recognized the knife at once, described so accurately in the story told to Bess. Peters knew that this was the same blade which had butchered a girl named Hassy, and with which Dawn had so viciously attacked McPhearson, causing Washington to mistake that man to be a woman. Brave and hardened as Peters had become over the years, the sight of that blade still managed to turn his stomach.

Now Peters was convinced that Dawn's tale was true. There was no need to exhume the bodies. But the truth of her story meant that Stronton's hope of finding his daughter was most likely lost forever.

Colonel Peters saw the look on Stronton's face, long and sullen. He had spent all those months searching for the man who had taken his daughter away from him. This quest had been the driving force that had kept Stronton going. And now the jour-ney was over, leaving him empty handed, and without hope.

Peters had confided in Stronton that there was more than enough information to indicate that the wounds McPhearson had suffered were sufficient to cause his body to be mistaken for that of a woman.

The Colonel was now convinced that Conger's story was true, and that an unlikely series of events had been the source of his misgivings. It was Conger's missing chestnut horse which Washington had discovered in the barn watching over the chickens that had sealed the matter. This was the final piece of a baffling puzzle, that along with the painful tale told by a young woman who had been rescued by a gallant stranger.

It was then that Peters got a sudden flash of inspiration, and maybe the chance for Stronton to find out the fate of his daughter after all. It was a long shot to be sure, but it would be worth the effort. He passed the word for Sergeant Gregg.

"Sergeant, we will be returning to the fort in the morning. You will remain here with five men of your choosing, and assist Mr. Washington in properly setting up his home here. A well is to be dug, and a proper shelter constructed. Feel free to use whatever means and materials you have at your disposal to complete the task. I fully expect the work to be completed and your return to the fort in two weeks time. Is that understood?

The Sergeant was surprised and delighted by this assignment. This was a man who loved to work with his hands, and with a hand picked crew, the work was certain to go well.

"Take what you'll need from the pack animals. We came here as a burial detail, but it seems now that those shovels will be put to a much better use. Your men will have to live off the land---it will be a good exercise for them. Be sure to provision for this man and his family whenever possible."

Sergeant Gregg saluted, and with a broad smile on his face went off to choose his volunteers. Peters then turned his attentions to Stronton, standing alone and silent, several paces away.

"General Stronton, I am sorry for your loss here. I know full well that finding this man McPhearson was the key to your efforts toward finding your daughter. However, just as I am privy to information which assisted us in verifying the identity of the bodies found in the burned out house, it is possible that same source may have knowledge of your daughter, and perhaps hold a clue as to how and where she might be found. It seems the United States Government has need of your services in getting some dispatches to this same individual, and that any and all information you can gather while there is yours to use as you see fit. Are there any questions sir?

Stronton had fully intended to begin his journey back east the next morning, hoping to somehow revive a trail that had long gone cold. He looked into the Colonel's eyes and saw both wisdom and hope. He was a shrewd one, that

Peters. Stronton made a mental note never to play poker with this man.

The troop moved out shortly before dawn the next day. Sergeant Gregg already had his men busy laying out the well. He had spoken with Washington concerning the rebuilding of the house, and was duly impressed with the plans the man had drawn up for that very project. One of the men was busy at the fire burning an epitaph into a piece of wood rummaged from the barn. As fate would have it, this would be the only marker that would ever grace the gravesite up on the hillside. Always the master of details, Colonel Peters himself had ordered the inscription to read as follows:

RHEN LARSON AND WIFE   June 1866

Two days later, as morning found the sun creeping over the eastern horizon, a lone rider dressed in buckskins, and with a spare mount in tow, was already far to the west of Fort Davis, fulfilling his role as a courier of important documents which required the signatures of one William Conger, and of a young woman never thereafter to be known as Catherine Larson. The predated documents had been drawn up at the Colonel's direction, and dealt with the sale of Will's chestnut horse with outfit, and the transfer of ownership of the Larson farm to one Josiah Washington, currently charged as caretaker of the aforementioned property, at the request of the Government of the United States of America. And for Stronton, it meant a chance to speak with the young woman who may well have been the last person to see his daughter alive.

chapter 9

THE WEATHER WOULDN'T change. It was hot and dry, just like the day before and the day before that. The heat bounced up off the dry grass like a second sun. Even breathing was difficult. Staying near the river provided ample water, but was also taking Conger much further south than he had intended to go. Landmarks and creeks indicated on the crude maps he had put together with the help of the teamsters proved elusive. Sometimes things just weren't there, and most of the streams had dried up and filled in with grass. Shade was becoming increasingly rare, even close to the river, and the dry grass did not set well with the riding stock. It was not yet noon, but Conger decided to pull off the trail and hole up under the shade of a young cottonwood which grew alongside the now smaller and shallower Cimarron River. They got down and watered the livestock. It was still morning and already they were both worn out.

"Dawn, I don't mind telling you that I'm more than a little bit concerned. According to this map, the river is going to play out soon, then we have deserts and mountains and then more desert. I had intended to head for Colorado sooner or later, and I'm thinking that as there is nothing really waiting for us in Santa Fe, that this might be as good a time as any to head that way. Anyway, I'd really like your opinion on the matter. I need to know how you feel about all of this."

Fact was, Conger just didn't know. Were he alone out here he would have more than likely taken off in that direction a long time ago. But having Dawn along changed everything. He cherished his wife, and knew for certain that if all he found on this trip west was her, it would have been more than worth it.

Dawn didn't respond at first. She sat there and played with a stick in the soft river sand instead. After a time she stood up and walked over to Ooh-luh, and shared some gentle words in her native language. It was as though she were talking to a child. Then she turned to Will, and spoke her mind.

"Mr. Conger, I thank you. It means so much to me that you would seek my thoughts on matters such as this. In this way I truly feel like your wife, and not just your woman, as so many other women are forced to feel. I agree, this route is not getting any better. We're going, but not really going anywhere. Remember what you told the people in the wagons about not having a destination? Well, right now I think that means us."

Conger listened. She was right. How can anyone know when they've arrived when they don't know where they are going? They needed to stop right where they were and make some real plans before going any further.

So they stayed put during the heat of the day, and rested in the shade of that cottonwood. They drank cool water and grazed the stock on the soft green grass near the river bank. They decided to leave the next morning before sunrise, and ride due north for the Arkansas River, which according to the map was several days ride north. Riding in the early morning and in the evening, and staying out of the sun during the heat of the day seemed to be the best plan.

It was three days later that Conger figured they were somewhere near the southern border of Colorado. But as they had not yet met up with the Arkansas, he wasn't really sure where he was, or if this river really existed. Despite the heavy rains of the day before, the land remained parched and dry, with more and more brown finding its way into what had once been an endless green landscape. The water in the few streams and creeks they ran across flowed more slowly now, if at all, and usually had a foul smell to it.

There were wagon tracks aplenty, along with the tracks of the stock that had pulled them. Every so often there would be a grave along the way, marked with a crude wooden cross or a stacking of stones, mute reminders of just how fragile life could be out here in this beautiful desolation.

Now Conger was a man of ideas, and one of those ideas developed itself into an awning for the animals during the heat of the day. Copying something he had seen outside of Mullit, Conger rigged two tent poles into something like a stretcher, with a canvas in between. It could easily be set up as a sun shade and packed away easily. Dawn's big black horse had to kneel down to get under it, but all I all it seemed to work out just fine.

They had used up most of the deer that Dawn had dropped several days before. Will had smoked much of the venison to help make it last as long as possible. But dry meat added to a body's thirst, and rationing water would soon become a necessity unless things changed quickly. Two of the large canteens were already empty, and the sky did no look like rain. Instead, it just looked endless. At least the stars were pretty at night.

It was two days later until Will and Dawn finally reached what they figured to be the Arkansas. But expected relief quickly turned to disappointment, as the river banks ran dry, with only a few shallow pools spread about here and there to show where water had once flowed freely. The source of the river seemed many miles west from this spot, and from the looks of things, offered slim hope for any better luck. Conger got down and led Pumpkin to what little water he could find. Dawn did the same with Ooh-luh. The mules had already found the water they needed.

Conger was undecided. If the Arkansas had dried up they were in real trouble. They could go back, there was water behind them, but go to where? The maps indicated water ahead of them, but that was a gamble as well. Will paced as he thought things out. This was serious, and different from the kind of decisions he had been forced to make before. Captain Conger had made life and death decisions on a daily basis for years, but that was war, and he had few options then. Here he had Dawn to think about. His enemy had changed. Before it had been flesh and blood, men like himself. But here the enemy was the earth and the sky around him. And he knew he was already outnumbered.

But he was well read, and he knew that any man who tries to fight the land is destined to lose in the end. He must learn to live with the land, with the elements, with the limitations his surroundings placed upon him. To be blind to the power and will of nature is to invite defeat and death.

Dawn was standing beside her mare, watching her husband pace and fume over their circumstances, knowing full well that her presence there was most likely the source of his indecision. She cherished his willingness to ask her opinion on things that affected her, but she was wise enough to know that there could only be one head of the family, and she knew that William was the only one she trusted with her life.

Still, behind every successful man is a woman prepared to administer a good swift kick in the pants as needed from time to time. After all, every now and then it was necessary to just throw the dice and charge headlong into whatever the future would hold. She decided it was high time to kick.

"William, we need to get going. It's a long way to the mountains, and I don't wish to ride forever. While I intend to spend the rest of my days with you, at least for as long as you'll have me, I don't intend to spend them here."

With that she got back on her horse and waited for him to do something.

He probably should have kissed her right then and there, and he would have too, if that blasted horse of hers wasn't so darned tall. Besides, he was too busy trying to deal with the realization that she had actually addressed him by his first name!

So he took her suggestion and mounting up, pointed Pumpkin due west, along the banks of the dried up Arkansas river, and straight into trouble.

Mirages exist in the desert. Sometimes clouds can be mistaken for mountains. They had ridden about three hours from the last watering stop when Will saw a grove of trees. He figured it to be an hallucination of some sort. He had seen them before out this way. But Dawn saw it, too. Right before them in the middle of the parched brown land stood an oasis of beauty, green and alive! They rode on ahead, praying that the image was somehow real.

Coming closer, a small lake came into view, and the river itself started showing signs of life as well, although still no more than a trickle. Conger could not imagine how this lake came to be here---it was not mentioned on any of the maps drawn up by men who had been out this way as late as six months ago. Something had to have happened to change the landscape, but what?

The water in the river was now ankle deep, and they went ahead and watered the stock. Will dismounted and walking a few steps upstream, filled the canteens. It wasn't the best water he'd ever tasted, but it would do. At least it didn't smell like rotten eggs.

Suddenly Dawn stood up on her mare, looking back to the east. Someone was there, and she said as much to Will. After a few moments she sat down again, obviously troubled.

"Mr. Conger, I believe we are in great danger here. Someone has been tracking us for some time now. I cannot yet see them, but I have heard their prayers. They are strong with the spirits, and have called upon the earth and the wind to help them. We cannot hide from them. Our only hope is to get to the great mountains before they reach us. We must hurry."

Will heard what she had said. There might have been a time when he would have discounted her words as nonsense, but he had seen her in action before, and found truth in her words. He would listen now. The lake was over a mile wide, but he wasn't sure of its depth. In this dry expanse, quicksand was a real danger. Going into the water was not an option. They would continue west toward the river's source, and then turn north. The next water was said to be that way, and he knew that the canteens would not stay full for very long. So it was that the journey continued on, in the heat of the day, with a pursuer close behind, and the safety of the mountains still very far away.

Whoever they were, they weren't friendly. The riders were fanned out, staying back about a quarter mile, and riding as though they were herding their quarry. That quarry was Will and Dawn, and those mules, and that magnificent black horse. The pursued knew not where they were headed, but it was obvious the pursuers knew this place well. They would be patient and run their prey down, for they had plenty of time.

Dawn once again stood atop her mount to look back, and at once sat down again. These were natives, not whites, just as she had suspected. There were eight that she could see, but there figured to be more nearby, possibly waiting in ambush just up ahead. The lake was to their left as they hurried west, with only sparse rolling scrub and prairie to the north. There was nowhere to run to, and their time was running out.

Conger appreciated their predicament perhaps even more than Dawn, but from a different perspective. He was cavalry, and cavalry tactics were different. He was being pursued by a mounted force, more than likely native to this country, with all the advantages a local force would enjoy. This was not in his favor.

However, Will knew he probably enjoyed the advantage of greater firepower, what with the arsenal of rifles and pistols he had at his disposal. Not to mention the dead shot ability his young bride had already demonstrated.

But dead men pull no triggers, and he knew that if he went down she would be on her own out here in the middle of nowhere. And worse than that, what if she…

Conger cleared his mind. He couldn't be thinking about that sort of thing, not here, not now. He had to make a choice, and he would have to do it soon. He had to do it now.

"Do you trust me?" Dawn was surprised by his words. They stopped riding and looked upon each other for what seemed and eternity, even though it was only a matter of seconds.

"Tell me what you want me to do." There was no hesitancy in this girl---she was gritty and strong and ready for anything.

"Do you think you can hit the farthest one at this distance?" Will would have to admit she was a better shot than he was, and right then he was saying just that.

"Not with the repeater, but maybe with the Sharps---yes, I think so." If she was scared or worried, she didn't show it.

How did she know about the Sharps? It had been his father's gun. His brother didn't want to keep what he called an 'antique', so Will brought it with him out west, thinking it might prove useful. The Sharps was not as quick to use as the newer cartridge models to be certain, but its .54 caliber slugs could take out a target at great distance. Perhaps she had somehow seen a gun like this in use somewhere. No matter, now was not the time to argue about it, maybe later.

They dismounted, and Will made quick work of pulling out the big gun along with powder and shot. He had picked up extra rounds at the Smith's store back at Mullit. Dawn watched closely as he expertly loaded the weapon, with a little extra powder for distance.

She would be using Pumpkin as a gun mount, laying the horse down prone to act both as a shield and a steady platform for the fighting which was to come. Pumpkin, a cavalry veteran, knew what was expected of her and responded to Will's command without hesitation. Dawn patted the horse twice, and speaking softly in her native tongue, carefully laid the barrel across the saddle and began to sight in on the fast approaching pursuers.

These were Indians, there could be no doubt, but of a kind that neither Will nor Dawn was familiar with. It was quite obvious by the way they were being stalked that these fellows were not following them to make an even trade for horses and blankets. That is, of course, unless one would consider trading bullets for horses an even trade.

This enemy approached in an inverted 'V' formation, with the point the furthest away, and the ends in a flanking position, and coming ever closer. In the end they would complete a classic pincer move which would then surround and overwhelm their quarry. Conger recognized the brilliant and time-honored tactic at once.

Will decided that the best way to inflict as much damage as possible was for Dawn to hit the target furthest away first. Will rightly assumed that this was their leader. He hoped that this would create enough confusion as to allow them to escape. The secondary targets would be those riding closest to them, who by now were well within reach of the Colt repeaters. If they could drop two or three in the first volley the advantage would be theirs. Dawn lay patiently behind Pumpkin, quietly sighting in her target, checking her elevation, and gauging the light afternoon breeze. Will stood nearby with rifle in hand, waiting for Dawn to open the show. The riders were still closer now, their muscular bodies shimmering in the hot sun. The time was now. She fired.

They were Sioux, and they were in no hurry. The chance encounter with what they assumed were two careless white men was going to turn a disappointing hunting trip in to a great triumph. Their leader was indeed the rider who was furthest away, just as Will had suspected. 'Wolf that Runs' could see clearly see his quarry as well as direct the movement of his warriors from that vantage point. He had the eyes of the eagle, being the first to see the whites with their mules, and that big black horse which would give him great stature standing beside his lodge.

But he mistook the movement of the red horse as it went to the ground, assuming that it had fallen or gone lame. He also assumed that the man lying along side on the ground was there to tend to the horse in some manner---perhaps to remove the saddle. Dressed as she was, and at this distance, he could only assume that Dawn was a man.

The big .54 slug plowed into 'Wolf that Runs' just under his jaw, ripping a gaping hole in his throat and throwing him backwards off of his horse and onto the dusty scrub below. Before the others heard the report of Dawn's shot, Will had already opened up with the Colt, quickly relieving two horses of their burden, and sighting the third target, first one side, and then the other.

The Sioux reacted too slowly. They had been lulled by the certainty of their success and were unprepared for the sudden onslaught which was cast upon them. Turning to their leader, they found him lying lifeless on the ground, and then the one who rode beside him fell from yet another shot from great distance.

Dawn had watched Will load the Sharps the first time and learned quickly. She probably used a little too much powder for her second shot, but the results were just as deadly. In a matter of seconds, only four of the pursuers were still mounted, one badly wounded, riding swiftly away from these white men and their guns. It would be some time before they would be willing to venture back to collect their dead.

Nothing needed to be said, but Will's emphatic "Let's go!" underscored the need to put distance between themselves and their attackers. A few minutes later Dawn stopped, and standing back atop of Ooh-luh, carefully scanned the empty horizon. The pursuit had ended. This meant that there were no others ahead of them, waiting in ambush. At least none connected with this bunch. She shared these thoughts with Will, who wisely took her words to heart. He was learning.

But Dawn was only partially right, for not far behind the retreating Sioux were four other warriors, traveling swiftly and with purpose. These two groups met head on, and following a brief burst of gunfire, and the detailed questioning of an unfortunate survivor, the four Washahzes continued their westward trek, close now on the heels of the Spirit Woman who rides the great horse.

chapter 10

HOURS OF SAMENESS and moments of terror, such was the world Will and Dawn had ridden into. Could it have been only a week since they had fought for their lives there by the lake? Eyes stayed alert for danger, and yet the days had come and gone without incident. They discovered that the lake on the river had been the work of some overactive beavers who had managed to dam up the water and create the unmapped lake. Conger rightly figured that the heavy spring rains would most likely wash out their efforts, and the river would once again run free. It was a cycle which had gone on for as long as there had been beavers, trees, and streams.

They camped next to the river near a thicket that offered some scant shelter for the livestock, but with a ready supply of fresh cool water, and fragrant green grasses and wildflowers. The stock joyfully drank, ate, and rolled to their hearts' content.

At Dawn's insistence Will went about making a fire, as she seemed overly eager to make a good hot meal for the two of them. She asked Will to set up the tent and cots, something he had not done for several nights now, fearing the presence of hostiles lurking nearby.

But tonight his bride seemed at ease and comfortable in her surroundings. The far away mountains were becoming clearer on the western horizon, and she could be found dismounting more and more often to gather plants and flowers she found along the way. Her mother had taught her well in the use of the plants and herbs that were found there in the Virginia wilds. Some of these native plants seemed very similar to those she had known back home, while others would require closer inspection.

The sun had set long before their dinner was ready, and the stars had begun to form their endless canopy in the sky. This was a land of great beauty, and the two of them shared a feeling of 'home' for the first time since their journey together began.

She had shot the rabbit from horse back while it was in a dead run, without so much as slowing Ooh-luh down a step. Will had been good enough to retrieve it. The rabbit was delicious, and was accompanied by some greens mixed with dried beans. Dawn looked up at the stars and then quickly stood up and walked slowly over to where Will had set up their bedding for the night. Will was intrigued by the sudden change in her manner, and was beguiled as Dawn softly asked Will to come and join her over by the tent. She then surprised him even more by handing him one of the Colt rifles, and then, unholstering her side arm, stepped purposely toward the thicket. She pointed her pistol and spoke in her best Southern accent.

"Please do come to the fire and join us. And remember to keep your hands up high where I can see them, as I would hate to be forced to shoot you before you've had your dinner."

Conger had been surprised by her actions, and even more so as a tall dark haired man in buckskins walked slowly out of the thicket, hands above his head, wearing a big smile on his face.

"Mr. and Mrs. Conger, if I'm not mistaken." The deep Southern drawl of this dark stranger caused Dawn to hold a little closer on the trigger, immediately fearing that this man might be a partner of Jacob's come to take revenge.

Will's gun held steady as well. "Alright, who are you and what do you want here?" He could sense tension in Dawn's posture, and was paying very close attention here. He had no idea how she knew this man had been there, and wondered why the stock had not reacted to his presence, even though he had been right among them.

"My name is Stronton, and I carry dispatches from Fort Davis. Colonel Peters sends his greetings and apologizes for the inconvenience I most likely will have caused you, appearing unexpectedly like this. But I am here not only for these dispatches, but because I need your help. I am looking for my daughter, who was kidnapped by a man named Jacob McPhearson, and has not been seen since. Unless I'm mistaken, you are Catherine O'Dell, daughter of William and Rebecca O'Dell, of Virginia. I believe you knew the late Jacob McPhearson, and I hoping against hope that you have some information, anything, that could help he find my daughter. She'd be about your age, Ma'am."

Dawn shuddered from the suddenness of it all. Once again, and in the middle of nowhere, she had been discovered. This man was certainly from Virginia, there was no mistaking the voice. He knew their names, and apparently knew Colonel Peters as well. But somehow his being here all seemed too preposterous to be true. Dispatches? To whom, and for what purpose?

Looking the man over, Conger had a hunch, and decided to go with it. This fellow's appearance could not hide his military manner, and the snap down holster could have come from only one place, as most men found them to be cumbersome. Besides, if this man had intended to do them harm, he certainly had his chance before now. Will decided to do it the way Peters would have done it, and lowering his rifle, held out his hand in a gesture of friendship.

"Good evening sir, and welcome to our fire. I am William Conger, formerly Captain with the Illinois Sixth. What outfit were you with?" The man smiled in recognition, but kept his hands firmly in the air.

"I am Brigadier General Henry James Stronton, formerly of the Army of Virginia. Pardon me for not accepting your hand sir, but your wife here has ordered me to keep my hands in the air, and I fear she might up and shoot me were I to move without her permission." He was looking Conger straight in the eye.

"I assure you she would, and I apologize for putting you in such an uncomfortable position." The two men were having a little fun with this, but in truth, Will was not yet quite certain about his wife's opinion of their guest.

Dawn had been looking closely at this man's eyes, and saw something familiar there. She moved in closer for a better look, gun still unwavering. "What is your daughter's name?"

"Her name is Ginny. She has long dark hair like yours, and a smile that can light up a room. She loves to sing, and often taps her finger on the table to keep the beat as she does. She giggles like a little girl, and is always happy and a joy to be around."

Dawn took a deep breath, and lowered her pistol. "Please put your hands down and join us by the fire. Help yourself to some dinner. You are welcome here." Dawn's accent had vanished. She was filled with thoughts and memories from long ago. Dawn had known this girl.

Conger read over the dispatches, along with the papers he had lost when his chestnut gelding had run off with his saddle bags. Meanwhile, Dawn sat with Stronton by the fire and talked of Ginny, and what little she knew of her.

"When I returned home from Lynchburg, Ginny and another girl named Hassy were already living there. Apparently there had been several young girls who had lived in the house over the last few years, at least since my mother died. Jacob had told these girls that their families had died in a fire, and that they were to be placed in wonderful homes with people who would love them as their own. Hassy wasn't buying any of it, and had run away twice, both times being caught by trackers with hunting dogs. Jacob made an example of her and had her killed." Dawn was not about to tell Stronton any of the horrific details of Hassy's death, not wanting to plant that vision in this poor man's mind, if in fact the same fate had befallen his daughter.

"So when did you last see Ginny?" The tension and worry in this man's voice was evident, as he could hardly get the words out without shaking as he spoke. Any doubt Dawn had about the genuineness of this man and his story had left long ago. This was a man desperately looking for his lost child.

"I managed to run away two nights later. I went downstairs on my way out, hoping to take Ginny with me, but she was already gone from her room, along with her things, I didn't hear her leave, and I don't know for sure what became of her. But I do know of a man who might. He was close to Uncle Jacob, and did all of his legal dirty work. His name is Judge Bennet. I am certain he is up to his neck in all of Jacob's dealings, and if there is any record of where your daughter went to, it would be in his care. Most likely he does not know that Jacob is dead." Stronton could tell by her manner that she was holding something back from him. She had already explained that McPearson was her Uncle, and thus the family connection. Like Peters, Stronton knew there was much more to the story, like what all had taken place out on the farm, but he was a gentleman, and was not going to pry into this young woman's troubles.

The papers Stronton was carrying were varied and useful. One introduced the Brigadier, and vouched for him and his character, asking only that Dawn use her own best judgment as to what, if any, information she might be willing to share concerning any knowledge she had of Ginny and her whereabouts. The second document transferred ownership of the Larson farm to one Josiah Washington, a former slave, with all rights and responsibilities thereof. Another was a bill of sale to be signed by Will, giving ownership of what had once been his chestnut gelding to this same Washington fellow. At least now he knew where that runaway horse had ended up. There were other letters and papers, and a brief note of greeting for Dawn from Bess.

One document was intended solely for Dawn, and she had to read it over more than once to grasp the true significance it held. In the end it made perfect sense, and meant freedom from her troubled past. She would sign the paper, bearing witness to the deaths of Rhen Larson and his wife, who would remain unnamed, now buried side by side on the small hill overlooking the farm. She had spoken to Bess before of her former life as 'Catherine' being dead now to her, and now it would be a matter of record.

While Will and Stronton carried on about the war and the engagements they had fought, Dawn went over to her packs and brought out parchment and pen. After a few minutes she had worked up enough of the ink powder for her needs, and in a few short lines, severed her final link to her life back in Virginia, hoping at the same time to create a fine and lasting legacy to the place she had once called home. She signed her name as 'Catherine O'Dell', for the last time.

Bringing the finished parchment over to the fire, she gently handed it into the hands of Henry Stronton, with a tear welling in her eye, and a bright smile on her face.

"This is for you and Ginny. I know I will never be back there again, and there is no other living heir. I have dated it last year, and signed it by the name I was known by at that time. Have Colonel Peters witness the document. Then have him write up a death certificate for Jacob McPhearson just prior to that date, so there will be no question of ownership. Have the Colonel and Bess sign off as witnesses. No court in the country will be able to refuse it."

The certainty in her voice and the determined look on her face was all that Stronton needed to understand the full impact of this gift. His own place had indeed been burned to the ground. It had never amounted to much anyway. He was humbled.

"You will always be welcome there, Ma'am. We will care for your family's graves, and put up a marker for your father as well. We are forever in your debt."

Dawn then took pen and paper over to Will, and reminded him of something which was long overdue. "You need to write that letter to your brother now. This man will be able to get it close to him on his way back to Virginia. You promised to do this a long time ago." She was right, and he sat down and got to it without argument. Much of what he had seen and done on this journey was unfit for a letter home. But the news of his wonderful wife named Dawn was certainly the best news he had enjoyed in years.

While Will wrote, Dawn sat down next to Stronton and explained in detail a plan she had cooked up. It was involved and detailed, but if it was done properly, and with great courage, it just might work. Stronton was forced to take notes. Later, Will joined in with some of the letters he had found in Jacob's saddlebags. It was well past midnight when the plan had finally come together. Dawn then excused herself, and walked on over to where her great black horse was lying on the soft grass. She curled up beside her and wept softly for her childhood long since lost, for her wonderful parents, the trust and friendship of Rhen, now gone, and for the gift of answered prayer named Will Conger.

Later on William laid a warm blanket over the sleeping girl, still snuggled beside her gentle friend. Her young husband would sleep nearby. And somehow during the night, neither was awakened as the stern looking man in buckskins rode out of camp, heading east, armed now with newfound hope of finding his lost child.

The four Washazhe watched closely as the man in buckskins rode out of the camp that night, his business with the Spirit Woman now finished. Guns had been trained upon him during his visit, ready to stop any move that threatened her or her servant. It was their appointed task to keep her safe until which time she would perform the ceremony to free the wandering soul of Tall Tree, and return his spirit to their people.

They had done well when they caught up to her just outside of Mullit. It was one of their rifles that shot the drover in the back as he went to fire upon the girl. Shots fired into the nearby tree had warned them in advance of the ranch riders who bore down upon that place, allowing them time to escape discovery. They had killed the wolves that had picked up the scent of the deer meat despite Dawn's efforts with the travois. They had nearly failed after briefly losing the Spirit Woman's trail during the heavy rains when Will changed direction, and came up on them again only after Will and Dawn had driven off the attack of the Sioux warriors.

A place for the ceremony would need to be found soon, as they would soon pass beyond the ancestral lands of their people. In two days time the moon would rise. This would mark the time. They must not fail.

chapter 11

THE MOUNTAINS WERE in clear view now and the land had once again turned dry. Conger's map showed them being very near the Platte, but in truth, Dawn's words had come back to haunt him. He was headed for the mountains alright, and there they were, right in front of him. But then what?

He was certain winter would be difficult this far north, and while he had counted on game to help sustain them, he'd seen precious little of it in the last few weeks. He was certain his lovely wife had seen more than him, for she had the eyes of a hawk, but still, she had said little about it. He really hadn't planned this part of the journey out very well at all. Will would need to discuss this with Dawn that night.

Truth was, Dawn hadn't seen all that much game either. Every other day or so there was a rabbit or a stray deer for dinner, but she had seen few targets. Luckily her every shot accounted for a kill, but what would happen when there was nothing to shoot at? She decided to speak to Will about it that night at the campsite.

The livestock had fared surprisingly well so far, due in part to excessive care and fussing over by their owners. The oats and corn had long ago played out, and the grasses had gone from green to brown to everything in between. Everyone, man and horse alike, had been losing weight as of late, except for the mules that is. Mules will eat anything.

Once again the spirits spoke to Dawn Flower, and she knew that others were close by. She did not stand atop her mare this time, for she knew they would not be visible to her. She knew now that it had been their prayers that she had heard upon the wind, not those of the ones who attacked them back by the lake. Once again those prayers were heard, and the Spirits were not opposed to their wishes. It would happen very soon now. Her being here was no accident. They had been led to this place, and had been protected on their journey until now. They could not escape what had been planned for her.

That night she again insisted on a tent with the cots, and a warm fire. After dinner, when the stars stood in their assigned places in the heavens, Dawn excused herself as though to deal with personal business, and walked behind the horses to meet with the one she knew was waiting there.

He was dressed much like Tall Tree and his followers, but with a look of strength and wisdom which was missing in the others. She knew this man was a leader, and that he was there with a purpose.

No words were spoken. Signs and gestures were all that was needed. A few minutes later, Dawn knew exactly what was expected of her, and what she would be forced to do to save her husband's life.

She walked back to the fire to clean up after the meal. Will noticed the change in her manner, but said nothing. She would tell him what she wanted him to know, when she decided it was time. He went to check on the horses.

Dawn's watchers were patient but firm. She would have to do something to get Will out of the way, or he would be killed. She pulled a bag of herbs from her pack and started mixing a familiar potion. Once, back in Virginia, she had used these leaves to save herself from her husband. Tonight, she would use them to save her husband from her.

Will was convinced that things were secure for the night, and came back to the fire. Dawn had a special surprise waiting for him. He smelled the delicious aroma and knew at once that she had made his favorite---hot sassafras tea! Dawn drank sparingly, while Will downed cup after cup. She had made it for him only once before.

It wasn't long before he found himself growing tired. In fact, he was having trouble staying awake. He lay down against his saddle, and watched as the fire blurred, and then was gone. Conger was now in a deep sleep, and was unaware as strong arms lifted him up and took him away from the fire.

Minutes later Ooh-luh knelt down to allow her closest friend to mount up, and following the words of Dawn's native tongue, the big horse carried Dawn and her worldly belongings away from camp, and into the night. She would not return.

Will woke up hours later, and knew that his world had changed. She was gone. He did not need to look around to confirm what he already knew. A little over two months now they had been together, day and night. Right at that moment he felt her absence just the same as he would feel her presence.

He lay face up on his cot under the tent. He had not lain down there the night before, and had no idea how he got there. As strong as she was, Dawn could not have lifted him, yet there he was. Last night all seemed dim and distant. They had enjoyed a dinner of prairie hen and some beans as well. She had made a special pot of sassafras, Will's favorite, and seemed to enjoy watching him drink cup after cup. She smiled at him, and sang a tune he had heard her hum many times before. But this time there were words to the tune, words in Cherokee he assumed, as he couldn't understand a word, but it was beautiful and lyrical and wonderful to hear.

His head hurt---not like from his fall from the horse those many weeks before, that had long since healed, but rather from a stuffiness in his ears and nose. He didn't understand it, but somehow he knew it had to do with that sassafras tea she had brewed up. But why?

Conger reached for the tent pole and pulled himself up to a standing position. The campsite spun for a few seconds as he fought to catch his bearings. He saw at once that Pumpkin and the two mules were still there. The sun was just coming up over the horizon, but even in the half light, he couldn't help but notice that the massive bulk of her precious Ooh-luh was gone as well.

She really had gone then, taking her packs and her horse and left him behind. There had been no struggle, no warning, no shots fired. No abductor or wild beast could be blamed. Off to the southwest Will could hear distant thunder---a long-awaited rain. But it would wipe out her tracks, and make following her nigh impossible.

Follow her? Why should he follow her? She had left him, drugged him and left him. If she didn't want to be there, why should he care? After all, he had started this journey alone, and had absolutely no intention of picking up a bride along the way. What was he doing with this girl anyway?

Then he looked down at her cot and saw a carefully placed bundle, wrapped in oilskin. He recognized it at once, knowing that it held her family Bible, the most cherished of all her possessions. She would have never left without it unless...

He knew at once why. His self doubt and pity were immediately replaced by desperation. Within minutes he had struck camp and had his little parade on the move. The big horse's tracks were easy to follow, and there were others alongside. The rain was skirting to the south and he would have no trouble following the trail. Wherever she would go, he would follow. He now understood that he would never be whole without her. Mules in tow, he picked up the pace.

Dawn rode with an empty face, her heart filled with sadness and loss. Twice now she had drugged her husbands, to escape from one, and now to save the life of the other. She was alone now, and realized that she might not have long to live. If only she had not made all that big brag to the Washazhe that night. All that nonsense about claiming Tall Tree's spirit and threatening to change them all into coyotes! Now look at her, alone and defenseless against these warriors. She did not even know where they were taking her. They had ridden on through the night, under the light of the full moon. The destination seemed to be a long way off.

But at least she had protected William. He was such a good man and deserved to live on. She had drugged his tea, for she knew he would fight to save her, and be killed in the effort. She had sung a song while she waited for him to succumb to the drug. The words were directed to the Washazhe saying that they needed to wait until her servant slept before she could go away with them. They had honored her wishes, and even gone so far as to carry Will to his cot under the tent. They did not disturb the mules, or his horse, or even his weapons. They were there only for her.

Dawn was not at all sure what fate awaited her, but understood that once she released Tall Tree's spirit, they would have no reason to keep her around. She wished now that she had brought a weapon of some sort---the derringer, or even a knife. If they intended to kill her, at least she could make a fight of it. These were Indians, and yet right now she felt no kinship with them. There had been a time when she had clung to her Cherokee roots, shunning the white man's world in any way possible. But now, after all she had been through with William in these past months, she felt only as a creature of the earth, not as a member of any tribe or group, neither Indian nor white.

She had been taken away from her happiness, and was being led to a place she knew not where. Dawn was in the company of three Washazhe warriors. She could not know that a fourth, a shaman of the tribe, was miles away, preparing a place for the ceremony which would restore the spirit of Tall Tree, and remove the cloud of doubt and darkness from his people.

Ooh-luh was a brave horse, and powerful, but was not considered fast as horses go. Dawn could not outrun her captors. All she had were her wits, and the hope that she somehow could find a way to elude these men, or trick them into letting her go free. Those hopes faded the farther they rode.

Pumpkin would have gone faster, but with the burden of the mules to contend with, Conger was unable to increase the pace. The tracks of the big black horse were easy enough to follow. In fact, Will considered the possibility that such a poorly hidden trail would lead to an ambush. He should have been more careful, more aware of his surroundings. But right then, he just didn't care. He wanted Dawn back from whoever had taken her, and he was itching for a fight, rifle at the ready. He pulled the lead rope a little harder.

Dusk of the next day was upon them as they finally reached their destination. Light from a glowing fire cast unholy shadows upon the stone walls which surrounded this place. There was no warmth here, no welcome for the weary traveler. This was a place of darkness and sadness, perhaps chosen for that reason, or perhaps simply chosen unawares. Even the light of the full moon was hidden by heavy cloud cover.

The fourth Washazhe sat near to the fire, his shadow looming large against the rocks behind him as darkness overtook that edge of the encampment. The riders dismounted, continuing the silence which had accompanied their journey. Dawn was led to a small enclosure, something like a tent, but more of a blind. Garments had been laid out for her, including a dress of white doeskin with intricate bead work, and a shawl of finely woven cloth. These appeared to be garments of honor and distinction, representing the finest craftwork of their people.

The warriors stepped away as she changed. She knew it had nothing to do with preserving her modesty, as these men lived open lives in the close company of many others. The appearance of her unclothed body would cause only the slightest sense of curiosity among them, if any.

No, they had gone to prepare themselves for the ceremony to come. They too changed into garments more suited to the occasion, regaled in beadwork and feathers, with ceremonial tools and weapons as well. Special foods had been prepared, and arranged in an intricate and detailed manner. All had been made ready. Dawn stepped out from the blind, beautifully adorned in rich clothing, her long dark hair flowing across her shoulders in the light evening breeze. Her mind was busily forming a desperate plan, rough and futile perhaps, but still a plan. She would watch for her chance.

The warriors were seated in a ring around the blazing fire, with the shaman facing east, and a place presumably left empty for Dawn, facing westward. She noticed that while two warriors sat to her left, only one sat to her right and got an idea. She opened the ceremony in Spanish.

"I thank my brothers of the Washazhe for the preparations they have made for this ceremony. These things are pleasing to me, and the garments you have provided are well-suited for my work here." Dawn became troubled as no words were spoken in response to her greeting. Could it be they did not understand the words of the Spanish? She truly doubted that, as these tribes traded widely with others to the south, and were known to be skilled in English, French, and Spanish as well. There had to be another reason for their silence. This treatment smacked of rudeness.

"You will release the soul of Tall Tree now." It was the voice of the shaman, still seated, but not letting his gaze fall upon her. In fact, none of the Washazhe was looking at her, averting their eyes as though she were not really there.

And then she understood. It is considered unholy to look into the eyes of a sacrifice, lest it steals your soul and takes you with it to the land of the dead. The garments she was wearing were not those of honor, but rather intended for the sacrifice of her life after she had restored Tall Tree's spirit. A shudder ran down her spine as she understood the gravity of it all. If she refused, they would torture her as needed until she spoke the words that freed the warrior's soul. There would be no mercy, no turning back. The die was cast.

"I will require the aid of my servant." She then spoke softly to her closest friend, and the great black horse walked softly over to the fire, kneeling gently beside her, and causing the warrior to her right to jump away, careful not to find himself under the weight of the horse's massive frame. The men might not have been looking at Dawn, but they were now to a man watching that big black mare, convinced of its power, and of the mystical bond between the two.

Without further ado, Dawn then reached down in front of her, taking a fistful of sandy soil in each hand. She then tossed the soil into the fire, first the left hand, and then the right. Then she stood, and raising her hands to the heavens, proceeded to sing the song of Jack and Jill in a mixture of English and Cherokee. The result was an unintelligible maze of language which the men before her could neither interpret nor understand. Adding movement and gestures, and a few more handfuls of sand, Dawn put on a pretty good show. After all, this was all for them. She never really had any sort of control over Tall Tree's soul, and wouldn't know how to do such a thing if she had wanted to. The whole charade, along with the coyote story , had been to frighten the young men into taking Tall Tree's body back to their village, and making it possible for her and Will to get away.

"The ceremony is complete. I have returned Tall Tree's spirit back to your people. He will no longer wander in darkness. I will now continue on my quest to the great mountains, to make sacrifice for the people. Walk with honor, and do not further hinder me from the task which I must complete." She then quickly climbed aboard Ooh-luh, and giving quick instruction, had the great horse stand upright, all the time hoping that her luck would hold.

Forceful words from the Shaman sent the warriors into action, surrounding the mare, and moving to lay hands upon the girl. Her chance to escape was doomed.

And then the fire exploded!

Flames and embers blew across the encampment, searing flesh and clothing alike. Gathered around the horse to prevent the girl's escape, the warriors took the brunt of the blast, and thereby sheltered Dawn and her mount from the worst of it.

Conger's toss had been perfect. It had cost him his sock, but the amount of powder needed for a blast that size required some sort of container if it were going to make the distance to the fire. The resulting explosion was nearly instantaneous, and a whole lot bigger than Will thought it would be.

The chaos that followed was all that Dawn needed to escape her captors. Desperate words were spoken, and the great horse surged forward, and spinning around, trampled two of the would-be captors.

The Colt rifle was already in action, dropping the leader and the Shaman in a matter of seconds. The other two were already on the ground, one with a broken arm and the other knocked senseless. Dawn knew the sound of that rifle and rode straight for it, overjoyed that William had come for her. But her reunion with her rescuing knight was once again not at all what Conger had figured it would be.

"Give me the rifle and cover me!" She took the Colt into her hands and rode swiftly back to the remains of the fire, and spoke in her native Cherokee to those who could still hear her.

"Cowards of the Washazhe! Did you believe my servants would allow me to be harmed by your betrayal? Hear my words. From this day forward, each time you hear the cry of the coyote, within one cycle of the sun, one of the people of your tribe will die. You have angered the spirits of the earth and sky, and betrayed their servant, and you must now accept your fate." Amazingly, this time she really meant it, and somehow had the feeling that she had the power to order such things. Dawn had never thought in these terms before, and she was amazed at the changes which seemed to have suddenly happened within her.

With the mayhem at the fire behind them, Dawn and Will rode quickly west, or at least what they thought was west, as it was completely dark now, and low clouds were hiding the moon and stars. They stopped for the night only a few miles away, as the terrain had become too treacherous to travel in the darkness. Conger would not sleep at all this night, but he was not alone, as nearby a coyote called sometime before midnight, answered by his companions some distance away.

As prophesied, the Shaman died from his wounds the next morning. All in all, only one of the four Washazhe warriors ever made it back to their village, haggard and worn, and telling of the frightening power of the Spirit Woman, and of her magical black horse.

chapter 12

DAWN HAD NOT yet awakened as the sun began to peek over the eastern horizon. She looked serene and lovely in the white dress with the beautiful beadwork. Ooh-luh was awake, but was not stirring so as not to awaken her closest friend lying against her massive frame.

Will smiled, knowing that the partnership of horse and girl was one that he could never come between, nor would he ever try. Pumpkin and the mules were already awake as well, sampling the local grasses accompanied by an occasional stomp. Nearby some native birds had begun their daily business, singing to one another and announcing the new day.

Conger thought about a fire, and the coffee that would go with it, and then recalled the wonderful breakfast they had enjoyed at that little cantina in Mullit. They had come a long way in a short time since then, and all that was not just simply the distance they had traveled. He had grown up a bit on this trip, and had to admit that he really didn't care for all this traveling as much as he thought he would.

He had not yet seen it all, this vast and amazing land, but he had seen enough for now. He had it in his mind to stop all of this nonsense and settle down somewhere, at least for a while, and put down some roots. He was going to have to talk to Dawn about it, and see what she thought. It wasn't safe for her wandering around out here like this. In fact, she seemed to have been in danger much of the time he had known her, despite his better efforts. He really loved this girl, and knew it was up to him to protect her. Riding around aimlessly like this no longer made any sense.

"Mr. Conger, we probably need to be moving on now." Will wasn't really startled by his young wife's sudden appearance by his side, or by the soft gentle way she had spoken those words to him. But he had yet to understand how she could move about so silently, as though her feet did not actually touch the ground as she walked.

"I thought you were still asleep. I didn't want to wake you." Conger was speaking quietly as well. There was every possibility that their pursuers were nearby, hoping to avenge the events of the night before. They were not that far from the ceremony site, as traveling in the dark had seemed too treacherous. Still, the place they had camped was surprisingly suited for the task, even more so as Will had chosen the spot in the dark, with no landmarks or view of the countryside to guide him.

They rode on to the west, but the mules were uncomfortable and contrary. Saddles and packs had remained on the livestock through the night, given that they might have to be up and running at a moment's notice. Conger regretted the need for such rough handling. Of course, Ooh-luh never wore a saddle, and Pumpkin, being an army horse, was used to difficult circumstances. It was the mules that were fussing, and Conger knew he needed to get those packs off and be about some badly needed rub-downs. That meant that today's ride would be relatively short, as soon as they could find a place with adequate water and good grass.

Trouble was, Conger had no idea where that might be. They were far north of the river now, and following Dawn and her kidnappers, Will hadn't paid much attention to where he was headed. The land had become rocky and broken with trees and flowers the likes of which neither one of them had ever seen. Furthermore, they seemed to be riding slightly uphill now, and ever closer to those enormous mountains.

Dawn had changed back into men's clothes along with a wide-brimmed hat. Luckily she had purchased several out-fits in Mullit, and had replacements for the ones she had left behind with the Washazhe.

"Where did you get that dress you were wearing?" Will couldn't think of anything useful to say about the previous day's events, and he was not of a mind to give her a bad time about drugging his tea. He was much too happy just to have her there with him that he was not about to spoil the moment. He had tried to say nothing at all, waiting for her to open the conversation, but his Welsh just wouldn't stay quiet.

"They had me wear it while I went about performing a ritual to free that big Indian's soul. It's very comfortable and very nicely made." She stopped speaking then, not wanting to talk about it any more just then. In truth, she was so incred-ibly grateful for his rescuing her---again---that she didn't know what to say or how to act. She knew she could never feel free to complain to Will about anything, ever, for the rest of her life. It bothered her more then when Will said nothing more after that, lost in his thoughts, but seemingly not about her. They rode on.

It was just past noon when Pumpkin's ears went up, and she looked over toward the south. Ooh-luh looked too, and the mules spoke as well. A small herd of very large elk came out of a thicket hidden among some gray boulders. Conger rode on ahead to look the place over.

There was a spring, and a pool of water ninety feet or so across. There was shade and grass and flowers. He quickly rode back and got the others. Packs flew off of tired backs and the stock enjoyed the cool water of the spring. As would be expected, within minutes Dawn had her clothes off and was playing joyfully in the fresh clear water. Conger stood watch, rifle in hand, for even the Garden of Eden had its snakes.

They spent the better part of the day there. Dawn pre-pared a delicious luncheon while Will stayed busy fussing over the livestock, cleaning weapons, and refilling their stale water supply. He also spent a considerable time scouting around the area, aware of the tracks of the creatures who frequented this place, and the dangers staying there could bring, especially at night, when the big cats came out to hunt.

So it was that with a few hours of daylight left, the Conger party wearily packed up again, and headed further westward and away from the lovely little oasis. They would need to find another place to stay the night, and the next, and the next, with the mountains and their destiny looming ever closer, and still no idea where they were headed.

Many days of hard riding brought Stronton through the gates of Fort Davis once again. A change of horses and a few hours rest were all the man needed. The signed dispatches were delivered, and new ones were drawn up, following the instructions given by Dawn as they had made plans by the camp fire. Bess was called upon for her penmanship skills, and using some of the documents provided by Conger from out of McPhearson's saddle bags, the hair-brained scheme cooked up by the former Catherine O'Dell, and with her knowledge of her Uncle Jacob's operation, had about a fifty-fifty chance of working. It would all be up to Henry Stronton now.

Sergeant Richards whipped up a pack with several days' rations, while Whittle supplied the Brigadier with two strong mounts for his ride back east. After a planned stop at what was now the Washington farm, and delivery of the deed, Stronton was free to ride back east, except for a brief stop near Lexington, to hand deliver Will's letter to his brother James. Stronton's orders were to turn the two horses in at any army post, if and when he saw fit.

It was a race against time, and against all odds. His mind was on Ginny, and a judge, and the things he would have to do to find her at last.

Once Stronton had given his report, Peters took action on matters of special importance. Credence had been given to the documents Dawn had provided, including careful instructions on the kind of paperwork the Brigadier would need to execute the plans they had dreamed up. Bess got busy with pen and ink while the other documents were signed and countersigned as needed. The Colonel was heartened by the cleverness and generosity that Dawn had shown in deeding the family farm to Stronton, and in planning a death certificate for Jacob McPhearson. At least that was one he wouldn't have to falsify.

A few days earlier Durbin had been escorted back to his place, along with his horse, having recovered sufficiently to make the journey. Surprisingly, his farm had somehow been spared during the raids, and except for a few dead chickens, most everything was intact. The army escort stayed behind for a couple of days to help put things in order for the still-healing Durbin.

Browner had also left the fort under escort, but in a very different manner. Having been found guilty of concealing evidence, and being an agent to horse thievery, Browner was banished from the fort along with his hand tools and livestock. All other equipment was confiscated and already in use by other members of the garrison. Browner started to argue the matter, but the threat of a hanging softened his tone. He left quietly in his wagon, and headed for Mullit.

Peters also received the first shipment of those repeating rifles he had asked for. Following Conger's example, he had protective leather sleeves made up for each man, and personally oversaw instruction for the loading of the cylinders.

The Italian family had decided to stay on after all, and the man began plying his skills as a barber and basket maker as well. One of the soldiers had already been calling on his oldest daughter.

Bess stayed busy as always, but often stopped to think about that nice young couple who had slept in their bed and blessed their lives, wondering just what had become of them, and hoping they might come back and visit some day. But her thoughts were interrupted, as yet another group of wagons was rumbling through the gate for a brief stopover on their way west. She hurried out to greet them.

As for Will and Dawn, the trail had provided another week of uneventful days and nights, with only a light rain off and on to break the monotony of it all. The rolling wooded landscape around them was certainly breathtaking. But with the need for constant vigilance for game and dangers as well, there was little chance to sit back and take it all in. They were very near the mountains now, and Conger was thinking more and more about that pretty little spring they had visited just a few days before. With a little work it could make for a very nice home site. There was plenty of game, good water, and provided a reasonably defensible position if a few improvements were made. To the north was a pretty good looking stand of timber, and with the aid of Dawn's big horse, it wouldn't take long to build up a suitable shelter for man and beast alike.

Summer wasn't all used up yet, but Conger knew that at this elevation, winter could be pretty rough out here if one wasn't prepared. His map showed settlements to the south of where he figured they were, and maybe if they headed down that way soon enough, they could stock up on the provisions they would need to see them through 'til spring. The more he thought about it, the better it all sounded.

Conger pulled up early that evening at a likely looking place, and thought of just how he was going to try to talk Dawn into going back the way they had come from and settling down in what he believed was the perfect spot, even if it was only until next year. The tiredness in Dawn's eyes convinced him that she was travel weary as well, and would maybe be open to the idea.

Will decided he would say something to her that night after supper. It looked like rain again, and the tent and cots were already up and ready for use. After checking on the stock one last time, Will came to the tent only to find Dawn softly snoring away. Well, he sure wasn't going to wake the girl up just to talk about some crazy idea he had cooked up. Besides, he was just as tired as she was. He would simply talk to her about it over breakfast the next morning.

He never got the chance.

chapter 13

THE WELL-WORN BROWN horse pulled the rented carriage up to the two story brick office of Judge Otis Bennet, as though it knew the place, and had been there before. This structure had somehow remained untouched by the fires and utter destruction which had ravaged so much of downtown Richmond, and was now in use by those who benefited most from the comings and goings of the post-war legal process. Much money had changed hands here.

The driver of the carriage, a tall, dark distinguished looking gentleman, pulled a sheaf of papers out from his inside coat pocket, and looked them over one last time to double check their contents, hoping that all was in order. He was clean cut, and well dressed in the most recent eastern fashion, and while not so showy as to be called a dandy, the appearance of wealth and station in life was unmistakable.

The transformation of Brigadier Henry James Stronton from buckskin to suit coat had been successful enough, yet somehow the frightening fearsomeness of the man who had ridden through the gates of Fort Davis could not be so easily hidden. He only prayed that he could play his part well enough this day. Everything depended on it.

Dawn Conger had remembered his daughter Ginny. She had looked for her the night of her escape from the family farm, and the clutches of her Uncle Jacob. Thinking back, Dawn had recalled a brief exchange between McPhearson and the Judge shortly after their sham wedding ceremony at which the Judge had presided. She heard the girl's name mentioned and something about a payment long overdue. Based on what she had seen, and what she had learned of her uncle's dealings, she reasoned that Ginny must have been given to the Judge as payment for services rendered. Since Ginny was nowhere to be found, Dawn assumed that the Judge must have taken her with him as he left for home that evening. It was a long shot, and sketchy at best, but Dawn figured that Judge Bennet was Stronton's best chance of locating his daughter.

Dawn had cooked up this clever scheme while sitting by the fire with Stronton, and papers and letters had been drawn up using the documents Will had found in McPhearson's saddle bags as a guide. Now it was up to Stronton to successfully impersonate one of Jacob's known associates, supposedly with a debt to collect. There would be no margin of error.

Of course, Stronton would have preferred a full-on frontal attack instead of all this play acting and subterfuge. Dawn had rightly warned him that the Judge would be surrounded by a small army of men who were heavily armed and ready to do his bidding at any time.

Stepping down at last, Stronton tied the lines off to the ring post, and latching the gate behind him, proceeded to walk down the flower lined brick path and up the steps to the door marked only with the number 27. Sweat trickled down his neck, not only from the heat, which was bad enough that day, but from the reality that this entire matter could go very wrong, very quickly, and in so many different ways.

Nearby were two men, seemingly busy working in the garden. Both men wore the unmistakable look of those who would kill at the slightest provocation. Stronton was certain they were armed, and could tell at a glance that they would be dangerous with any kind of weapon. The man he was impersonating this day was known to be very dangerous as well. He hoped he looked the part.

The pull of the porch cord brought a finely dressed black man to the door, charged with the task of accepting visitors into this private office space. Despite the fine clothing, he too had the look of an assassin. This could prove to be a very difficult place to get out of alive. Stronton spoke first, taking unto himself the identity of another man.

"Good afternoon. My name is Rue French, here for my appointment with Judge Bennet. The Judge's reply to my inquiry instructed me to be here at this time."

The doorman quickly took Stronton's hat and gloves, and motioned him in to the parlor. "Yes sir, Mr. French, his Honor is expecting you. Please make yourself comfortable. I will inform his Honor of your arrival."

The parlor was finely appointed, with rich fabric adorning the furniture, and a beautiful flowered carpet lying thick and full upon the brightly polished oak floor. It was apparent that the Judge lived well, and lacked for nothing in what was still a war-scarred city.

Shorter and wider than his guest, Judge Bennet waddled out from his office at once, and offered his hand to Mr. French, knowing his visitor by name and reputation only, having never met the man face to face.

"Please step into my office. I don't mind saying that it's a bit awkward having you here like this you know, but having read your note, I understand your need for conducting this business firsthand."

Stronton followed the Judge into his book-lined office, again furnished in the finest of materials, accented by a beautifully crafted mahogany desk.

"You live well sir." Stronton's deep Virginia drawl could not be mistaken as anything else, and simply added to the confidence the Judge enjoyed that he was indeed dealing with the right man.

"Ah, the spoils of war, my friend. The Yankees hereabouts have been very generous in allowing for the preservation of certain unclaimed items from the abandoned buildings and houses here in Richmond. I have, in fact, a warehouse full of such finery at my disposal, which will bring a handsome price in the months to come. Richmond shall rise again from the ashes, and the rich like to live well."

"Judge Bennet, at the risk of seeming impatient, I feel it is in our mutual best interests that we conclude this business as quickly as possible. The sooner I return to Charleston with my package, the better."

"You are right of course, Mr. French. In your note you mentioned a letter you hold written by Jacob McPhearson, and the reward he has offered you in return for services rendered on his behalf. Might I see the letter sir, that I might authenticate the writing and signature therein?"

Stronton drew the letter from his coat pocket and tossed it carelessly over to Bennet's side of the desk. "If you can read Jacob's scrawl, you're a better man than me. Just tell me where to find the girl, and I'll be on my way."

Judge Bennet unfolded the letter and studied it carefully. As expected, it had been written in the maddeningly careless handwriting style which seemed to mirror most every aspect of McPhearson's life. It was authentic alright, right down to the nearly illegible finger mark at the bottom back side of the page.

"One last thing, Mr. French. Jacob mentions in this letter a wound that you suffered as a result of your saving his life. All of this seems perfectly in order, of course, but I must be certain. Perhaps you would be kind enough to show me the scar from the aforementioned bullet wound."

Stronton hesitated. The entire matter of a gun battle on an Ohio river sternwheeler, and French's subsequent wound had been his idea, designed to add credence to the ruse. The General had indeed received a nasty little bullet wound to his left side in the last days of the war, and it was taking its fine time healing up. Applying a little bit of lady's rouge, made the wound seem more recent than it actually was. The fact that it was still tender to the touch did not have to be faked.

Stronton had gone through enough stalling and posturing already, and was growing impatient with this phony Judge and his endless delays. Besides, he thought he might just be smelling a rat in the room. Stronton decided to take charge here, just as the man he was impersonating was known to do. The General stood up, and unholstering his LeMat, pointed the barrel straight at Judge Bennet's ample midsection.

"I will oblige you, sir, on this one last curiosity of yours, but only as a courtesy to our friend Jacob, as you are not fully acquainted with my way of doing business. But any more delays, and I shall give you a scar identical to my own to firmly convince you who you are dealing with." With that, Stronton pulled up his shirt, displaying the still angry-looking welt on his side, gun still in hand.

"I apologize, Mr. French. Please forgive me for being overly cautious. You must understand, I have not heard from Jacob for some time now, and this is all rather unusual." It was the Judge who was sweating now, and regretting his last inquiry. The utter viciousness of this man French was well-documented, and he knew he had played his hand as far as he dared. He knew French was not a man to anger.

"Allow me to assure you, Judge Bennet, that the last time I saw Jacob he couldn't have been better. Seems he was chasing down some girl and was headed out Kansas way or some such. Our trouble on the riverboat didn't allow much time to catch up on old times. I was fortunate to run into him when I did."

"Based on this letter, the good fortune was all his, Mr. French. Jacob owes you his life, and I, my gratitude. The agreement will of course be honored. I noticed that you drove up in a carriage. We can take it to my house, if you don't mind. It's only mile or so from here, and in a very fine neighborhood, I might add. The girl in question actually lives there in my home as part of the wait staff. She's quite pretty, you know."

Stronton's heart skipped a beat with the knowledge that his daughter was still alive, and close by as well. He had to somehow hold it together, and stay in character. This was agonizing. He spoke up, playing his part again.

"And the money? That's five hundred in gold he promised. Don't try to tell me you keep that at home as well." Stronton had almost forgotten about the gold.

"You are indeed the very scoundrel Jacob told me you were, Mr. French. I find it interesting that even though we have never met before today, I feel as though I know you quite well. You can put that gun away now, I have no intention of crossing swords with a man of your reputation." The Judge then opened the bottom drawer of his desk, and carefully pulling out a pistol, laid it gently on the desk top. He then proceeded to pull out five heavy bags of coins, and laid them down just as gently. He then returned the pistol to the drawer, and closed it. Stronton's gun had not moved.

On the way to the Judge's house, Bennet entertained Stronton with a running commentary of downtown Richmond, and of the frantic rebuilding process that was underway. He proudly indicated those projects that he himself had a hand in, and boasted of the profits to be made there. But he had not finished with the quizzing of his mysterious guest.

"So tell me, Mr. French, how is it that you came to decide upon this girl in particular? Many lovely girls have come through our hands in the last few years, you know." The Judge found this particular detail troubling, as this girl had been given as payment for work the Judge had done from time to time, not that he could really complain, as his association with Jacob had made him a very wealthy man. Still, this was somehow unlike Jacob, and his way of doing business.

"I told McPhearson what I wanted. I simply described what I had in mind, and he said he knew a girl that fit my order to a 'T.' He even told me her name. The next day he wrote up that letter, and told me where and how to find you, and that you would see to it. He went on ahead west, while I stayed in Cincinnati until I could travel again. I figured I'd stop off here on my way back to Charleston. You ask a lot of questions mister."

"Forgive me. It's just that I've enjoyed having Ginny around these many months. She's such a nice girl, and she just brightens up my household, especially with the way she's always singing. I'm an old man now, and I don't have much use for womenfolk these days. You'll be a lucky man to have her, Mr. French."

"Sounds like it." Nothing else was said between them.

Stronton had insisted that the girl not be allowed to see his face or be aware of his presence until the transfer was complete. The Judge thought it all just another precaution that French was so well known for in all of his dealings.

The truth was, that while Stronton was nearly shaking in anticipation of a reunion with his daughter, to have her recognize him at this time, and among the armed throng that Stronton assumed lived there at the Judge's home, would surely mean death for both of them. He just couldn't take the chance. Dawn had told Stronton about the way girls and stolen goods were transported in specially designed caskets, so as not to arouse suspicion. By insisting that Ginny be transported in this way, Stronton not only lessened the chance of a face to face meeting before he got her away to safety, but also helped to reassure the Judge as to French's identity, as Jacob had entrusted very few with the knowledge of his manner of secret transport.

So it was that, upon their arrival at the Judge's house, Ginny was forced to drink a strong drug mixed with a shot of whiskey. Within minutes the drug took effect, and Ginny was deeply asleep. She was unaware of being placed into a brown wooden casket, specially designed with adequate ventilation to prevent suffocation. The casket was quickly carried outside and placed in the back of the carriage. The few personal items the girl kept had been hurriedly stuffed into a carpetbag and loaded up with her as well. The entire exchange took place in less than fifteen minutes, a testament to the ruthless efficiency of Jacob McPhearson and his smuggling network. Stronton didn't bother to wave goodbye as he drove away. It was all he could do to keep the horse moving at an easy gate, when in his heart he wanted to race away from this place and take his daughter home again.

It was near dark and many miles away when the carriage stopped at the farmstead of Ben Chalmers. Stronton was simply known as the 'General' in these parts, and Chalmers had served alongside the Brigadier for many a campaign with the Army of Virginia. No request for entry would be needed at this home, or many others like it, as the welcome mat was out for Stronton day or night, and always would be.

If Chalmers was surprised or hesitant at the General's arrival, it didn't show. Stronton had shared his plan with no one east of Fort Davis, and Chalmers could only wonder as to why the General would ask that the casket be taken inside. Without hesitation, Chalmers and his son helped with the box, and laid it gently by the fireplace. Chalmers' wife stood back in the corner as the lid was opened, wondering why the General would disturb the dead in this way.

Peering in, the General wept as he carefully bent down and lifted up the sleeping girl, holding her close in his powerful arms once more, just as he had so many years ago. She was older now, and much more a woman than the little girl he had left behind as he rode off to war. She looked like her mother.

Mrs. Chalmers rushed over, seeing at once that the girl was indeed the long lost Ginny, whom she had watched growing up. A bed was hurriedly made up close to the fire, and Ginny was gently placed upon it. Still drugged, it would be morning before she would wake up to know all that had happened, and of her father's meeting with the unsuspecting Judge who until that day had been her captor.

Stronton sat there beside her, tears of joy still flowing, the months of searching now finally over. Holding Ginny's hand, he spoke out loud a prayer of thanks for his daughter's deliverance.

Somehow, despite being so heavily drugged, Ginny heard the voice she had known so long ago. She opened her eyes and looked into the face she cherished. "Daddy?"

Then she smiled, and squeezing his massive hand, fell back to sleep, a beautiful reunion waiting for them both come morning.

The phony paperwork had succeeded after all. It seemed Bess Peters really could duplicate anyone's handwriting if she put her mind to it. She had done it to her husband often enough.

chapter 14

It was Pumpkin who spoke first. A chorus of whinnies and stomps quickly followed. Morning had just begun to peak up over the hillsides, when Will and Dawn woke up with a start. Hearing the horses, they grabbed for their weapons.

In the distance was a fire, now two fires, now three. These were cooking fires, with people walking nearby. The light increased as the sun continued its western journey. Dawn sat her rifle down, and advised Conger to do the same. Those weapons, as lethal as they were, would serve no purpose this day, except to get them killed.

Already a large group of horsemen, at least thirty in all, had ridden up from seemingly nowhere. These were Indians, to be sure, but unlike any either of them had ever seen before. Their faces showed no emotion, no feeling. No weapons were brandished, no sign of threat to be seen. Then, one among them addressed Dawn in Spanish.

"Come with us now. Ride your horses."

There was no room or place for argument here. They were helplessly outnumbered, and would have to follow whatever instruction was given. It was clear that they had no choice.

Having been told to leave their belongings and pack animals behind, Will saddled up Pumpkin, while Dawn gave instruction to Ooh-luh. Two of the riders had already dismounted and seemed to have been assigned to guard the Conger campsite. Nothing was touched.

As they rode, they saw what must have been a dozen fires or more, with hundreds of people there, men and women alike. Will was certain that they had not been there the evening before when he made camp, and marveled at how such a large group of people could move so close by without his noticing.

But then, Dawn did that to him all of the time, and would suddenly be right up next to him without warning. That still amazed him. Will was just as amazed to see that Dawn seemed to have no concern on her face whatsoever with the events which were transpiring. He had not understood the Spanish words which had been spoken, but Dawn had already mentioned to him that those words, while understandable, seemed to be spoken in a much more formal and distant manner of speaking than what she was familiar with. The words themselves seemed quite old, somehow.

The ride was short. The lodging where they stopped resembled the drawings of tip is she had seen of the Sioux, but were more box-like in design and seemed far less roomy. They got down from their mounts, and yet there seemed to be no surprise or comment made as to the way Ooh-luh bowed down to allow Dawn to dismount. It was as though they had seen it all before. Conger considered the possibility.

They walked over and sat near the fire as instructed. A young girl, about ten or so years old, Will guessed, presented them with wooden cups filled with a warm broth. She smiled and bowed as she spoke, but Dawn could not make out the words. Minutes later, a blanket moved from the opening of the shelter, and a very old man came out, supported on one side by a much younger man of great strength. The resemblance was strong between them, and he very well could have been a son, or more likely a grandson.

The old man was helped down by the fire, a blanket placed beneath him to cushion the cold hard ground. He had no expression on his face, but his eyes were bright, and seemed somehow to be smiling.

A word was spoken, and the young girl brought forth a bundle of antelope skin, carefully tied with leather strips. It seemed ancient. The old man motioned for Dawn to come and sit beside him, and as she did, he unrolled the bundle, revealing a carefully drawn map, heavy in detail but without words or numbers of any kind. He spoke to Dawn very slowly in Spanish, a Spanish of long ago. She listened carefully, and followed his gnarled finger as it indicated a route to be taken, and a direction south and west from where they were now camped. They spoke together for some time.

Conger had no idea what was being said, but certainly did not feel as though they were in any danger here. The broth was excellent, and he would have loved to have had more, but fearing it might be an insult to ask for seconds, he just sat still and tried not to look overly concerned about anything, even though he was.

For starters, he had no idea who these people were. He also had no idea just where he was. He knew he needed a bath and a shave, and wondered if that might be the reason no one was standing anywhere near to him. Just as well, he thought. Still, he felt naked without his rifle, or at least a pistol. He did have his clasp knife.

Then, without any ceremony or signal that Will could detect, Dawn stood up, and walking back over to him, quietly asked him to stand up and follow her back to the horses, walking only behind her.

"Please don't say anything or ask any questions, Mr. Conger. We are among friends here, but they believe that you are my servant, and that you take orders from me. It is best that we play along with that idea for the time being. Please trust me in this."

Well, Will remembered that she had once said there was a horse in a barn where no horse could be seen… He had no real good reason not to do as she asked, so he did. A servant, of all things! Of course, looking back, there had been nothing about 'to love and obey' in their wedding vows. He figured that most married men came to understand that part didn't really apply to their women folk except when it suited them anyway. He would just stay behind her as they rode back to their campsite and keep his mouth shut.

In less time than it took Will and Dawn to strike the tent and pack up the mules, the entire Indian contingent was loaded up and moving south. The fires which had burned brightly only minutes before could no longer be seen, not even smoke showed where the fires had been. The group of riders which had come for them earlier now surrounded them, acting more like a protective escort than a threat. Conger had many questions to ask his young bride, and an explanation was in order to be certain. But the look in her eyes reminded him of her wish that he remain silent. So he quietly rode behind her, pulling the mules along, just as was expected of a servant.

What he really wanted right then was some coffee and a decent breakfast, but he realized that wasn't going to happen this morning. At least she couldn't keep his stomach from talking.

Conger was amazed that such a large group of people, and horses as well, could move across the landscape so quietly, and leave behind so little sign of their passing. He cautiously estimated there to be close to two hundred individuals traveling with them, all moving in single file columns. Outriders came and went, reporting each time to the powerfully built man who had earlier helped the old one out of the dwelling. Will could not see the older man anywhere, and assumed that he was not riding a horse.

For her part, Dawn was not nearly as calm and collected as Will had been led to believe. She knew they were traveling to a place, south and west of their current location, and that the journey would take many days, possibly weeks. She was now traveling in the identity of the Cherokee Spirit Woman, and the old one had told her that the Spirits had spoken of her coming. It would be his responsibility to lead her safely to the place she was to dwell among them, to her home in the far away mountains.

And so, this large group of men and women had come to this place on orders of the old one, to fulfill the wishes of the Spirits, and to lead her safely home. It was understood that their journey would lead them through the lands of their ancient enemies. It was hoped that by moving swiftly, and in great numbers, that their travels would go unchallenged, and without bloodshed.

At the end of the first day's travel, Conger finally had a chance to talk to Dawn and find out just what was happening to them. She really didn't know all that much, and had not asked many questions, as it seemed to be understood that as the Spirit Woman, she was all-knowing, and had no need to ask questions. She told him what she knew.

"They call themselves 'The People of the Mountain', along with another name I don't understand. What we see here is but a very small part of the entire tribe. The old man that we met at the fire is called Anhna, but I could not find out the leader's name, you know, the strong one. I am not sure of their relationship, but they look very much alike. I have no idea where Anhna learned Spanish, but it is in an old style, and difficult for me to understand. But it is good that he does, as I cannot make out anything they are saying in their own language. It is very different than anything I have heard before." Food was brought to the tent of the Spirit Woman, and provisions were made for Ooh-luh as well. Conger and the rest of the livestock were on their own, fitting of the servant's role. Dawn quietly giggled at Will's discomfort with it all.

The days went by uneventfully, finding them traveling through breathtaking vistas and along mountain passes that seemed to climb straight up to the heavens. Dawn was raised in the mountains of Western Virginia, and was far more prepared for traveling at this elevation than was her husband. Will, a native of central Kentucky, had never been all that much higher than the barn loft.

It was well into the second week of their travels that they found themselves riding into a small valley, shaped like an oblong serving bowl. Suddenly, one of the outriders galloped through at great haste, seeking the strong one with frightening news. But the report did not need to be given, as the hillsides above them were filled with riders, who raised their voices as one, in threat, and menace to those trapped below.

The travelers had not gone unnoticed after all, and their willingness to protect the Spirit Woman would very soon be tested. There would be no escape.

chapter 15

HUNDREDS OF MILES to the east, and worlds away, another group of horsemen, about a dozen in all, sat silently on their mounts, grim-faced, and waiting in the predawn light to begin the fearsome task that lay ahead of them. Once again they wore their military gray. Here was but a remnant of what had once been the Great Army of Virginia. Still, the fire of certainty kindled this day as it had before, with a firm conviction in the honor of their cause, and the necessity to succeed.

But this time the enemy was not the Yankee blue coats of the North, but rather the rag tag murderers who squatted on the ancestral home of O'Dell, bringing their unique filth to what had once been a place of happiness.

Brigadier General Henry Stronton once again sat at the head of his troops, gathered this day as volunteers to follow the command of the Great General, and to rid Virginia of this nest of vermin. No mercy would be shown this day, no quarter given. None would be allowed to escape death's wicked hand. Jacob McPhearson had been the first of this evil lot to die, and he would not be the last.

Ginny Stronton had proved an excellent source of intelligence for the campaign which was about to begin. The information she gave, often horrible and sickening in the telling, spoke of conditions of cruelty and slavery, and vicious assaults on captives and prisoners alike. These reports worked to harden the General's heart, and caused him to approach those dwelling at this farmstead in a very different manner.

At first he had intended simply to run the bunch out, and rid the territory of them. But upon hearing of the acts of torture and shameful treachery inflicted upon young girls such as his own daughter, he knew that unless this gang was stamped out once and for all, they would someday return to cut his throat, and hers, in the days to come.

They must all then be destroyed, as swiftly and silently as possible. Their bodies would be disposed of down a nearby mine shaft, long unused, and well-suited for the purpose.

The silent signal was given. A handful of skirmishers went ahead of the horses. There would be no rebel yell this day, no reckless charge into the fray. Next the horsemen moved into position, surrounding the house and outbuildings.

Surprise and stealth won the day, as in a matter of minutes the ordeal was over and done with. Seven bodies lay dead, six men and one woman, all known as vicious murderers. None of the defenders so much as got off a shot. One girl, beaten, and half starved, was rescued, with hopes that somehow she might be reunited with her family and returned to some semblance of a normal life.

In far-away Richmond, a smaller group of Gray coats, chosen for their skill and cunning, had already completed their pre-dawn raid on the home of Judge Bennet. Three young girls, known to Ginny, had been rescued, and were on their way to a safe house outside of town. The Judge's thugs had found themselves in the hands of men who were far more skilled in the art of war than they. Their worthless bones would later be found in the rubble of the Judge's burned out house, the fire having spread too quickly to be extinguished.

The body of Judge Bennet would not be discovered until the next day, found hanging by the neck in his splendid office, a suicide note nearby, admitting to his acts of piracy, and naming his accomplices. As a result of this evidence, many more hangings would soon take place, and many more young girls set free.

It seems Ginny Stronton had a knack for duplicating handwriting almost as good as the Colonel's wife. It was necessary of course, as the Judge would have never written such words of guilt and remorse on his own, even if asked nicely.

Soon enough, the O'Dell home would once again be a place of laughter and happiness, and the graves of Catherine's ancestors would be surrounded by flowers, and honored with tender care. Henry Stronton kept his promises.

While the battle in the east had been won, the battle in the west seemed hopeless. Will and Dawn both understood that a fight between old enemies was about to take place there, and that unless some sort of divine intervention occurred, the People of the Mountain looked to lose the fight. They were badly outnumbered and, being trapped in this valley, at a definite strategic disadvantage.

"William, have your guns ready. This may go very badly for us all. But right now I need you to trust me. Someone is speaking to me, and I know what I must do." Dawn looked him square in the eye, and smiled, and then mouthed the words so that only he could see, "I love you."

Conger simply smiled back. That was only the second time she had ever addressed him by his first name. Despite the threat of conflict soon to come, his thoughts were on her, knowing he couldn't have found a better woman.

The warriors near Will were grouping up and forming ranks, preparing for the onslaught that was to come. Shouts of defiance and death echoed from the hilltops surrounding them. Against such overwhelming odds, this conflict could only have one outcome. The certainty of hundreds being slaughtered or made captive this day was apparent for all to see.

With a few quick words from Dawn, Ooh-luh knelt down, allowing Dawn to dismount. She called for some of the nearby women to assist her, as she quickly disrobed, and rummaging through her packs, once again donned the beautiful white deerskin dress the Washazhe had insisted she wear for the ceremony to free Tall Tree's soul. The dress had power, not to be unleashed until this moment in time. Suddenly, Dawn was transformed, and seemed to glow with an amazing radiance.

Dawn remounted her great horse, and with her hair blowing freely in the fresh rising breeze, she slowly and purposely rode out alone to stand below where she assumed the leaders of their adversaries were gathered.

Conger made no move to stop her, or to ride along with her. The Sharps was already loaded, and extra cylinders for the Colt rifles were at the ready. He couldn't stop them all, but he could certainly even the numbers out a bit before he was finished.

Ooh-luh walked steadily forward, as Dawn Flower, once again chanting words of her native tongue, called upon the spirits of her people to rise up and assist her in this, their hour of trial. Then, asking Ooh-luh to stop, Dawn proceeded to stand up upon her horse's massive back, and stretching her arms up to the heavens, sang out a cry of power, summoning the spirits of the earth and sky which surrounded her to come to the aid of these people who had obeyed the will of the wind, and had brought her to this place.

The voices on the hilltops became silent, as they beheld the powerful beauty of this woman in the glistening white garment, her voice somehow carrying across the land. Suddenly a wind came from the west, and a rumbling tremor, deep and dark, came echoing across the mountains. As it continued, it became stronger, as though a thousand drummers were beating an unnatural cadence of power and warning.

And then it appeared: a cloud, dark and more threatening than any had ever seen before, turning day into dusk in a matter of seconds. It came running down upon them from among the mountain peaks to the west, like a great bird with wings widespread---an omen of doom.

Feeling the power of the moment, the faithful began a chant of their own, many falling to their knees, with arms held high in tribute, beckoning the spirits of earth and sky to protect them in this moment of peril. Most of those lining the hillsides chose to ignore the fast approaching cloud, confident in their overwhelming numbers, and loudly regaling those who knelt below, in what they considered an act of surrender and cowardice, and a plea for mercy. Loud voices mocked the chant they heard, as they renewed their war cries.

Then, as if in reply, came a massive voice of thunder, like the very voice of nature itself, replying to the taunts of those who would not pay homage to the powers which stood above them, with an unnatural echo which rolled and circled again and again in a deafening crescendo. With it came the wind, swift and powerful, pushing trees to their sides, and hurling great clouds of dust into the air. The mockers on the hillsides now were forced to deal with their frightened mounts, who being far closer to nature, understood the peril they were in, far more than the men who sat upon them. The horses bucked and ran, their handlers working feverishly to control them. The great voice of thunder spoke again, as the chants of hope and prayer became stronger, evoking the protection of the very fabric of life itself.

Dawn Flower, daughter of Flower Song, and keeper of the gifts of the Spirits, stood unwavering, seemingly unaffected by the winds which pummeled the land around her. She stood, arms outstretched to the heavens, dark hair blowing wildly, her white garment glowing in its own radiance amid the darkness of sky and dust. Her chant continued, unshaken, and the spirits answered once more.

The unexpected appearance of this woman in white, and the powers of nature that she seemed somehow to summon, were unnerving enough. But now, for these would-be attackers, the strategic advantage of being gathered on the surrounding hillsides became their undoing. A single bolt of lightening, white hot, and massive, struck down their leader, causing man and horse to explode in a cloud of fire and flesh. Others, being nearby, fell burned and screaming in agony, blinded by the brilliant light. Now lightening was striking all across the hillsides, again and again, falling upon these warriors like spears from heaven above, easy prey and vulnerable, standing on the high ground, with no shelter, no place to hide.

The rout was complete. The battle this day had been won, not by the strength of men, but by the power of nature which surrounds them, rising forth when summoned by those who live in peace with the land which nurtures them, and gently use the gifts that nature provides.

The sound of pounding hooves, and the cries of agony echoed, as this all-devouring cloud seemed somehow to pursue the attackers as they ran from those shafts of lightening more numerous and terrible than any who were there had ever witnessed before. And yet, through it all, no bolt of lightening, and not so much as a drop of rain had fallen upon those who had called upon the spirits for aid. Even the wind, ferocious and mighty, was felt only as a gentle breeze by those huddled in the valley below.

The sky brightened as the storm moved on. The People of the Mountain stood in amazement at what had occurred, the story of which would be told and retold for years to come. They had been delivered from certain death by the power brought forth by the Spirit Woman, who they themselves had been entrusted to deliver in safety.

But at this moment, their voices were hushed and still in reverence, for there before them remained the girl, her arms outstretched, standing tall and beautiful on the massive back of her great black horse. But she didn't move or speak, appearing now more like a carved figure, still and lifeless.

Conger lay down his weapons, and slowly and carefully walked over to where Dawn stood. Her eyes were closed, her head still turned to the sky, and her outstretched arms unwavering. He saw that the great horse was also transfixed, as if in some sort of trance, unblinking and motionless.

There was now a streak of white through his wife's hair that had not been there before. Will had seen what she had done, and had experienced the fury of nature around him. Something mystical had happened there that day, something that had happened to Dawn as well.

As high up on the horse's back as she was, Conger could not reach her to bring her down. But before he would motion for another horse to be brought by, he decided to speak to her first.

"Dawn Flower, this is William. You need to wake up now. It is time for us to go.

We need to leave this place. It is not safe for us here." He had spoken to her like a father to a child, very much as he had back at the Larson farm, so very long ago.

Dawn's eyes did open. She looked down at Will and nearly lost her balance. Now the horse began to move as well, and trembled on shaky legs. Dawn knelt, and then slid off the horse's back into Will's awaiting arms. She said nothing, but closed her eyes again and folded her arms around her husband's neck, and fell into a deep sleep.

chapter 16

"WHAT DO YOU remember?" It was three days and a night since the miracle in the valley, and Dawn had at last awakened. She looked puzzled as Conger gently tipped a wooden cup of cool water to her lips. She seemed confused and frightened as she beheld the face of a stranger, someone she did not recall having ever met before.

For Will, the joy of having her awake and responsive again was quickly tempered by the distant look in her eyes. It had been days now, and he had feared that he might never get her back. As amazing as the events in the valley had been, and the miracle of all their lives being spared, the thought of losing this girl was a greater torment than death itself for the man who had found her at her most desperate moment. But at least now she was awake. That was something. The old one had been summoned. The People eagerly awaited the great words of wisdom they expected to hear from this woman who could call on the spirits of heaven and earth at will, and bring destruction to their enemies.

Dawn was awake now, yes, and sitting up, but she looked around in confusion. The face of the man holding the cup seemed somewhat familiar, but without form and substance. The people around her were not of her family, and the words they were speaking were not familiar. Nothing they were saying made any sense.

The horse! It was her sister! Perhaps she too was a horse. She knew she could talk to the horse, it was her friend. And so she spoke to the horse, in a language that only the horse among those around her could understand. Ooh-luh responded at once to the familiar voice of her closest friend, knocking well-wishers over left and right in an effort to get close to the girl.

Anhna, the old one arrived at last, and seeing Ooh-luh's concern spoke softly to her, and the horse was calmed and knelt beside the girl, much like a great dog. Anhna then turned his attentions to Dawn, and noticed the confusion in her expression. He smiled, and lifting up her hand, spoke to her, once again using the ancient Spanish that Dawn had heard him use before.

"Dawn Flower, you are called. Do not be frightened by what you see and hear. You are still in the realm of the spirits, and you see us all as spirits, and not as men. Your journey on this earth has not yet ended, and you must now come back through the veil, to rejoin us here in the land of the living. Tomorrow you will see the home which has been promised to you. You must finish this journey to fulfill your destiny. Close your eyes now, and call upon your mother's name. She will show you the way."

"Flower Song, Mother, I promise I will return to you again." The words had been in Cherokee, and no one there knew what she had said, excepting Conger, who had read her mother's name in the family Bible, and had heard her mentioned as Dawn had spoken of her family. Of course Anhna would know---he seemed to know all things.

Dawn opened her eyes once more, and saw her beloved William, and reached for him at once. She had come home to him once more, and the joy of their reunion was witnessed by all. A spontaneous song of rejoicing rose up among the People, as Dawn stood once again among them. A bedlam of happiness soon overtook them all.

But it wasn't going to be all that simple. It was apparent that Dawn had experienced a great ordeal. She was physically weakened, and had trouble walking, and keeping her balance. It turned out that Dawn did not remember any of her experience in the valley, not even the putting on of the white deerskin dress, which she still wore.

Dawn was astonished and disbelieving of the reports of her role in turning back their attackers, and the display of nature's power which seemed to have been brought on by her evocation. She had no memory of standing on Ooh-luh's back, or of the winds, or the clouds, or of the lightening which vanquished their enemy.

There was reminder, however, that she couldn't dispute. A look into a quiet pond showed the reflection of a lovely young woman who now had a streak of white in her hair, from the root to the tips. Those around her saw it as a mark of honor and power. But as for Dawn, she thought it made her look something like a skunk. She would see what she could do with it at a later time. Meanwhile, she would remember to wear a hat.

That morning they crossed into lands controlled by their own people. A large vanguard of horsemen was there to meet them, to ride as escort for the homeward-bound caravan. The old one had promised Dawn that she would see her new home the next day, but she seemed bewildered by it all.

After a comforting meal, and a cup of warm broth provided by one of the women, Dawn fell back to sleep. They all agreed that she had earned her rest. She had now become a legend. News of the Spirit Woman, and of her deeds of greatness were already being told and retold at the campfires of the neighboring tribes, of friend and foe alike. Her presence here in the mountains had changed the balance of power here among the mountain tribes. That power would not go unchallenged.

Conger figured he knew his young bride pretty well, at least as well as you can get to know someone living elbow to elbow day and night for the last three months or so. There wasn't much about her that he wasn't highly familiar with, good, bad, and in between. He truly loved her.

But that night, he wasn't real sure just who that girl on the next cot was. She looked like Dawn, except for the white stripe in her hair, but didn't seem to act like Dawn. Her way of speaking seemed different, not so much in the way she sounded, but in the way she put her words together. She seemed now to hesitate when she spoke, as if she were translating what she was trying to say.

And she had stopped snoring! Her snoring was never anything like his, and was actually kind of cute to hear, but he missed it now. And she hadn't moved in her sleep. She simply lay down, took a deep breath, and did not move again. She was always known to flop around like a fish as she slept. And she was almost always up before he was, but not this day. It just didn't seem right somehow.

Worst of all, Dawn had hardly spent any time with Ooh-luh, who had always been her closest companion. She clearly was not herself. Will wondered who she had become. And this was to be the day that she would see her new home. Conger assumed it would be his new home too, but he really only had a half-way idea as to what this was all about. What little he knew had come from Dawn, and she wasn't making a whole lot of sense lately.

Conger let Dawn sleep while he put the coffee on, and took the livestock down for water. Lately Ooh-luh came along with the others without being told. Will had noticed a subtle change in the big black horse as well, possibly due to the sudden change in Dawn's behavior.

Breakfast was on, and the coffee was almost ready. Conger was just sitting there considering his situation and frying up some pan bread. And then, just as she had done so many times before, Dawn was suddenly standing next to him, with a big grin on her lovely face.

"So, what are you fixing for breakfast today, Mr. Conger?" The playful look in her eye and familiar ring to her voice were like a tonic to the worried young man. He jumped straight up, and taking her deep into his arms, held her tightly with no intention of ever letting go again. She was back!

Conger actually lifted the girl off the ground in his happiness, and setting her back down, felt a tear of joy run down his cheek. Dawn saw the tear and gently wiped it away, accompanied by a tear or two of her own.   For the longest time, they just stood there and stared at one another, much like they had done on the dance floor, on their wedding night. That seemed so long ago now. It was a magical moment.

Breakfast was burning and the coffee boiling over when they finally broke it up and got back down to the business at hand. Conger salvaged the coffee, he liked it best boiled anyway, while Dawn got busy putting together a new batch of pan bread. They both giggled like children over the mess they had made. It was a good time.

They were just cleaning up when a delegation came walking over to their tent. Anhna was not among them, but their powerfully-built leader, whose name Dawn still did not know, and had purposely not asked, was the one out in front. He gave a palm up greeting to Dawn, which she returned, and then handed her a roll of parchment. Dawn unrolled what turned out to be a map, different from the one she had seen on the first day, and complete with words written along the margin, along with very specific landmarks indicated.

Visible at the bottom of the map was a rock, seemingly large and shaped like a broken tree. The leader pointed to the rock on the map, and then turning to his right, indicated the very same rock sitting little more than a mile away, clearly visible from where they stood. Without saying a word, his sign language made it clear that Dawn and Will were to ride together under this rock, and follow the path which the map indicated. They had come to the place at last.

Dawn couldn't make heads or tails out of the writing, given the age of the manuscript, the ornate hand in which the words were written, and the ancient Spanish words which were being used. It looked as though there were several points indicated on the map either as landmarks for guidance, or for indicating some significance to that particular location. This map had been expertly and beautifully drawn, but its accuracy had yet to be verified. Something troubled Dawn.

"Where is Anhna?" She had spoken in Spanish, not knowing if this one spoke that language or not. She used hand signs to emphasize her words, hoping to somehow be understood.

The big warrior stood there for a few seconds, seemingly unable to digest the meaning of Dawn's question. Then he smiled, and using his finger to tap a mark on the parchment, indicated a place far along the pathway which was shown on the map.

"Anhna casat." He nodded and turned to go away, and then stopped and turned back again. Will and Dawn had no idea what the man was saying, but the gestures were unmistakable---they needed to go---now.

chapter 17

THEY HAD BEEN well into mountain country for weeks now, and having been aware of the gradual uphill climb, Conger knew that the elevation here must be much higher than back in Kansas. The air seemed light, and sometimes it was difficult to catch his breath after doing something as simple as saddling a horse. As no one else seemed to be bothered by it, he figured that it was something you just had to get used to over time. More mountains could be seen in the distance, and more behind those. He had never seen anything so high up, and wondered at how a fellow could get through a place like that.

They were already packed and moving toward the big rock. Dawn had become quite talkative again, and babbled on and on about the map, her encounter with the strong leader, and her asking about the Anhna. These people had brought her here at great risk, and they were aware of her coming long before she got there. Therefore, she felt obligated to see this place that they insisted was there waiting for her, and to follow the path indicated on the map. She had no idea what this place was, or how far distant, but she was excited by the newness of it all, and was eager to go.

So was Conger, almost. Following a map going to somewhere, drawn up by someone, and being recommended by people he didn't know, and who didn't even speak his language, was not a good reason to throw caution to the wind and go charging uphill into the unknown. And yet, it wasn't that much different than sitting down with a bunch of teamsters and drawing up his own map of places he himself had never seen, with much of the information coming second hand or based on stories they had heard.

Still, these people had done them no harm, and had even put themselves in harm's way to guide them to this place. There must be more to this than met the eye. Well, he had come west looking for adventure, hadn't he? Yes he had, and there she was riding that big black horse right in front of him. Will knew that as long as he was with this girl, his life would never be dull. All things considered, he had to honestly admit that he couldn't have done better if he'd tried.

It looked like the whole tribe was there at the opening where the rock bent over like a broken tree. It formed something like an arch that seemed to lead straight into the mountain. Conger really didn't care much for caves, and hoped that wasn't the kind of destination these people had in mind. Still, the map showed things that seemed far away, with a forest and water indicated. There had to be more than a hole in the wall.

Will numbered the crowd at least a thousand or more. He had gotten pretty good at numbering large groups of individuals during the war. They chanted and sang as one, and threw freshly-picked flowers along their way. It was like a coronation procession for a queen. Riders from the tribe rode along with them, but stopped short at the big rock, intending to go no further. Looking back, Will noticed that no one was following the mules as he continued to ride on. This was a journey meant for the two of them alone. They entered the coolness of the cave with Dawn and Ooh-luh leading the way. Will pulled out his rifle.

The cave got deeper and darker. Soon the sound of distant thunder, a thunder that never seemed to end, came echoing against the granite walls. It was as though they were riding into the gaping mouth of a great beast. It was nearly pitch black.

Then Dawn screamed, and she and her great horse completely disappeared.

Will had only heard Dawn scream once before, that had been on that fateful day at the farm, where he had found his lady in deadly peril. His reaction then was his reaction now. He gave Pumpkin a frantic kick, and releasing the mules, rode into the breach with reckless abandon, prepared to do battle with whatever foe he might find. He was certain that once again Dawn's life was in peril.

But there was no mighty beast awaiting him, no vicious adversary ready to do battle. Instead, Conger rode smack-dab into a thundering waterfall, hidden by a turn in the cave, and found himself suddenly on the other side, waist deep in water, with only his smiling bride and her great black horse there to greet him. She sat there laughing out loud, drenched from head to toe, and pointing playfully at her equally drenched husband. Will sat there on Pumpkin, dripping wet, and couldn't keep from laughing as well.

A minute or so later, Jack and Jill came out from under the waterfall dry as a bone. It seems there was a clear path behind the waterfall and off to the left, that only someone as smart as a mule knew how to find.

After taking a few minutes to wring out their clothes, and get their bearings, the journey continued. The waterfall did not appear on the map, nor did the cave, only the rock. Ahead of them a stand of pine trees, different from any that either of them had seen before, filled their view as far as they could see. The waterfall had formed a pool which in turn fed a stream which seemed to disappear into the forest. The pines were on the map, but bunched as tightly as they were, it was impossible to see what lay ahead. Here and there tall mountain peaks could be seen through the trees, rock-faced, and touching the clouds.

With no landmarks to guide them, they could only follow a vague direction through the fragrant pine forest. So far, so good. The mountains seemed close by, here on both sides, but the tops now were no longer visible. Dawn decided to let Will take the lead here, while she and Ooh-luh brought the mules along. Hearts beat rapidly in the strange and unknown land, much of it unlike anything they had seen before.

They saw birds, some familiar, others not. No other creatures were visible, but the sounds and calls they made were unmistakably new to them. This place seemed to be teeming with life. They were following something like a pathway, possibly a game trail, that Conger figured had been in use for many years. The pines were thick and tall, with very little sunlight penetrating the canopy.

And then as suddenly as the forest had begun, it ended. It was as though there was some sort of barrier that would not allow the forest to go on beyond that point. Will was amazed at the abruptness of it all, and guessed that they had ridden a little over two miles since the waterfall. He decided to add that calculation to the map next time he had the chance.

As they adjusted their eyes to the bright noon sunshine, they found themselves gazing at a huge basin, miles wide, and seemingly without end. The grasses here were a brilliant green, with tall wildflowers, and large-leafed trees scattered about in groves. The stream seemed to have reappeared out from the side of the mountain. There were deer and elk in the distance, and in great numbers. Conger recalled reading about the 'Illysian Fields' mentioned in ancient Greek texts, a place of great beauty set aside for heroes. This was such a place.

Dawn got down and pulled out the map. Will joined her on the lush grass as they gazed together in amazement at what lay before them. The livestock in turn wasted no time in sampling the plants and grasses around them, much better fare than they had endured for the last several weeks.

A few of the landmarks mentioned on the map were now visible, with many more undoubtedly much further away. It was while Dawn was pointing out a particular rocky outcropping, that it happened. It was all so sudden, so unexpected, that they both sat frozen, and stared in disbelief.

The valley, the entire valley, and the mountains surrounding them had suddenly shimmered before them. It was like a reflection in a pool of water, that moves and changes when a pebble is dropped into it. And then, just as quickly, it all moved back to its former self, as though nothing had happened.

Will immediately noticed that the livestock did not seem to have been affected, or even aware of the event, munching along happily as though nothing had happened.

"Dawn, did you see that?" All Will had to do was to look at Dawn's face to see the answer. But he wanted confirmation to know that he wasn't going daft.

"Yes, William, I did see it, and I was hoping you had seen it too, and for the very same reason. It seems as though the light plays tricks here, just like the mirage we both saw just before we met up with the Arkansas River." But there was no conviction in her words. That had been no mirage, and they both knew it.

"Maybe we should go back. Maybe we shouldn't be here after all." Will regretted the words as soon as they came out of his mouth. But there it was. Dawn's response would surprise him.

"Go back to what? This place is as good as any, and a whole lot better than most of what we've seen in the last few months. There is nothing back there for us. Anhna told me that this is a magical place, strong in the spirits. That is why they brought me here. I want to stay, and I want you to stay here with me, whatever happens."

Conger hadn't thought of it that way. But the girl was right. They really had no other place to go. The sad truth was that he had never had a chance to plan for a place for himself and his bride. He had just figured on seeing the land on his own. But without her help, he probably would have had his hair lifted by now.

They had stopped there long enough. Mounting up, Dawn took the lead as they continued on. Conger kept his rifle at the ready.

Landmarks came and went. The twin trees, the round boulder, a slash of quartz on the side of the mountain, and the small cave, all appearing as indicated. It was well into the afternoon now, and there was plenty of map left to explore. Conger knew that, even as wide as the valley appeared to be, darkness would come suddenly with those tall mountain peaks surrounding them. He figured they'd best be looking for a place to spend the night. The stream appeared again, winding its way through the valley, an oasis of flowers and trees along its banks. And then there was a bridge.

This was the first man-made object they had encountered since they had entered the valley. Even from a distance, its structural beauty was unmistakable. It reminded Conger of some of the arched bridges he had seen back east, built in the early days of the colonies. But those had been of stone, and this appeared to be built totally of wood. The timbers looked heavy, and had been carefully hewn. The structure arched gracefully over the water, beautiful and ornate in its simplicity. The wood itself gave off a reddish hue, unlike any wood Conger had seen before. The closer he got, the more impressive the bridge became. He was about to say something to Dawn about the questionable safety of a structure as old as this looked, when she and Ooh-luh proceeded to trot right on over the bridge without any concern whatsoever.

Will started to scold his young wife for her carelessness, and then wisely decided to just be still, and cross the bridge as well. Chances were that if it would hold Ooh-luh's massive weight, it could certainly deal with Pumpkin and a couple of mules. Always the strategist, Will had learned long ago that some battles are won by not fighting them at all in the first place. This tactic seemed to work in marriage as well, and for all the same reasons. He was learning.

An outcropping of rock blocked some of the view for a time. This was a large rock which had slid off from the mountain above, and was not on the map, more than likely occurring long after the map was drawn. The next landmark simply showed the face of a woman wearing a shawl. Even with the artwork being rough and worn, she seemed very pretty, with a serene and gentle smile. Conger couldn't help but notice the uncanny similarities that face shared with that of his own lovely bride. It had to be a coincidence of course, with the drawing having been made so very long ago. Still...

Conger was about to suggest to Dawn that they needed to stop soon and make camp, as there were only a couple of hours of daylight left. She was a good thirty yards ahead of him as she rounded the rock fall, when suddenly she stopped short, and stared in awe.

There, on a slight rise above and to the left, right where the picture of the woman marked a spot so mysteriously on the map, stood a house built of stone, large and strong, with what looked like a large stone barn standing nearby. Will caught up to the place where Dawn sat and stared, and then he too sat and stared.

Their faces showed their amazement. And while the appearance of a house where none was indicated was surprising enough, it was even more uncanny that there was a light shining through the window, and smoke curling up from the chimney.

The stone house was well-crafted, and of a design which seemed to blend in with the mountains which surrounded it. Sitting up on the rise as it did, the dwelling had a commanding view of the valley below. There was an abundance of pine trees near the house, but it seemed to enjoy ample light from the afternoon sun above.

Dawn felt drawn to this place, as though she had been there before. A pathway, dim and not recently used, ran up the hillside to the house. Ooh-luh turned and walked up the path without instruction from Dawn, as if the horse was drawn to this place as well. As she rode closer, Dawn could see a figure standing in the doorway.

Conger had not seen the path, and had to turn around to follow his wife, who was already near the summit. For some reason or other Will assumed that he and Dawn would be the only ones here, and was not prepared for this massive structure of stone, let alone a fire in the fireplace. Dragging the mules along, he was unable to catch up with Dawn and Ooh-luh and her long strides. But his rifle was at the ready, and despite all of the positives, he wasn't sure he trusted any of this. Still, the absolute stunning beauty of the place could not be denied. He caught himself holding his breath.

The figure in the doorway of the house was now clearly visible to Dawn---it was Anhna, the old one. But he was no longer stooped over and frail as he had been before. Now he stood strong and tall, and much younger. He smiled as she approached.

Ooh-luh knelt, and Dawn walked quickly over to the doorway, and into the welcoming outstretched hands of Anhna. She then sat down with him on the tall grass in front of the dwelling, still holding his hands in front of her, as he spoke.

"Dawn Flower, this is your home. It has been waiting for you for many years now. There is much that has happened to you that you do not understand. I can only tell you a little, as much of what I would say is of things you already know, but have not yet accepted to be true. You must first believe, and then you will understand."

"You have always been the Spirit Woman that you claimed to be that night by the fire with Tall Tree. You have been protected by the spirits since you were very young. Your mother gave you two names to protect you from the white man's world. She gave you knowledge of the earth so that you could escape the clutches of the evil one named Jacob. The strong man from the north hid you on his land, but the evil was strong, and would find you again. Your cry to the spirits was heard long before you voiced it, and the young man lost his horse so as to walk into your life at the very moment you most needed him. At the fire, your courage and cunning were there for all to see, and the owl was sent to speak for you and put fear into the hearts of those who had come to harm you."

"Even those who were sent to reclaim Tall Tree's soul were entrusted to protect you on your journey here, first when the evil men trapped you at the stream, and later as wolves had found your trail with the deer meat. Even your trusted friend Ooh-luh was sent years ago as a gift to become your companion, and to aid you in your escape when needed."

If Dawn was amazed at Anhna's knowledge of the events in her life, it didn't show. Instead, she was spellbound and comforted by his words, being for the first time at peace with the feelings that she held inside.

"Your mother stood with you atop the great black horse as you called upon the Spirits of the earth and sky. It was she who helped hold your arms outstretched, and who kept you from falling until your young man could reach for you. She knew at the moment you were born who you would become, and has never left your side. She will always be near you."

"I must go now. My work here is finished. Inside this dwelling are many things which will help you along on your journey of life. Remember this one thing, and hold it in your heart---you have no powers except for the powers the spirits bring to you. You must use those strengths only to help others, and never for yourself. Only in this way will the people be served. The young man has been brought to you to be your protection on this earth. Love him, and cherish him, for he was chosen for you many years ago, and was kept safe during the white man's war for the good of us all."

"I will return and visit with you from time to time, as the need arises. Tell your children about me, so that they will not fear my presence, for I too dwell in this place of magic." With those words, Anhna disappeared before Dawn's eyes, first as a mist, and then as a gentle breeze blowing away from the place where she had seen him seated just moments before.

Conger had watched Dawn sit down in the lush grass in front of the dwelling, and hold out her hands, seemingly to touch something. She did not speak, but tilted her head back, and closing her eyes, swayed softly as though moving to the sound of music. Conger could see no one there with her. As far as he could tell, she had been completely alone there the entire time.

Dawn suddenly moved, and standing up, looked around curiously. She seemed disoriented, but was smiling and satisfied. Will moved to stand beside her.

"Anhna was here and spoke with me. I now understand who I really am, and what I am to do. You are my protector, and my friend. I put my life completely in your hands, Mr. Conger. And I thank you for loving me the way you do. I could never live without you."

Such a speech could only be answered in one way--- Conger took the girl in his arms and kissed her. Their embrace lasted for several minutes. The beauty of the afternoon, the gentle breeze, and the overwhelming feeling of homecoming had brought their unlikely journey to a remarkable conclusion, with the promise of wonderful days to come.

Filled with joy, Conger lifted his bride up into his arms, and proceeded to carry her over the threshold and into the house. They giggled together at the wonder of it all, and then stopped short, startled, as someone was already inside the room, seated in a rocking chair, wrapped in a woven light red blanket. The figure spoke.

"I've been waiting for you." It was the young girl who had brought them their cups of broth on the morning they had first met Anhna. She sat in the rocking chair, fresh faced, and with a wonderful smile which seemed to light up the room. Will and Dawn were very confused.

"Welcome home. My name is Annahe. Anhna is my grandfather, and I have been sent to teach you the ways of this place, and to answer the many questions you will have as the days go by. I am here to serve your needs in any way that I can."

Now Conger was more befuddled than ever. He had been happy to see this place, and was more than willing to give it all a try. But he had figured to be alone here with his wife, and to finally get to enjoy their togetherness, not to have some little ten year old girl running around and getting in the way. He started to say something about it, but was cut off short by the girl.

"You need not worry Mr. Conger, as I will not be in the way here. I will respect your privacy and not interfere with your intimacy together. But I too am one with the spirits, as is Dawn, and I have much of life that I need to learn from her, just as she learned from her mother before her. Besides, she will need help with the child she is carrying."

Dawn stood there and stared at Annahe in disbelief. Then she broke into a big grin, and the girls joined hands and danced around the room in a moment of absolute spontaneous abandonment. The resulting chatter seemed destined to go on for hours.

Will took a deep breath, and sighed. So, he was going to be a father! Well, he'd spend time thinking about that later. Right now he needed to get the packs off those poor animals and look into bedding them down in the stone barn he had seen earlier.

It seems that Will Conger's western adventure had just begun.

END

www.ingramcontent.com/pod-product-compliance
Lightning Source LLC
Chambersburg PA
CBHW060053150626
46556CB00017BA/300